SEEKERS

SEEKERS

APOCALYPSE IN EDEN BOOK 2

ANN SWANN

WordCrafts Press

To Crystal Vanmeter
Thank you for all the encouraging messages.
You kept me writing.

PROLOGUE

August or September

I'm writing this from the road. I've lost track of days. For a while, I had another notebook where I tried to keep up with things like time, but I must've left it somewhere along the way. It's all right. I picked up this new spiral yesterday. Everything is free now. Free for the taking.

That's the problem, you see. The Takers. When the sky ripped open and dumped them into our midst, I lost my parents and everything I'd ever known. My little hometown of Eden, Texas, became a ghost town. Worse than a ghost town, it became a mausoleum—no; it became the set of a horror movie, gory and surreal.

The Takers dropped through sky holes in a thunderous rain of slime that stopped everything that wasn't underground. My mom died in the library where she worked—probably from the ear-splitting pulse of energy—I found her body in the Comparative Religions Room, but I haven't found my dad. He's still out there, somewhere. I'm sure of it. He left me a note in his car. That's why I'm on the road.

My name is Jack Lewis. I'm fourteen going on fifty. I've seen and done things I never would have thought possible. And I may have lost my family, but I gained a dog named Snake and a couple of strange friends named Turq and Carlos. There was another, but we lost him in New Mexico. The same place Carlos got burned.

This is the longest, strangest trip I've ever been on—and yes, I did mean to reference The Grateful Dead—Dad was a music teacher and a vinyl record collector. I know all the classic rock. And here's the thing about my dad and me; we have this amazing musical connection, that's why I ~~think~~ ... *know* he's still alive. In addition to the note he left, I also keep hearing his songs. Especially when I'm in trouble or have some heavy decision to make.

The bad thing is, the tunes have slowed down recently, and that scares me. So, I improvise. "Truckin'" is one of Dad's favorite Grateful Dead songs, so I keep it going in my mind, and it helps to keep *me* truckin'.

But wow. Life is completely different since the rip. I live it, but I hardly believe it. What I wouldn't give to just go to sleep tonight and wake up tomorrow in my own childhood bed back in Eden, Texas. Of course, that will never happen. This isn't a dream or even a nightmare, this is just—now.

CHAPTER ONE

Jack

We came on across the dry land in our second Chrysler 300 with our trunk stuffed full of food and water. Every time we saw a market—or a farm with a greenhouse—we stopped to investigate and took whatever we could store and carry.

Snake stood for hours with his back paws on the floorboard and his forepaws on the broad console between the front seats. Turq, the turquoise-shirted Taker who had saved me from a painful death, occupied the shotgun seat to my right. He was my wingman. Carlos, my buddy the Harley rider, lay in the back seat on a mound of pillows and quilts, still healing from some of his burns even after all these weeks.

Thad, the attorney from my hometown of Eden, Texas, perished in the firestorm we started in New Mexico. That's also where we picked up Turq. We lost an attorney but gained a monster. Some would say we made an even trade. I wish Thad was here to appreciate the joke. He had a wicked dark sense of humor when he wasn't drinking.

My mind wandered back over the last few days. The monotonous sand-toned landscape wanted to sing me to sleep. The hot air punching through the wide-open windows wanted to roast me.

We'd all grown accustomed to riding in the first car with no windows at all, thanks to the battle at the buffalo jump, so even though we'd picked up another Chrysler in Levelland—silver this time—we sometimes rolled down the windows instead of running the AC.

Carlos said the wind rushing through the car made him think he was back on his Harley before the battle that almost killed us. It made sense to me. Without radio or music of any kind, the sound of prairie wind probably seemed the same as riding on a motorcycle.

I stuck my head out the window to test my theory and to try and stay awake.

That's when I saw the tall man in the distance. He stood beside a gray Dodge Challenger that had seen better days. His long scraggly hair fluffed around his face like cotton candy. His skin was pale.

Night traveler, I thought. *No sunburn. No tan. Why's he out in the daylight now?* I had learned to be suspicious of everyone and everything.

I let the Chrysler slow.

He appeared to be filling the Challenger's gas tank from a red and yellow plastic container exactly the way we'd been doing.

We were still a little way off, but on this stretched ribbon of earth, it was easy to see the man and his task.

"Whaddya think, Snake?" I said. "Good guy, or bad guy?"

My four-legged buddy whined in response. I believe he understands everything I say even though he is stone deaf. I'm convinced he has DESP. Dog extrasensory perception.

Turq turned his multi-faceted, garnet eyes toward the man.

"It looks like a man, not a Taker," I said for the benefit of Carlos lying prone in the back seat. "He has hair, for one thing, no bald skin with sin words floating."

Turq never spoke, but he did gesture from time to time, and he seemed to have a special rapport with Snake, as if they were on the same invisible wavelength.

Not for the first time, I wondered why the creature was always silent. As I thought about it—something I had plenty of time to do—I realized that all the Takers were silent. That was one of the things that made them so deadly. They made no noise other than the *shushing* sound of their bare feet on pavement. When whole groups were on the march, that smooth clamor was chilling.

That's not *the only sound,* my subconscious insisted. *They make others. You've just forgotten, put it out of your mind for self-preservation.*

The first time I'd seen the Takers was when I made my way up from the Eden Middle School basement and peered outside to see what had caused the freight-train noise and sudden lack of power. I didn't know it was the sound of the universe splitting open. I assumed it was a killing storm. A tornado.

When I reached the school doorway, the horrific sounds had stopped, along with the heavy rain, but the parking lot was full of wide puddles of silvery liquid shimmering violently each time a monster arose, dripping, almost fully formed.

They all looked alike, no toes or fingernails, no ears, nothing to even distinguish their gender. Mostly they looked like ugly wax dolls waiting for an artist to carve in their features. And then I saw their shiny garnet eyes and black-slashed mouths. Their sharp silver teeth weren't visible until they opened those mouths wide enough to bite off someone's arm or head.

They all had the same bald heads and automaton gaits.

But the strange part, if it could be any stranger, were the black-lettered words that writhed beneath their translucent skin like worms in a shallow riverbed.

I called those internal tattoos their "sin words" because the ones I could read spelled out things like murder, rape, and robbery. But I couldn't always read the words. Many were in languages I didn't recognize. Maybe even languages that don't exist anymore.

When the creatures first arose from their sticky puddles, it had sounded like thousands of leeches being pulled off the earth's wet skin. The acrid odor of ozone had filled the air. Electrical power no longer existed. Everything in our town had been coated in a thick layer of slime. Including the electrical poles and transformers.

But the creatures themselves were silent.

Until they began to feed.

That became apparent when they yanked moaning survivors out of dead cars and stabbed them onto broken tree branches and fence posts, hanging them up to bleed out like slaughtered hogs. That's when the slurping, gulping, gargling noises began. The awful sounds were loud in the Takers' throats as they devoured the flesh and entrails of their victims. The sounds were so horrible I was almost glad when the screaming would cover it. And the screaming always happened; after all, the monsters only ate the ones that were still alive …

Now, here we are, a small handful of survivors, rolling up on a *man* beside the road, the first live person we've seen since we lost Thad.

I shook my head and glanced at Turq. He—I thought of him as male because he was so large—stared in my direction as if looking inside my head.

"Are you reading my thoughts the way Snake does?" I tightened my grip on the steering wheel.

He rotated his eyes away and raised one hand, tilting it in a very human back and forth motion that said, *maybe, maybe not.*

I laughed and looked back at the road. That was the first sign of humor I'd seen from the thing. It made trusting him that much easier. Plus—and this was the biggie—he'd saved my life and joined us of his own accord.

As a Taker, he had set himself apart almost immediately by donning this turquoise shirt. Several other creatures had also found articles of clothing to wear.

Back in Eden, I had stumbled upon an entire congregation of these Turq-Takers filling the pews in St. Stephen's church. What a surprise that had been. Not knowing any better, I had run like a scalded dog. Now I wondered if all the clothed ones were good, like Turq. If we came across them on down the road somewhere, would they join us? That would *really* be a motley crew.

I waited for a burst of Dad's music to invade my brain the way it always did, but nothing came other than the Grateful Dead song I'd been conjuring up all day. I'd grown so used to feeling connected to him through those blasts of unexpected moldy oldies that I now realized I'd been taking the music for granted.

Now that the tunes were few and far between, I really missed them. None of the songs I thought up gave me magical guidance the way they had before. The ones I conjured were just skull notes bouncing inside my head.

That worried me. If the music was gone, did that mean Dad was gone, too?

I had so many memories of him belting out the words to all these songs as we worked on the car, or when he was in the shower—echoing all over the house—or anytime he had a grill-spatula in his hand, that I must've absorbed every one of them through osmosis. Probably the same way he'd absorbed a lot of them from his own parents. He'd also shared them with his music students at Eden High School where he taught.

Now, I missed all that, and missed having the tunes shoved into my brain unexpectedly, to help me make decisions. *But what if they weren't forced upon me? What if the tunes were there all along, waiting for me to need them?*

I didn't like that train of thought. I'd much rather believe Dad was sending them to me somehow. Projecting them at me. It didn't seem far-fetched anymore. Not when compared to everything else that had happened.

Question of songs unresolved, I slowed the car to a crawl as we approached the Challenger. "So, Snake, do we stop, or do we wave and go on?" *As if we could afford to pass up another human in this desert wasteland.*

I gripped the wheel tighter.

The man turned to face us. Something about him disturbed me. It may have been the way he didn't seem surprised to see us. As if—somehow—the joke was on us.

My right hand naturally went up in greeting.

The dude simply stared and then turned back to his task, gas can tilted against the Dodge. A dark thought occurred to me. *Maybe he's wondering how much fuel is in* our *tank.*

Carlos curled upward from his blanket nest, propping himself on one elbow. "You stopping?"

"Yeah," I said. "Can you see him?"

Carlos grunted an affirmative. "Yeah. Ugly gringo, pouring gas."

"Yeah—"

The *cha-chunk* of the shotgun being pumped told me Carlos also had misgivings. I recalled the day Thad and I had found him roaring down the road on his Harley.

Attorney Thad, the hero we'd lost at the buffalo jump firenado, had been a little leery about the butt of that shotgun visible under Carlos' rolled-up blanket. But even in my fog of pain, from a newly broken arm, I'd recognized him. My own ESP had told me he was the one we'd been looking for.

"Ready," he said now. He pushed the tip of the barrel out the back window.

I let the Chrysler coast up alongside. "He's got a passenger," I said. "You see him, Turq?"

The Taker remained immobile. That's when it dawned on me that the tall man's gaze was focused on Turq, not on me. *Of course.* I should have known that was why he stared, but I'd grown so used to my new buddy, and so *not* used to seeing other humans—except for their remains—that I'd forgotten how strange my little crew must appear.

Snake began to rumble deep in his chest, like an attack motor warming up. We'd stayed at the half-demolished shell of the Bitty Sloan house long enough for his broken leg to heal—with the help of antibiotics from the deserted horse farm down the road—but that fiery battle out at the buffalo jump had aged my deaf canine protector. He no longer tried to charge headlong into the fray like before, now he sat back a little bit. Studied the situation.

"Bad guy, Snake?" I asked again, knowing full well he couldn't hear me.

The dog's muscles stiffened, preparing for launch.

The pale haired man raised his hand at last. But it wasn't that which drew my attention. My foot smashed the brake to stop the car completely.

Snake lost his balance.

"Dude!" Carlos squawked. "You nearly made me shoot 'im!"

I couldn't help it. I gaped at the car's passenger.

"Cade?"

My voice broke as if I'd never gone through puberty.

CHAPTER TWO

Cade

The tall man glanced in at his passenger.

The younger guy leaned across the seat and looked at my face. Then he flung himself out of the Challenger and ran around the front of the car. "Jack?! Is that you?"

I shoved the gearshift into park and stumbled out. We crashed together. We'd never hugged or touched each other in affection before, not in all the years we'd been friends, but now we hugged as hard as brothers. He was scrawny. Not just a lanky prankster anymore, now he was skin and bones.

"I can't believe it's you," he said.

I released him, and we shoved backward, embarrassed at the same instant. "I thought you were dead. I saw your leg sticking out from behind the bleachers in the gym."

Cade shook his head. "It was Rusty Garza. We had the same Adidas, remember?" He glanced down at the new Nikes on his feet.

Snake interrupted our reunion.

We both glanced toward the Chrysler. We could hear the big dog growling above the quiet hum of the car. The Taker seemed to be looking somewhere in between Cade and the tall guy and just for a second, I caught a glint of sunlight off the tip of the shotgun barrel still sighted out the back window.

I yelled back to Carlos not to shoot. We'd started the whole firenado back in New Mexico with a few gas cans, a shotgun, and a Bic lighter. A crazy image of Thad's face as he sailed off the buffalo jump popped unbidden into my head. It was accompanied by a snippet of Blind Faith's "Can't Find My Way Home." I welcomed the music because it mentioned home, and standing here before me was the biggest chunk of home I could imagine. Then it hit me—that was Dad's music. It had come at me unbidden. Dad's music was *back*.

"Am I dreaming?" I asked. "Hallucinating?"

Cade laughed, slung his straight dark hair out of his eyes, and shot a sidelong glance at our Taker. "Hey, Jack," he stage-whispered. "You got a monster in your passenger seat. What're you doing, man, holding him for ransom?"

I laughed a little. "Nah. That's Turq. He saved my life. Pretty much saved us all."

The look on Cade's face was beyond priceless. His friend must have also heard me. His eyes already on Turq, he lowered the gas can in slow motion. The shadow of a cloud moved across the highway like an omen.

Blind Faith continued to play softly in my head. In behind my thoughts that way, I couldn't make out every word. I knew most of them by heart, though, and I remembered something about coming down off a throne. But what could it mean? And why did the music suddenly come back with the appearance of Cade?

I searched the moving clouds looking for the sky holes. Many had been sealed up by the swarms of black locusts, but a couple were still visible. They looked like repairs in pale worn-out blue jeans.

Cade followed my gaze toward the sky. "Have you seen that black shit that pours out?" he asked.

I nodded. "I think of it as our salvation." I realized how that sounded, but I couldn't help it.

"You're kidding me, right?"

"Hell, no. We used it to take care of a whole platoon of Takers up in New Mexico. It Hoovered 'em right up and took 'em back to Purgatory."

Cade held up both hands and took a step back. "Hold on, Jackie, just hold the freakin' phone." His face had changed. Something had happened that I didn't understand. "You fought a whole platoon of these things and *won*, and now you have one riding shotgun?" His smile disappeared. "What are you, King Turd of Crap Mountain?"

Ahhh, there he is. There's the old Cade. He didn't believe me, so he had to mock me. "C'mon, man," I said. "We had to survive." I looked back at my motley crew. "You must've been going through the same stuff."

He took another step backward.

This felt strange. I thought we were thrilled to find each other. What happened?

The tall man stood motionless beside the Challenger, waiting.

I wondered if Carlos still had his shotgun trained on the guy's chest. If so, it would be a miracle. He hadn't been able to sit up for more than a minute or two at a time since the fire.

Once again, Cade followed my gaze. "That's Hal."

The guy nodded, and that seemed to goad him into action. He placed the gas can back into the trunk of the Dodge, then strode toward me, hand outstretched. "Hal Kennison," he said.

I shook his hand, uncomfortably aware of my somewhat-boyish grip. "Jack Lewis."

Hal almost smiled. His lips curved upward for a moment, then relaxed. "You two really know each other?"

I rubbed the back of my neck, trying to figure out *their* relationship. "Believe it or not, Cade's been my best friend since elementary school."

The man's face showed his disbelief. "You're pullin' my leg." It seemed a mocking reaction just like Cade's had been a few seconds earlier.

"S'true," I said. "Believe it or—"

He held up his hands as if in surrender. "Yeah, I believe you." He put his hands down. "I was just messing with you. Cade has actually mentioned you a time or two. Said y'all went through a lot together—" This time, the guy's voice sounded normal. "Just hard to believe you both survived. And now," he swept his arm out to include the lot of us, "here we are."

"Yep," I said. "Here we are." I cleared my throat. "You know, after the Covid pandemic, I thought we'd pretty much seen it all. 'Course we were only what—eight, nine years old?" I looked to Cade for confirmation.

He nodded and slung his long hair back again. "Remember how some people got so pissed off 'cause they had to wear masks in public?"

I nodded.

"We didn't care," he said. "As long as we got to ride up and down the street on our bikes, wearing masks didn't bother us. We were bandits." He tossed his head again. It seemed to be a new thing; something he'd never done before. It reminded me of the first days of the virus when all the barber shops were closed, and his mom tried to cut our hair.

"Hey, Cade, remember that haircut your mom gave us?"

A grin crossed his face. "Fixed us right up, didn't she? For some reason, we both had bald spots, right about here." He touched the side of his head, and for a moment he was my old friend again.

It felt like seeing a ghost. The last time I'd seen his face that way had been right before the world fell in, back in the middle school gym, when he'd urged me to go down to the basement for more crepe paper.

"I still can't believe it's you, man." My voice came out a little huskier than I'd intended. I shuffled my feet and glanced at the sky.

He slugged me on the shoulder. "And I can't believe it's you, Jackie-boy. Can you imagine me looking through all the bodies hanging in those sycamores around the school, searching for you?"

"You did?" That surprised me. I remembered the gore, the stench. I had given those trees a wide berth, riding my bike down the middle of the street to avoid them, and still the smell had nearly melted the rubber off my wheels. I had a sudden memory of Snake sneezing and shaking his head as we went along.

Hal wandered back to his car, climbed halfway into the driver's seat, and sat with the door open.

I lowered my voice. "I can't believe we both survived. We lost so many to the virus. And then when we finally got back to normal—"

"Yeah," Cade nodded. "I know what you're about to say. We barely had time to recover and then *boom*. Armageddon." He pinched his fingertips together and blew across them as if blowing dandelion seeds into the breeze. "All my family—*poof*—gone."

"Your parents *and* your grandparents?"

He dipped his chin. "Yeah. You know, the virus got one grandma, this mess got the other. Now they're all gone. Parents and grands. All of 'em."

"Got my mom, too," I said. "But Dad left me a note in the Mustang." I stood a little straighter. "That's why I had to come back to Eden, to see if he's still around. We, uh, sort of got run out of town last time."

"Where'd you go?"

"Kansas, New Mexico."

Cade looked at me with a question on his face. "Both places?"

"No." I realized what I'd said. "Kansas is a small town *in* New Mexico. Long story. I'll tell you about it later. Have y'all seen any of the old farmers since this happened?" It was something I'd been worried about, wondering if crops would still grow now. The grocery stores had lots of canned stuff, but I worried what would happen when that ran out. Most of the fresh stuff was long gone. Frozen stuff, too. "It's rained some since the rip, hasn't it? Surely the slime has washed away."

"Haven't seen any of the old guys," he said. "No crops, either. We've been eatin' canned stuff."

"Yeah," I said. "Same. Except for a couple of greenhouses along the way."

Cade lowered his voice to match mine, "It hasn't rained much at all. I wish my grandparents were still here. They'd know how to restart things, plant some stuff. You know?" He looked down at the ground. "My folks probably would, too."

I let my hand fall to my side. "We might have to get a book on gardening. Veggies, sugar cane, potatoes. I miss French fries." I stopped talking because I knew I could never force myself back into the Eden Public Library. In my head, it was now Mom's tomb. Maybe we could get one in the Eden High library. "You know, you saved my life at school."

Cade's chin came up. "How's that?"

"By sending me down to the basement that day, remember?"

He held his head very still, like Mom—and now me—when a

migraine struck. "Of course, I remember," he shrugged. "I snuck down there, too. Then the lights went out."

"So that's how we both survived."

He nodded. "I was gonna scare you. Give you a good jump. You were so twisted up about Dee and that dance. Thought I'd loosen you up a bit."

I glanced at the sky again. "At first I thought you were the *cause* of the lights going off," I said. "It did scare the crap out of me—"

"Yeah," he interrupted. "Me, too." He shoved his hands in his pockets and studied the tops of his shoes. "I started to yell for you, then I thought 'that son of a gun is on to me, *he* turned out the lights to try and beat me at my own game.'"

A laugh bulled its way into my throat and out of my mouth before I could stop it. "So, you kept quiet thinking I'd got one over on *you* for a change?"

His face reddened.

I looked over at Turq. "Man, don't we wish it had been that simple?"

"Yeah," Cade said. "I stayed down there in the basement until the noise finally woke Coach from his stupor. You know he kept his hooch down there behind the old sports equipment?"

I nodded.

Cade continued, "I watched him stumble out from behind the equipment with a baseball bat. He took a swig from one of those high-dollar thermos things, to get his courage up, I guess, and then he went right up the stairs. Never even knew I was behind him."

Scratching the back of my neck, I pictured that in my mind. "I must've already made my way up by then. I was looking out the front window when Coach came around the corner with his bat. But he didn't get far. A Taker yanked it away and beat him to death with it." I watched the memories like a home movie in my head. "That's when I ran back to the gym. Saw Dee in the basketball goal." *The image of the rhinestone headband tangled in her black hair popped into my mind, but I shoved it aside.* "Thought I saw your leg sticking out from beside the folded bleachers—"

"Rusty," Cade said. "Those stupid Adidas." He took one hand out of his pocket, slung his hair off his face. "I ran the *soles* off mine."

Glancing at the horizon, his voice fell. "I saw what happened to Coach, too. I was still holding that side door open, the one near his office. That's when I got as far away from school as I could. Ran straight home, then to all my cousin's homes." He looked at me from the side of his eye. "When daylight came, they'd all marched on. That's when I came back, looked through the corpses. Looking for you."

"I had to get home, too." I indicated the car with my chin. "Found old Snake lying half-under Mr. Granger's house. Remember him? Grouchy old guy in that corner house, always kept the dog chained?"

Cade leaned down, peered inside the front windshield. "I'll be damned, Jack. That really Snake? I thought he was deaf. And mean."

I nodded. "He is deaf. But not mean. Just protective. At least I think that's why he's so trigger-happy with those pit bull jaws." Was I giving Cade a warning? My oldest friend? "He was the first living thing I found aside from *them*." I glanced at Turq when I said it.

"Yeah," Cade said. "I saw a lot of *them*, and a lot of dead bodies. Couple days after the rip, Hal found me. I was just walking along by that time, trying cars to see if any would start."

I laughed. "Let me guess … none did."

He shook his head, embarrassed. "Right. But Hal had the Dodge. Found it in Beau Jackson's dugout. Remember he had that old dugout on the edge of town?"

"Sure. Everyone knew he sold weed out there. Don't remember this car though."

"Hal said it was in the back of the dugout. Guess he kept it hidden. Maybe used it to make deliveries or something."

"Maybe so." I looked at the car a little closer. "That was smart thinking, going out to Beau's house. It took me a long time to realize I needed to look for a vehicle underground."

"Yeah, if Hal hadn't been one of Beau's regular customers, he wouldn't have known about it, either." He stopped talking and glanced at the Chrysler. "Looks like you got a nice one." He motioned back at their car. "This old Dodge ain't even got AC. Gets hella-good gas mileage, though."

"Looks fast," I said.

"A couple days after Hal picked me up, we went by the school again … I just couldn't believe I'd survived, and you hadn't. We even went by your house but apparently there'd been a fire."

I nodded. I didn't want to talk about that. Didn't even want to picture it. The memory of Kevin's body bleeding out on my mom's Irish lace tablecloth would live in my mind forever. Right there with Dee's sparkly headband.

On the other hand, I *needed* to hear about the fire. I hadn't been there for that part. All I knew was the little bit Thad told me, and I had been so angry at him at the time, I hadn't even asked any questions. But this was Cade. My best friend in the whole world. I could trust him to tell me the truth. Right?

"Did you go inside my house?"

He hesitated, cut his eyes at me. "No, man, there's nothing left but ashes. Burned to the ground, the ones next to it, too. No fire department anymore. Wonder it didn't burn the whole town. Know what I mean?"

I knew what he meant. I'd started one hell of a fire out on the prairie myself. For all I knew, it could still be burning. "Yeah, I know what you mean. It's just, you know, I'm still looking for my dad." Blind Faith's song "Can't Find My Way Home" surfaced again.

"I saw the Mustang in the high school parking lot. But I haven't seen him." He stopped, flung his hair, spoke a little softer. "I found my folks in the mulberry tree out front of our house. Both of 'em." His voice crumbled a bit. "My mom loved that tree."

Shuffling my feet, I leaned toward him, uncertain how to express my sympathy. Our shadow-shoulders touched across the pavement. "I remember how she would spread out an old beach towel when we were little, make us sandwiches to eat in the shade." My brain conjured up more home-movie images of his plump mom and hardworking dad stripped of flesh, half-eaten entrails hanging—

"Just imagine how many dead bodies there would be if the virus hadn't wiped out so many old people before hand—"

"Cade—" I couldn't believe that's where his mind went after just telling me about the deaths of his own parents. But he'd always been what my dad called *unpredictable.*

"It's all right, Jackie-boy." He stepped back, away from my shadow. "At least *we* made it. And now that we've found each other, moving forward will be a lot easier."

I nodded. "We can travel together. I'm going to look around Eden first, then we're headed to Abilene. Remember my Aunt Edna? The one with the old missile silo?"

"That's *right*." His face lit up.

"I figure if Dad is still alive, he might've gone there. If he isn't there, I'm going to turn, head north, straight on up to Colorado where my grands live. Or lived." I stopped talking.

The summer sun baked the back of my neck. My hand went there, rubbing, feeling the length of my own streaky, uncut hair as I gazed down the road, squinting at the wavy lines of heat rising off the pavement. "You know, there's something you said, about the lack of bodies and the virus ..."

"Yeah?"

I tilted my head toward the Chrysler. "My buddy, Carlos, said something very similar." I saw Cade grin, and I knew I must've sounded like a librarian, like my mom. He'd always called me a nerd because my folks taught me to speak properly. It was only when I hung around him that my speech deteriorated into slang. Even I knew that about myself.

"Wha'd he say?"

I glanced toward the rear seat. "He said these Takers might be the first wave of an invasion from some other government—he's sort of a conspiracy-type—but I'm thinking this might be like the third wave. First the virus, then the Takers, now this *nothingness*."

"Damn, Professor," another of Cade's nicknames for me. "You just always thinking about shit, ain'tcha?"

I could tell he was exaggerating the poor grammar and profanity. He'd often done it to bug me.

"Yep." I ignored his sarcasm. "And since this happened—"

"—the apocalypse," he said.

"Yeah," I agreed. "That's what we've been calling it, too. Anyhow, since all this happened, how can we *not* think about it?"

For once, he didn't have a smart remark. "Guess you're right," he said. "Hard to believe we made it. The both of us. What're the odds?" His grin was so wide it nearly cut his face in two.

CHAPTER THREE

Eden

"C'mon." I pointed to the car. "Come and meet the rest of the band."

Cade laughed at our old private joke. We'd tried to start a band when we were twelve, but right away we'd butted heads. He wanted to sing even though he couldn't hit a note with a hammer. When I pointed it out to him, he got mad.

We didn't talk for nearly a week. Until the neighborhood pool opened, and we both found we liked ogling girls in bikinis better than headbanging in my folks' garage.

Later he admitted I should've been the singer all along. We both knew my voice was way better than his, but the idea had been tarnished. Somehow, we never got back to trying again.

"Third wave, huh?"

I shrugged, reached for my driver's door. "Just one of many theories."

Carlos had lowered the shotgun. The barrel now pointed at the floor. A sheen of sweat coated his forehead, a testament to the amount of effort it had taken to hold the big gun for that long.

"Carlos, meet Cade, my best friend since we were little kids."

Carlos stuck his left hand over the seat. It surprised me that he didn't lay the gun down completely, but even with the tremendous effort it took, he kept his right hand on top of it. "Good to see a face," Carlos said.

Cade and I both laughed.

I opened the back door and motioned for Snake to come. He stepped out on his tiptoes, his gaze never leaving Cade. I got the feeling he didn't trust my friend any more than Carlos did.

Reaching down, Cade rubbed Snake's head going directly to the smooth spot between his ears. "Good dog," he murmured even though he knew Snake was deaf.

Snake submitted to the attention. He didn't growl, but he didn't wiggle either. His body remained as taut as a bowstring.

I reached down and scratched his neck to reassure him. "He's one hell of a sidekick, I'll tell you that."

Cade laughed. "We have quite a crew here, don't we? Me, you, Hal, your buddy, Carlos, old Snake." He gave the broad head another pat. "And that thing." He looked straight at Turq.

"Come on." I walked around to the passenger side of the car. Turq opened the door and stepped out. He moved like a machine, which is what Carlos thought they were.

I looked up at the garnet-eyed face. "Turq, this is Cade, he's a friend."

Cade also had to look up. All the Takers were tall. And solid.

Hal watched from beside the open door of the Challenger.

"It's alright, guys." I tried to break the tension. "If not for Turq, I'd be hanging in a tree somewhere. One of 'em broke my arm, and Turq saved me. Tossed me back in the car with Thad, the man who had the first Chrysler."

Cade's mouth fell open before he could stop it. "Bro. You're shittin' me—"

I shook my head. "Truth." I held up three fingers in the Boy Scout oath. "I knew he was different because he'd taken to wearing this turquoise shirt."

Cade looked at the battered garment a little closer. "I've seen a few of them with clothes on, even ball caps sometimes."

"Yeah, I'm not sure why." I studied Turq's internal, floating, tattoos. They weren't sin words anymore. It seemed as if by saving me and my little band, he'd earned himself some new tattoos. Now the swimmy words said things like *Redemption* and *Forgiveness*.

"My mom was lapsed Catholic," Cade said. "She once told me

that sins could be reversed by doing good deeds." He snorted. "I think it was after I wrecked the riding lawn mower that time."

I nodded. "Maybe sorry isn't always enough. Maybe sometimes you have to back it up with something a little more substantial."

Carlos spoke up from the back seat. "You're both right." The shape of a crucifix glowed whitely in the hollow of his throat. It had appeared there after his real one was lost in the firenado. "I was also raised Catholic." He took a long swallow from his water bottle.

We waited for him to say more, but he just rearranged himself on his pillows, always keeping one hand on the shotgun. He seemed religious sometimes, but he didn't subscribe to the Purgatory-theory like the internet professor had said at the beginning of all this.

I asked Cade for his opinion on the idea that the things had dropped through a rip between the dimensions of Earth and Purgatory.

"Purgatory?" He raised one eyebrow.

"Just going by what Dr. D said on his web cast right before the power went off."

Cade looked at me and then at Turq. "What'd he say?"

"He said they were from a parallel dimension called Purgatory, and when the fabric between our two worlds ripped open, these guys fell through. Then they saw their chance to score some new souls. Apparently, you don't get to Heaven with a dirty soul."

I could tell Cade wanted to say something derogatory. He glanced at my face. Probably to see if I was kidding. "But Carlos doesn't think they're from Purgatory?"

"No," I shook my head. "Not at all." An idea began to form in my brain. "He thinks they were dropped from some high-tech space-planes or something."

Carlos laughed from his backseat nest. "Yeah, maybe China and Russia put their heads together and figured out time/space travel and just blasted them at us." He chuckled beneath his breath. "Like they did those brain-damaging sound effects in Cuba and DC. After all, China made the virus, too. Didn't they?"

Cade nodded vigorously. "Now *that* we can agree on. Even if they did just let it get away from the lab on accident. What were they doing concocting it in the first place?"

Turq seemed to be following the conversation intently. His multifaceted, garnet eyes took in everything. He didn't have ears, just small openings where they would normally be on a human.

"I need to teach him to talk."

Cade's face showed confusion.

"Communicate, I mean."

"That's a good idea," Cade agreed. "In fact, we need to start on it right now." He glanced at the dusty shoulder of the road. "The sooner we get him talking, the sooner we can figure out what's really going on."

I didn't think it would be quite that simple, but I did think it would be a start. On the other hand, Dad's Kansas song was in my head again. "Carry On Wayward Son." It seemed to be urging me to keep going.

"Yeah, let's figure a way to get him talking, soon. Right now, though, we're going to head on into town. Toward home." I glanced up and down the wide-open highway. West Texas. Not much around save pumpjacks, cacti, and mesquite. Plenty of room for the cars dotting the lanes, there were lots of them, but very few were wrecked. Mostly they were just stalled out from the paralyzing electromagnetic pulse of energy and the thick slime that had rained down, bringing us the Takers.

"Have *you* seen a lot like him?" Cade asked.

"Yeah," I nodded. "I've seen a bunch of them with clothes on. They're the ones who cleaned up the bodies at the library and around town."

Cade looked at Turq again. "I guess I didn't realize they were different."

It felt awkward. I wondered why he hadn't noticed them if he'd been here in town all along. But I didn't grill him. I just said, "Well, be glad you didn't learn about them the hard way like I did." I held up my crooked elbow.

"Right?! I guess I got lucky when I met Hal downtown. He just drove up in front of J&K Gun Shop to get more ammo for his

Ruger, and I nearly had a heart attack. I'd been stumbling along, wishing for a car."

Hal almost smiled. "Never can have too much ammo. I shot three whole magazines at those monsters." His eye strayed to Turq. "And they just kept getting back up."

"Yeah," I said. "Unless you take their heads off, they keep coming back just like zombies." We both glanced at Turq again. "But if they're only injured, then their pheromones call down the black rain and it covers them—and whoever is near them—and flies them all back to the sky."

"That's right," Cade said. "You gotta be super careful. That black shit nearly got me more than once."

I thought of the thick, dark river that had almost floated our entire car over the buffalo jump. "Yes. But it can also save you. With Turq's help, it saved us all. You just learn to manipulate it." I laughed at myself, again. "I think of it as recycling."

Cade ignored the recycling part. "Saved you, huh?"

I glanced at Turq standing there so patiently, not moving at all. "Yeah, black rain and Turq."

I turned and started back around the front of the Chrysler. Snake followed and leaped into the still open car door. It was time to move on.

CHAPTER FOUR

Jack

Where were y'all headed anyway?" I asked before stepping back into the driver's seat.

Cade shrugged. "Just south, no real destination." He called back to Hal. "Jack's going to Abilene. His aunt owns an abandoned missile silo there—"

I squinted at the sun, one hand on top of the car, the other on top of the open door frame. "It's been abandoned for decades. But it would probably make a good stronghold if needed. At least it's underground. She has a ton of stuff down there, too."

"A ton of food?"

Something in Hal's tone made me think of Kevin's girlfriend telling me she needed my mom's pain pills. "Maybe so. And we can pick up some in stores along the road." I kept my own tone intentionally light.

"Same old Jackie-boy. Always got a plan." Cade moved back around the Challenger, then glanced at Turq as if just remembering he was there. "I don't mind tagging along." He chuckled. "As long as your gray buddy doesn't mind." He inclined his head toward the interior of the Chrysler. "And Carlos and Snake."

I shook my head. "You're welcome to come. The more the merrier, right?"

"Right-o," Cade said.

Hal didn't say anything at all, just closed his door and started the engine. The thing was loud. I felt an itch to look under that hood, maybe take the car for a spin myself.

I slipped the Chrysler into drive, but in the back of my mind, Cade's words echoed. *"Same old Jackie-boy, always got a plan."* Was that right? Did I? Is that why I'd survived? I seriously felt like I'd been doing little more than fumbling around from one catastrophe to the next. Muddling my way through as Mom would've said. Besides, Cade had survived, too. I doubt he'd been planning ahead.

"Carry on Wayward Son," grew softly in my head. *Got it,* I thought. *Time to carry on.* I was thrilled to have Dad's music back again.

My new plan—I guess he was right; I did always have something in mind—was very simple. Food. Shelter. Survival. No more worrying about grades or girls or even college. Well, girls. I still thought about them all the time.

Yep. Same ol' me. *Ain't it cool?* That had been another of our stupid little sayings back in the day.

"Hey!" I yelled across the gap. "I'm going by the high school one last time before heading to Aunt Edna's. You in?"

"Sure," Cade yelled back. "I've been by a couple times, but not inside. Pretty spooky there."

I nodded. "I don't want to, but I have to see if Dad left me any more notes or anything." I didn't say I wanted to see if his body was there. I felt sure he could figure that out on his own.

Hal nodded, and I led the way on into Eden. The streets were deserted except for a few wrecks here and there. The fact that everything looked the same made my skin crawl. Like an episode of the *Twilight Zone* reruns on TV. Episode #5, guy goes back to his hometown after being away for many years and finds everything exactly as he left it. Frozen in time. As if he'd been the key that kept the clock running.

At 4th and Bryan, I had to look away. It was one of the main intersections in town, and there were several cars wrecked there. A couple still had bodies behind the steering wheel or in one of the other seats. They were the lucky ones—beginning to mummify, staring secretly out of their desiccated eyeballs, out of their near-fleshless skulls—they were the ones who had been killed instantly. If they had somehow survived both the crash and the ear-splitting hum of the EMP, the Takers would have caught them, dragged them to the nearest tree or signpost.

My gaze automatically sought the places a body could've been hung up to bleed. The tall pair of oaks at the ranch house museum down the block; the street signs on each corner of the intersection; the old-fashioned scroll-work sign at Deb's Doughnuts.

Only Deb's sign and the two oak trees still held remnants of people—probably because they'd been stabbed onto the branches through the ribs or caught up on a wrought iron curl by some bit of sinew dried to leather by the summer sun.

I muttered a prayer of thanks that it was impossible to recognize any of them. In my rearview mirror, I saw that Carlos had pulled himself up to see the town. He made the sign of the cross as we drove past the gory remains.

My family's home was only a few blocks away. I longed to drive by it, but Cade said it had burned to ash. No use subjecting myself to that. What I left behind the night I met Thad, that was bad enough to carry with me from now on.

A song tickled the inside of my skull but didn't come to the forefront. It bothered me a little. Like a piece of lettuce stuck in my braces when I was twelve. I pulled my belt and holster from under the front seat and the .38 revolver from the console. I felt like an idiot. Just a couple months ago I'd been looking forward to a learner's permit to drive a car, now I drove around armed to the teeth like a gangster. Or a bandit minus the mask.

I turned right on 16th Street, headed toward the high school. It only took a few minutes. Cade and Hal were right behind us. Going around small traffic jams was nothing now that all the people were dead. Medians and sidewalks no longer meant anything. Neither did lanes or driving on the right or one-way street signs. We drove where we needed to drive to get around the wrecks.

The high school sat on one of the overgrown practice fields rife with dandelions and tufts of wild grass. The chain link fencing had been knocked down in several spots, and there were rust-colored stains here and there on the sidewalk. The windows were cracked and broken. The whole place looked sad, a relic of another life.

The faculty parking area was on the backside of the building.

The red Mustang sat right where Dad had parked it that last, long day. Turq and I got out with Snake. I'd stopped short of parking right beside the car even though I'd been tempted. Leaning back inside the Chrysler, I pulled out my old long-sleeved western shirt that would cover my gun and holster. Not sure why I felt the need to cover my weapon, but I'd learned to go with my gut. "Knockin' on Heaven's Door" flared in my head. Guns N' Roses version. From one of the old *Lethal Weapon* movies.

I left the western shirt open over my t-shirt.

Cade climbed out of the gray Challenger. I could see the butt of an automatic sticking out of his waistband. We learned fast. He jerked his thumb at the Mustang. "I checked it last time I was here," he said.

I went over and opened the door anyway.

Nothing.

No new note. No new feeling. Not even the remnant of his aftershave, the one he claimed Mom loved because it made him smell like a lumberjack. I always thought that was a joke. Now, I might never know for certain.

I swiped the cuff of my shirt across my face. I could feel four sets of eyes watching me, five if I counted Snakeman.

"Nope," I backed out of the heated hunk of metal. "Nothing here, just like Cade said." The door screaked when I closed it.

I had to grab onto the frame for a second. I wanted this car. Dad and I had restored it together. It was my link. *If only I could make it run,* I thought. But like all cars not in underground garages, the engine had somehow been ruined by slime. I said as much to Cade.

He stared at the muscle car. "I don't think so," he said. "Not the slime exactly. That EMP, that's what fried the electrical system …" He chuckled, realized he sounded like me for a change. "Me and Hal examine a lot of cars here in town."

Nodding, I had an unbidden image of the two of them yanking bodies out of interesting cars so they could examine them.

Cade cleared his throat. "Anyhow, we have to go around front here." He motioned toward the corner of the building. "The faculty door was locked when we were here the other day. One of those that locks behind you when you go out."

I knew all about those. I'd encountered one at the middle school gym the night I made my escape.

We walked around, peering in windows before coming to the main doors and opening them to go inside. The stale air held only a slight stench of unseen corpses. We'd all encountered worse.

I took a few deep breaths and pressed my t-shirt around my mouth and nose. We should have had face masks or at least bandannas. They were everywhere for the taking.

Cade, Turq, and Snake followed me in. We went through the halls quickly. There were a couple of women in the office—what was left of them—and a man half-in and half-out of the bathroom, the swinging door eternally caught on his lower legs.

We hurried past them all. None of them were my dad. "C'mon," I said. "His music room is this way. I have to be certain he didn't leave me any other messages."

It was near dusk by now, high summer. The school was full of light and shadow, most windows in this area completely gone. Cicadas could be heard in the sycamore trees. I wondered if they were the thirteen-year kind, or the ones that only hatched out after seventeen years underground.

I glanced outside.

The trees were devoid of human remains, and I figured it was because of the Takers I'd seen dressed in clothing on the practice field that day. I'd thought they were trying to kill us like the ones at my middle school but now I knew better. They had cleaned up the outside but not the inside. I wondered about that.

And then I recalled how Snake had torn into several of them like a whirling dervish with teeth, and how the black slime had rained down from a sky hole, covering them before the unclothed ones made their appearance.

Now I put all that out of my mind as we climbed the stairs to Dad's classroom. "Can't Find My Way Home" played through my head. Thankfully the rip had occurred after school, so the building had been nearly empty.

The shadows dappling the walls from the trees outside reminded me of the long hall in my own school that last day. The gold and purple shards of painted glass from those broken windows—our school colors—had been laid out along the tile floor like a crazy stained-glass mosaic.

I didn't expect to find Dad. His Mustang note said he would look for *me*, that he'd survived and would find *me*, but since he never came, and our home was gone, I had to start back at the beginning.

The school was eerie, the perfect high school for a ghost town.

Hal and Carlos had stayed with the vehicles. Carlos could only walk a few steps at a time, but he had his shotgun. And I made certain to bring the car key with me since I'd seen Hal eyeing our trunk. He probably wondered what kind of food we had. The guy reminded me of a stray—always hungry.

Besides, I'd learned my lesson about trusting people. Thad had deserted me once. I didn't plan on ever allowing that to happen again.

None of us spoke as we crested the stairs. An *EDEN EAGLES* banner hung crookedly from the high ceiling. A gust of wind from a missing window sucked it into movement as we walked underneath.

I gathered my courage and trudged on. I wanted to ask Cade about other residents of Eden. Surely there were other people who'd been downstairs in basements, in cellars, even out of town when the rip occurred. Wouldn't they have come to see about their loved ones? This place felt like an unvisited tomb.

"Man," Cade said, as if reading my thoughts. "It seems like no one has been here besides me and Hal."

"Have y'all seen *any* other survivors?"

"Not really. If there are any, they must be hiding, you know."

I did know.

I thought back to that first awful day. The horrific freight-train noise, the silvery slime coating and slipping down inside *everything*. The Takers that rose from slick puddles, the sin words moving beneath the surface of their gray, translucent skin ...

I shuddered and pushed those memories aside.

Man up, Jack, I told myself, pretending it was Dad's voice. Carry on! The song swelled, and I did carry on, as always, even convincing myself the terrible memories were getting easier to bear, harder to recall, because I hadn't seen or heard any new killings since we'd been back.

I felt Cade's stare. Had I said something out loud? I took a deep breath through my shirt and continued through the halls.

We didn't talk. It felt like a tomb, so we treated it that way, stepping easy, making as little noise as possible. It was only after we got to Dad's room with its guitars strewn about—one still upright on its stand—that Cade let out an exclamation.

"Damn. This makes it real, doesn't it? Like your dad should pop up from behind that desk with a stack of music in his hand—"

"Yeah." I clenched my teeth. "It sure does." I moved through the space last occupied by my father as if walking through saltwater. I couldn't feel a thing, and yet I stayed upright and moving. "Help me look for a note or anything, then we'll go." I tried to ignore the song playing in my mind even though it was one of Dad's favorites.

His original note, in the driver's seat of the Mustang the day after the world caved in, said he'd survived because he'd been down in the high school's basement, just like Cade and I were at Eden Middle School across town.

"I'm going down to check out the basement," I said. I didn't want to. Not at all. With no electricity it would be as dark as Great-Gran's old outhouse—probably just as smelly, too. But it had to be done. If I didn't go down and check it out, after Dad's note said that's where he'd been, I'd regret it for the rest of my life. However long or short that might be.

One strange thought kept nibbling at me, though. Could we really be the only ones left in all of Eden—aside from Hal? There had to be others who'd hidden in cellars and basements, safe from the rip. There *had* to be.

But where were they? The only others I'd encountered had been the ones traveling with Thad the night they came to my house. When he found me later—after I had run off into the night with my dog like a little kid—he said they had made him leave for getting drunk. Later, I overheard him tell Carlos there had been a fire. Now, I didn't know what to believe.

All I remembered was Kevin bleeding out on the dining room table, and Marla, his girlfriend, yelling that she would kill me for causing Kevin to get shot.

Every one of those recollections slipped through my head as we made our way down to the basement. I pulled out my trusty Dynamo flashlight and cranked the handle, but Turq took it from me. He literally stepped in front of me and took the flashlight from my hand.

I saw Cade reach toward the waistband of his pants and then Snake was in front of him, growling.

"Turq?" I left his name hanging in the air in the form of a question mainly because that's how we'd been communicating, through one-word sentences and hand gestures.

"Problem?" I asked.

Turq took the light, pointed it toward the floor, then proceeded down the stairs in front of me. Snake looked at him and then at me, and then at Cade. I could tell he wanted to follow Turq, but for some reason he didn't seem to want Cade behind us.

I went with their instincts. "After you," I said to my best bud.

Cade moved his hand away from his waistband and followed Turq down the semi-lighted steps. Snake fell in beside me, and we brought up the rear.

But it was all for naught.

I couldn't even find the place where the musical instruments would have been stored. I assumed that's why Dad would've been down there. Instead, we found ourselves in the boys' locker room. It was lined with row upon row of gray metal lockers, a few hanging open to display their meager contents of practice uniforms and gym socks.

The entire place appeared empty. Until we turned the corner into the sink and shower area and three somewhat mummified bodies caught my attention. Two had been hung up on the shower heads, one pierced through the ribcage, while the second lay across the floor, the shower head having broken, allowing the body to fall. Ropes of flattened intestines were strewn about the tiled area like dark, ancient licorice.

But it was the third body that made us all gasp. That one was in pieces. It didn't look like any of the other mutilations I'd seen from the Takers.

This one had been pulled limb from limb. The head and spine sprawled across the line of white porcelain sinks, the arms and legs ripped off and scattered to the four corners. For once, there were no signs of cannibalism. The body had simply been torn apart.

I thought back to the day Turq wrested me from the Taker who had broken my arm. *This is what I would have looked like if Turq hadn't won that battle.* I rubbed my elbow and forearm.

Turq's flashlight played across the scene erratically. The jerky light and shadow made me queasy, but with his multi-faceted eyes, the Taker probably saw things much differently than we did. When he reached down and began to gather up the body parts, I was immediately reminded of how the ones I called The Cleanup Crew had gathered up the bodies in the library and the park, the day after the rip.

I wanted to tell him to stop.

I wanted to be a good person and join him in a show of respect for the dead.

I wanted to be a *man.* Death was death, nothing to be afraid of.

But I was none of those things. I was just a kid. I took the flashlight from his grasp and stood back as he picked up all three sets of remains and stacked them neatly against the far wall, one on top of the other, piece by morbid piece. It gave me plenty of opportunity to make certain my dad's face was not among them.

A slight sound of movement made me look around at Cade. His mouth hung open in an O of surprise, and his eyes were turned toward the stairs. It was obvious neither of us had made that sound.

In unspoken agreement, we tiptoed back. I couldn't help wondering if Dad had been down here before or after the poor guys in the shower—

"What *was* that?" Cade whispered.

I stopped directly behind him. "Did you hear it agai—"

"Shhh!" He threw up his hand.

And then we all heard it again. Except Snake, of course. But maybe he smelled it or sensed it because suddenly, he took off like a shot.

CHAPTER FIVE

Faith

I took off, too, still holding the flashlight, tearing after him behind the rows of freestanding lockers.

Bam, bam, bam, open locker doors crashed against their metal frames as something banged into them in its haste to get away.

Snake remained strangely silent except for the sound of his toenails. He didn't bark or even growl. As a result, it was easy to hear the stealthy sound of someone's feet slapping the concrete floor.

I thought of the shoeless, toeless Takers, but their feet made more of a shushing sound. Not a sound like this.

Trying to keep up with Snake, I slung myself around a corner, wishing I'd brought the shotgun instead of the pistol.

"Bro," Cade said when he saw me holding the gun down beside my thigh.

I handed him the flashlight and shushed him with a finger to my lips. Then I motioned toward the opposite dark corner where I could see the outline of Snake standing guard in front of a stack of boxes. His taut muscular body resembled a statue carved in old marble. I knew I could walk up and put my hand on his back, feel him quiver, but would that spur him to attack?

Instinct took over accompanied by a few words from Kansas. *I hear ya Dad. I hear ya.*

"C'mon out," I said. "We all know you're there."

Cade played the flashlight across the flat surface of the boxes. When the light hit it just right, I glimpsed a slight silhouette crouched behind the stack. "We won't hurt you," I said in a softer tone.

No response.

Snake whined.

"Don't worry," I called out, a little louder. "This is just my dog, Snake. He's on guard. He's deaf. He can't hear you, but he can see you there." I laughed under my breath. Didn't mean to but it just slipped out. "We can all see you. Might as well come on out in the open. I swear, we're friendly."

The person pushed a couple boxes aside, and a bare foot caught a corner of the light.

Then Turq stepped up beside me.

I'd forgotten all about him.

The movement stopped as the person froze.

"It's okay!" I called. "Look, he's with us. Even the dog knows it's okay." I crossed the few steps, stuffing the gun back into the leather holster on my belt. I held out my empty palms. "See, it's okay. We're all friends." When I said that, I had a sudden image of the night of Marla and Kevin. I'd thought *we* were all friends, too, at first. But that was then—this is now. In for a penny, in for a pound, as my Gran always said.

Kansas continued urging me to carry on. *Okay, okay,* I thought, as I waited for the person to come out, but Snake gave up on all that waiting. He simply strolled into the shadow cast by the cardboard tower.

"Hey," a female voice whispered.

And that's when I knew it would be all right.

I stepped into the shadow and leaned down to touch Snake's head to get his attention.

When I straightened, a startled girl about my own age peered up at me. Her eyes were nearly invisible behind smudged and cracked glasses, but I could tell she was scared. Her body had made itself as small as possible in the cardboard trap.

I held out my other hand. "Jack Lewis," I said. "This is ol' Snake, the best dog in the world."

She smiled, and life took on new meaning.

"Faith," she said. "Faith Adams."

She put her hand in mine, and I pulled her gently into the open.

Cade shined the light at her face, and she threw her other hand up like a vampire shunning the sun.

He laughed and lowered the Dynamo. "Sorry."

"It's alright," she said, blinking.

I became aware for the first time how long my hair had grown; how filthy it must be. What I might smell like. Lumberjack? Probably not.

Snake pushed his head against the girl's leg, and I saw her hand go to the spot between his ears, and then it found its way down his bull neck until it landed on his collar. Her fingers curled under it the same way mine always did when I needed him to stay with me.

He leaned into her blue-jeaned thigh.

I didn't know if I'd gained a friend or lost one. "He sure likes you." I smiled to show her it was fine by me.

Faith smiled back. "Thank God."

Snake gazed up at her with adoration in his brown marble eyes. I wondered if he could feel the vibrations of her voice. Somehow, he seemed to know when she spoke. He switched his gaze to me and leaned into her a little harder.

I patted his back.

Cade stepped up and held out his hand. They introduced themselves to each other, but her eyes did not meet his. I realized I was watching her every move.

"And this is Turq, short for turquoise because well, you see—" I pointed to his filthy shirt. My mind was temporarily overcome with the memory of the pure turquoise haze that had led me to the edge of the buffalo jump back in New Mexico.

Cade's voice invaded my recollections. He was questioning Faith. Trying to find out where she had come from. "Did you go to school here?"

The girl's eyes never left Turq's face, but she shook her head slightly. "No." She looked up at me. "But when I arrived, Eden seemed like a good place to be." She closed her lips, then changed her mind and continued. "I was looking for some water. I'm kind of embarrassed, but I wanted a shower. I thought this might be like my school, back home. In Lewiston." She glanced around. "I've been in here for a while. Looking for shoes, too."

I motioned for Snake to come. He followed, and she was forced to come, too. "Lewiston, Texas?" I asked.

She walked with her fingers still curled under Snake's collar. He was tall from the boxer part of his mix, and she was on the short side, what my mom would have called, petite.

"Yes. It's only a couple hours from here. I, um. You know. Thought Eden sounded pretty cool."

That struck me as odd. "How'd you hear about it? I mean, we grew up here, Cade and me." I grinned. "And old Snakeman." I'd tell her that story later if she seemed interested. Right now, I wanted to know more about her. I think I wanted to know everything about her. Something about the way she looked up, with her head tilted down, made me think of Dee, the first girl I'd ever fallen for. She'd been petite, too.

A funny thought crossed my mind, I should be Jack Lewis from Lewiston, and she should be Faith Adams from Eden. Our names seemed jumbled.

We didn't talk anymore. Just concentrated on not falling up the stairs in the dim light of the flashlight. At the top, she hesitated. Who could blame her? We were a hell of a ragtag band. But it was only a few steps across the gritty field house floor to the double doors.

Always the gentleman, I opened one, and held it. "Those are our vehicles." I pointed across the parking lot.

Carlos almost fell out of the open car door when he saw us walk out with Faith.

She seemed just as awed. "You have *wheels*?" The wonder in her voice painted a picture of a Christmas morning, and her, coming down imaginary stairs in a short pink robe. *Damn, Jack, get it together, you've seen girls before.*

Yeah, I told my inner self, *but not since the rip. And not one with strawberry blonde hair.*

She sat down on the sidewalk and pulled on a pair of scruffy

Skechers. "I was trying on shoes in the locker room when I heard y'all come in." She held up her right foot. "These have had it."

Cade and I looked at each other. It had been downright spooky inside the empty school, and this wisp of a girl had been down there, in the dark, trying on shoes? We shrugged at each other. "I guess you didn't find any that fit?"

She laughed. "Nope. I think I was on the boys' side. I'm going to have to hit the mall, or Wally World if Eden doesn't have a mall."

"Wally World it is, then," I said. "But were you really staying in there? I mean the odor …"

Faith pulled a jar of Vick's Vapo-Rub out of her backpack. "I just put a smear of this under my nose." She smiled. "It felt good here. Sometimes I sleep in an empty house, but last night I slept upstairs in the music room. It wasn't too bad in there. The teacher had a closet with some sweaters and jackets hanging in it." She looked at the ground. "They made kind of a nice bed."

My legs almost buckled. "That's my dad's room," I said. "He was the music teacher."

"Woodstock," the old Crosby, Stills, Nash & Young song about children of God walking along the road, rose steadily in my head. "A child of God, going back to the Garden," I murmured.

"Yes." Faith said. "I love that song. Especially the part about how we're all made of stardust."

"And golden." I had to stop my hand from going to her hair, to touch it in the bright and slanting summer light.

She pulled my dad's favorite cardigan out of her backpack and pushed it under my elbow. "I'm sorry," she said. "I guess this might belong to your dad."

I took the sweater and allowed the faint scent of my father to drift into my nostrils. Somehow, it did not smell like death or lumberjacks. There was a moth-eaten hole in one sleeve. Mom would have stuffed it in the rag bag if she'd seen how weathered it had become. I raised my eyes to Faith's. "You keep it." I gave it back to her. "He'd want you to have it, I think."

She smiled, rolled it up, stuffed it back into her pack. Then she stood, ratty shoes tied, ready to go. "Did your dad survive?" Her voice was timid. "I mean, I saw boxes of stuff packed up, like he was moving things downstairs to storage or something."

I wanted to hug her for asking. "He did survive," I said. "Even left me a note in his car outside. But I haven't found him yet. We were overrun with Takers."

She nodded. Satisfied with my answer.

After making another set of introductions to Carlos and Hal, Faith decided to ride with us. I figured it was because of her connection to Snakeman. It had nothing to do with me. I tried to keep that in mind. The bad thing was that Cade nearly *begged* her to ride with them.

"We've got a whole unused back seat," he said. "Lots more room than Jackie-boy."

I caught myself frowning at the nickname. "I think she just feels safer with old Snakeman," I said. "We'll make room, no problem."

"He can hop in with us, too," Cade continued. "Give y'all a chance to stretch out a little." His grin was just like that day in the gym when he told me how he'd left me something in the basement. At the time he'd simply been trying to embarrass me with a porn site on his laptop, but of course it turned out to be the very thing that saved my life. Saved both our lives, come to think of it. Saved by porn. Gee, He does work in mysterious ways.

Still, I didn't like Cade's grin, I didn't like it then and I didn't like it now. Up until this point, I'd always made allowances for his bullyish-teasing, but not anymore. Shit got real as we used to say back in the day. Shit just got real.

"I don't think the Snake would care for the Dodge," I said. "Anyhow, we aren't going far." I glanced at the horizon. "Sun will be going down soon. We can find a place to hole up, build a campfire and roast these hotdogs." We'd found a generator-run freezer the day before at an awesome farmhouse near Lubbock. We couldn't wait to eat what we had taken.

The look on Hal's face was so transparent it was comical. I expected him to start drooling at any moment.

"Man!" Cade said. "The last time I had a hotdog was that cookout at your house, remember?"

"I remember," I said. But it was a painful memory now. Cade had eaten four charred dogs that day. Dad had laughed when Cade fell back on the lawn, pretending to be too stuffed to move.

It had been a normal weekend, a couple weeks before the rip, not too hot yet, but getting there. High, white, kid-drawn clouds in a pale-blue sky. Dad had the grill heated and ready to sizzle when the dogs and burgers hit it, and then a wasp had appeared like a tiny kamikaze. Dad finally swatted it with his spatula, and we'd all joked about adding a little extra protein to Mom's veggie burger.

There would never be days like that again. The old adage was true—you never knew what you had until it was gone. Blind Faith tuned up softly. "Can't Find My Way Home." Geez. I am here, and it's still not home. Not anymore.

Yet, it always would be. All my memories lived here.

I wanted to ask Cade if he missed our lives as much as I did, after all, he was the only human on earth—that I knew of—who shared at least some of my childhood. No matter what, we would always have that connection.

But I didn't ask him. We were too busy making room for Faith.

CHAPTER SIX

Jack

Carlos made room in the back. I know it hurt him to sit upright, especially with Snake in the middle of the big bench seat, but Faith didn't take up much space, and Snake was on his best behavior. I didn't see him trample her even once. And with her on the driver's side behind me, it was easy—kind of too easy—to glance in my rearview and see how she was doing.

Mostly she sat, looking out the window or resting her hand on Snake's broad back, but every so often—when she thought no one was looking—I caught her studying Turq and Carlos.

Cade and Hal were behind us, Hal still in the driver's seat.

I wondered if Cade ever drove. It had been the rite-of-passage we'd both been talking about for the last year or two. But for me, it had come and gone in the blink of an eye. In the blink of necessity's eye, that is. Necessity, the mother of invention.

An old, old Frank Zappa tune flitted across my brain, and I almost laughed out loud. The name of his band, way back in the decade of the sixties, was The Mothers of Invention. I could picture the crazy album covers in my dad's collection.

But I had never been a fan of his music. It was too weird for me. I mean "Don't Eat the Yellow Snow?" Seriously?

Dad thought that was so funny. He always said he'd been born a couple decades too late, and that's why he collected all the old rock and roll. I'd tried to picture my school-music-teacher dad as a hippie at Woodstock, high on weed, or LSD, but it wouldn't fly.

I think he just liked Frank Zappa's music because it was complex and unusual.

On the other hand, Sheryl Crow had also been a school music teacher, and she'd had a big hit with "If it Makes You Happy," which Mom had said was about crystal meth. People are strange—another of Dad's sayings, which I think he stole from a Doors' song.

I consciously turned off the musical past and began to watch for one of Eden's two motels. One was The Antlers Motel, the other was The Yucca. Both motels were located on Hwy 80 south of town. They were small and had been around since the beginning of time. I figured we could sleep in the rooms and cook on the grills out front. I made it a point to always carry a bag of Match Light charcoal in the trunk.

I guess Cade knew what I had in mind. He didn't seem at all surprised when I pulled into the near empty parking lot at The Yucca and stepped out. He and Hal pulled in beside us.

"Good idea," he said. "Better than sleeping on the ground or in the car."

I nodded. "It just occurred to me as we were driving. I've gotten used to avoiding towns and buildings, but Eden seems completely empty, doesn't it?"

"Yeah, Hal and I watched the monsters leave over a month ago. You know a big group of them cleaned up a lot of the bodies just like Turq did back there in the locker room."

"I know. It blew my mind when they did it at the library where Mom, you know …" I let that thought trail away and then continued, "They cleaned up the park, too."

Cade looked toward Turq. "Hal and I, we've been staying in my house, down in my dad's man cave. Only coming up for food and water." He shook his head. "But we heard the sound of them marching. You know that sound?"

I nodded. That *shushing* sound.

"We literally watched them leave. Don't get me wrong. I think there's still a bunch around, hiding somewhere, but we're careful." He leaned against the car. "We've been on the search for a place with a generator so we can be more comfortable." He let his gaze wander to the distant horizon. "Lots of little rural ranches out there. I'll bet some of them have generators that run on propane or something."

"Yeah," I said. "Like the one we found near Lubbock. I still can't believe that genny was still running. Makes me think someone was staying there. Which reminds me—are you and Hal really the only people left in Eden?"

He shrugged. "Far as I know. But I haven't searched every house. Basements are few and far between out here. Not like in Indiana and those northern states where my dad grew up. He said every house had a basement there."

I thought about that. "You're right. Probably a lot more people survived up there. But even here, the hospital has a basement, the courthouse has one, and I thought almost every school and church had them. Not to mention men like your dad who built his own home with a basement."

"Geez, Einstein, slow down. I never even thought about churches and shit." He made a show of pretending to take a toke. "Hal helped Beau out from time to time. You know, delivering the good stuff? I guess you could say we got lucky twice." He laughed. "Actually, Hal got lucky three times. When the rip happened, he was in a holding cell down in the courthouse basement. All the staff had gone home for the weekend except for one jailer and a dispatcher upstairs. He said she didn't make it, so after a little bit, the jailer took pity on him and the car burglar next to him and unlocked their cells. He said they all scattered to the wind—the jailer included."

"I wonder what became of them?"

"Hal said they didn't get very far. Both got caught trying to find a car that would start. He watched them, and then hid until the monsters marched on. The next day he got the Challenger and found me—"

"Dope," Faith said. "Figures." She dropped the level of her voice. "So, he's a dealer?"

I couldn't believe she was so bold. Or was it naïve?

"Just weed," Cade said. The question didn't seem to bother him. "Soon as Hal saw what was happening, he went back to get his dope out of the evidence room. He carried it in a Police duffel bag all the way to Beau's house to get the Challenger." He laughed happily. "Never had it so good. Couldn't have made it through these last few weeks without the ganja."

"Well, that explains why y'all are still in Eden even though it's a ghost town. No desire to leave, huh?"

His smile faltered. "Everything's different now." His mellow voice made me think he and Hal must've imbibed in a little ganja on the ride over. "Seems like the monsters cleaned up the town and then just left." He shook his head, eyes on the edge of unfocussed. "Almost like the bad guys came in followed by the good guys."

"Yeah," I agreed. "They cleaned up a lot of the mess all right." The bodies in the locker room shower appeared in my thoughts. They hadn't been cleaned up.

I wanted to ask Cade's opinion about that. He'd seen them, too. But he seemed ready to doze off. Instead, I said, "What will you and Hal do when the food runs out?"

Cade blinked slowly. "Then we'll move on."

I couldn't believe this was my old hyperactive buddy, the one who'd jumped off the roof and broke his arm, the one who couldn't sit still in class to save his life. Maybe he was coping the only way he knew how. Or maybe he should've had weed all along. That idea almost made me laugh.

But the bigger question remained. Where *were* the Takers? Where had they gone? We'd destroyed hundreds of them in New Mexico, at the buffalo jump, but if this had happened all over the world—and I was certain it had since no one had come to our rescue, and all forms of communication were still kaput—then where were the others? Where was the rest of the *world?*

Cade said, "Anyhow, we'll find a generator, grow a few veggies. Some more weed—we've been saving seeds—and Hal said he thinks the deer will come back, so we can hunt."

"I don't know. I haven't seen a deer, but I have seen rabbits and gophers. They live underground, so it makes sense they would survive. Guess we'll have to learn to hunt *them* if we want fresh meat."

I tried an idea in my mind before I spoke aloud, something my mom had always tried to train me to do—think before you speak. Finally, I said, "I wonder if Aunt Edna has a generator at the silo? She always said it would make the perfect bunker." I pictured the site in my head, but I couldn't recall ever seeing a generator.

Faith stood beside the Chrysler, Snake not far away. "Silo?"

I filled her in on the abandoned ICBM missile silo belonging to my aunt. "She's got over a hundred acres," I said. "And the silo is smack dab in the middle of it."

"Wow," Faith pulled a pack of cigarettes from her backpack. "I've actually seen those places online. One guy turned his into a fancy scuba diving thing, didn't he?"

"Yep." I couldn't believe she knew about them. Or that she was about to smoke a cigarette after questioning Cade's smoking habit. But I didn't push it. We all cope somehow. "Anyhow," I continued, "another dude made his silo into a really awesome recording studio." I thought of others I'd read about, but Turq had stepped out of the car and started to wander. I didn't want him to go too far without me. We'd made it a habit to check everything before we settled down each night. "But don't get your hopes up. My aunt's place is nothing like those. It's almost exactly like it was when the government sold it. Just a big empty hole in the ground."

Faith's eyes widened.

"It's the control center next door where she stores her stuff. That's where the people lived and worked. It still has office cubicles, a few desks and chairs, and it's two stories deep, right next to where the missile used to be."

Smoke hung around Faith's head like a halo. She seemed in awe that such a place existed. I excused myself and ran to catch up with Turq.

Faith came with me. "How do you get inside? I just can't imagine it. Are we really going there?" She took another drag on the cigarette. I liked the way she included herself in our plans.

"Yeah, I want to go see about her since I haven't found my dad. The note he left said he had made it out alive and that he would look for me, but then all hell broke loose, and the town was overrun. Cade says my entire house burned to the ground, so I'm sure he isn't there." I stopped talking, thinking about Thad and the women he'd left at my house. "Anyhow, I'm hoping my dad and Aunt Edna are holed up at her place. At the silo."

Snake wedged his head in between us. I hadn't even realized how close we were walking. Just then, Cade slung his arm around my other shoulder. "Damn, Jackie, I still can't believe we found each other."

"Yeah, me either." I elbowed him in the gut. "Doesn't mean you can paw me, though, pervert." I shoved him away, laughing like we used to do.

He tackled me and might've taken me to the ground, but Snake growled in a show of toothy uncertainty. I think he knew we were only playing around, but I also think he was warning Cade not to take it too far.

"Aww, hell now, buddy," Cade held his hand out to Snake. "We're old friends, Jackie, and me. Surely you remember all the times I walked past you chained up in that old man's yard, on my way to Jack's place."

"What's he mean?" Faith asked. "I thought Snake was your dog." She looked at me for clarification.

"He is now. But only because I found him half-way out from under a neighbor's house on my street. The old guy kept him chained up all the time since he's deaf."

Faith looked at the dog with an odd expression. "If he's deaf, I wonder how he found me in the locker room? I thought he heard me."

I shrugged. "I guess it's like they say—when one sense is gone, the others grow sharper to make up for it."

She laughed out loud. "Or maybe it's because I haven't bathed in a week or two." She ducked her head to the side, pretending to sniff her armpits.

I fell even more in love with her in that instant. Although, truthfully, I think I loved her the moment she stepped out from behind the boxes with her hand on Snake's head. "Speaking of bathing, wait till you see the sun-shower I picked up at Academy Sports the other day. It's just a plastic bag you fill with water and hang in a tree. Once the sun heats up the water, you stand under it, release the valve, and voila! Instant shower."

Cade leered at her. "And I'll be glad to help you with that, if you want."

A slight frown crossed her face. "Thanks, anyhow. I think I can manage."

I thought of her out in the open beneath a tree, naked, and my physical response was immediate. *Damn. That wouldn't work at all.* "I'll make an outdoor shower," I muttered. "We'll get the water good and warm and then put a blanket-tent around it."

Both of my companions went silent. Embarrassed, I went on, "Well, you know. For a little privacy. We haven't really had to worry about that with just Carlos and me." I glanced around for Turq again. "And the Turquoise One. He doesn't care about privacy one way or the other."

Cade gazed at Turq. "Why don't you call *him* a Taker, Jackie?"

I thought about it for a second. "Because he doesn't take. Not anymore. If anything, he does just the opposite. He gives."

We watched him disappear into the office of the motel. In a moment he came back out and held up his thumb.

"All clear," I said, returning his thumbs up.

Cade's mouth fell open.

"Be right back," I told Faith. I ran to the office and yanked all the keys off the old-fashioned peg board behind the desk. Each one was affixed to a green plastic fob. No digital scan cards here, no sir.

Turq had moved on to the first room on the left-side wing. I followed him and unlocked the door. Then we checked the other rooms, one by one, before moving on to the right-side wing. "After we get all the rooms checked, we can start the grill."

Cade made a goofy face and rubbed his palm in circles on his belly.

We found no bodies until we went around back. It must've been a light day at The Yucca. There were five bodies on the dry grass out back, but they hadn't been mauled or hung up in the pecan tree out front to bleed like they would have if they'd been taken alive. "I guess they ran outside to see what was causing all the noise," I said. "That's probably what killed them."

"Oh, poor things." Faith exhaled the last of her smoke. "I'll bet that old man and woman were the owners, and those other guys were customers." She glanced up at me. "I saw two cars in the front lot."

I nodded. "Makes sense to me."

"Well," Cade's tone was darkly gleeful. "Looks like there's plenty of vacancies. At least we'll each get our own room tonight."

It sounded wrong to stand there, laughing, looking at the remains of the owners and their guests, but I didn't say anything. I was used to Cade's sick humor.

I turned back just as Turq rounded the corner with the bag of charcoal in his hand. "I guess someone is ready to grill, and he doesn't even eat—"

"They rip people apart and eat *them*." Faith's mouth twisted to one side in a brief grimace. "It's hard to get used to seeing this one so ..." she pushed her chin at Turq. "Like this."

"I know." I looked at my gray friend. "But if you'd been there when he pulled me away from the one trying to stab me onto a tree branch—and if you'd seen how he took the other Taker down with an elbow to the head—it would be a lot easier to understand. A lot easier to accept."

She seemed in deep thought as we traipsed back toward the parking lot where the rusty iron grills were stuck, leaning this way and that, on square cement pads in front of each outward-facing door. "I think I might start calling you The Monster Whisperer," Faith said, under her breath, and then she glanced down at Snake. "Monster whisperer, dog whisperer, what next? What else can you do, Jack Lewis?"

My face grew warm, but it could've been from the heat of the late afternoon. "I hope I'm a girl whisperer, too."

She grinned and shaded her eyes with one hand as she looked up at me against the last rays of the summer sun. "Yeah," she said. "I think you are."

My heart did a funny little jig, and I puffed out my chest like one of Gran's old roosters. *Girl whisperer.* I liked that image. I really did.

CHAPTER SEVEN

The Yucca

Poor Carlos! When we finished checking all the rooms and went back to the parking lot, he lay prostrate in the backseat of the Chrysler with the doors open and his head on a pillow.

"C'mon, buddy." I helped him to his feet outside the car. "Let's get you out of the heat. Plenty of beds inside where you can really stretch out."

He held onto my arm as we made our slow way across the strip of brown grass to the sidewalk that ran the length of each wing. A large pecan tree stood at the corner of the office.

"Can I help?" Faith asked.

"Will you bring more pillows?" I glanced back at the car. "And some water from the trunk. There's a button on the lower left dash to open it."

Faith hurried toward the car. When she saw Turq set the charcoal down and start toward her, she stopped and looked back at me uncertainly. But he didn't pay her any mind. Instead, he came straight to me and slid one hand under Carlos' knees and one behind his back. He picked our friend up as if he were a groom about to carry his bride over the threshold.

We took him in the first room. "How about some free HBO?" I joked. "Or free internet."

"You're killing me, Jack," Carlos moaned. "I'll settle for a wet washcloth to put on my face—"

Faith stepped into the room. "Coming right up." She handed

me the pillows from the car, then ran to the bathroom, grabbed a washcloth, and poured part of a bottle of water on it over the sink. Then she brought it straight to Carlos and laid it across his forehead the same way my mom always did when I had a fever. "It's been a long day, hasn't it?"

That tiny gesture made me long to tell her about *finding* my mom in the library that day. I also wanted to know about her parents. For the first time, an old Beatles song bloomed in my brain.

"Something" wasn't one of Dad's songs. I think it was Mom's. She used to sway-dance around the kitchen when it came up on the playlist. The words talked about the way a woman moved and how it made the guy fall in love with her.

"I think he wrote it for the woman he loved," Mom said once, hugging a dishtowel to her chest. She was all about the Beatles and Simon and Garfunkel and Neil Diamond—

"Hey," I said out of the blue. "Do you like classic rock?"

Faith laughed at the odd question. "Sure, why?"

"Oh," I just wondered. "You knew that Crosby, Stills, Nash & Young tune, plus, you know, it's one of my things."

I felt the weight of Turq's many-faceted eyes, and I turned to see what the problem was, but he wasn't looking at me. He was looking at Carlos splayed out on the bedspread, cool cloth on his forehead, eyes closed, face nearly the same shade as his own skin.

He turned toward me ever so slightly and I saw one of his blue-black words float to the surface. Beneath his skin, the word *BUTTERFLY* flitted across his scalp and was gone.

I thought the word must be referring to Faith. She was the most beautiful human we'd encountered since this whole thing began. I did not let my mind slip down the twisty hall back toward Dee hanging through the basketball goal in the gym, but I did let it acknowledge the old Beatles song on its continuous loop in my head.

Faith whirled around as a shadow darkened the doorway, and I realized, too late, how we'd trapped ourselves in this tiny room.

My eye immediately found the window latch and at the same time, a heavy lamp to break the glass if the latch wouldn't open.

But it was only Cade. "Bro, we got the fire going."

Faith and I exhaled at the same time. Even Turq relaxed. He'd taken a half-step toward the door, ready to defend us all. Snake stayed beside Carlos. I didn't realize he had jumped up on the bed with him.

"Man, you startled us."

Cade laughed. I got the feeling he might have done it on purpose.

"Sorry about that." His eyes flicked to Faith again, just for an instant, almost like the word butterfly had flickered across Turq's scalp.

"C'mon," I said. "Let's go grill some hotdogs." Snake glanced at me over his doggy shoulder. "It's okay, Snakeman," I gave him a downward wave. "You can stay with Carlos."

He folded his heavy body into the space next to Carlos and laid his square snout on his friend's arm.

"He is really something, isn't he?" Faith smoothed her strawberry hair behind her shoulder and adjusted her cracked glasses.

I nodded. "He's kind of amazing."

Carlos opened one eye. "Thanks, guys. Ummm, make me a hot dog? With mustard?"

I laughed. "You got it."

The burned man gave a little salute, then let his hand fall to Snake's back. The dog sighed and settled in a little closer.

While I got the food from the ice chests, Hal and Cade moved a couple of wooden picnic tables together. Faith and Turq brought straight-backed desk chairs from some of the rooms.

"Just a nice little cookout," Cade said.

Turq looked at him as if he were speaking Klingon.

I held up the packaged hot dogs and cheese. Water dripped from the plastic. "That's about the last of our ice unless we make our way north and set up camp beside a frozen river." I said it in jest, but at the same time, it *was* a thought.

Until now, we'd been very lucky to find packaged foods, and even ice. After the firenado that burned Carlos along with so many of the Takers, we had driven back to Texas, taking our time, hitting every decent looking place along the way. We found so much food we couldn't even pack it all in the car.

Now, I kicked myself. Why hadn't we hooked up a trailer and packed it full of boxed and canned foods? Even dry goods weren't going to last forever in the closed and uncooled grocery stores. The Takers had done some damage along the way, but not that much. Mostly they just killed. The main damage to the grocery stores and other enclosed places was the fact that there were quite a few dead bodies decaying inside and it was summer. Plus, the mice and rats. They lived underground, and they would multiply. No doubt about it.

The smaller towns were better. At least some of the grocery stores weren't completely empty. And every now and then we would find actual greenhouses full of tomatoes and beans, cucumbers, and carrots. Some were overgrown, some sad and dry, and many eaten down to the roots by small, burrowing, animals; but it's true what they say, beggars can't be choosers.

Yes. Small, rural, towns were much better, safer.

One more reason to avoid large cities.

"Hey, y'all, I've got a question—where do you think the Takers are now?" I looked at Hal and Cade, and at Faith.

Cade stuck his first hot dog on a stick and poked it into the fire. I'd simply laid a few on the grill, but his way worked, too.

I opened a package of buns and checked for mold. The ones on top were okay, but the bottom row was iffy. I didn't mention it, just got out another bag and checked them, too.

"Hal and I watched a bunch of them march out after cleaning up the bodies."

I knew that already, but I wanted to hear more about it. And to find out what Faith might know, or think.

"Yeah," Hal said. "But the bad ones had already left the day before."

I wanted to hear more, but where was this old hymn coming from in my head? I didn't even know that song ... something about being close to Heaven. I shook my head to try and clear it.

"Still think it was just another wave," Carlos called from inside his room.

I laughed and slapped his hotdog in a bun, slathered it with mustard, carried it to him. "You feel like sitting outside with us?"

He was propped up against the headboard. The light had grown dim, the room full of sepia shadows. Outside the window, orange and pink streaked the upper sky deepening to thick yellow at the horizon.

"Yeah," he said. "Wish I had one of those lounge chairs."

"I'll look around. But in the meantime, how about I throw a couple mattresses out there?"

His eyes lit up. "It's a lot of trouble."

I ignored that and went to the next room, wrestled the heavy mattress off the bed and dragged it outside. Turq saw me and before I knew it, he and Faith had two more dragged up. "Just stack them up for Carlos. One on bottom and two more for him to lean back against."

Cade and Hal watched from the sidelines. I noticed the bag of chips passed back and forth between them without pause. In a moment, Cade wadded the empty bag and tossed it on the ground.

A rustling noise caught my attention, and I looked toward the bag expecting to see it uncrumpling the way those shiny bags will do. Instead, I caught another whiff of song—yes, it now had an odor—and a few more words about being closer to heaven, then a deep voice said, "Smells good."

I yanked my pistol free of its holster as the other part of my brain automatically calculated how many steps it would take to get to the Chrysler for the shotgun. It was much easier to shoot a Taker with a shotgun than a .38 but either one was better than nothing.

"Hold on, son," the voice said, and I swear I expected Chuck Connors to step out of the near-twilight-gloom holding his Rifleman's rifle. "I'm a good guy," the voice continued. "Human. Not one of *them*. I just smelled your cookout and had to investigate." The man finally took shape as he neared the puddle of light from the grill. Huge, he even looked like Chuck Connors or Cheyenne Bodie, one of those big heroic cowboys my grandpa watched on the old western TV channel.

"Hotdogs," I told him. "We've got plenty if you're hungry." From behind me, Snake had started to rumble. I couldn't believe he hadn't rushed the guy yet.

The "Closer to Heaven" song began to play softly again. The scent of Old Spice aftershave accompanied the music. It played through me just like the song. I wanted to look at Snake, see why he hadn't come up beside me the way he always did, but the *cha-chuck* of the shotgun grabbed my attention. I swiveled my gaze toward Hal. He appeared to be holding Carlos' shotgun from the car. *What the hell?*

"Wait a minute, friend," the big guy told Hal. "I'm not armed." He held his open hands up beside his smiling face. "I'm just a traveler, going down the road—"

"You walking, or driving? I didn't hear no vehicle." Those were a lot of words coming from Hal, and I didn't care for his sudden need to be in charge, or the fact that he'd taken possession of the shotgun while I was helping to settle Carlos. I also didn't like the fact that I hadn't *noticed* that Carlos didn't have it. That one was on me.

I turned my gaze back toward the big guy. The words of this new song alarmed me. "Closer to Heaven" could mean closer to death. I'd learned to pay attention to my musical intuition, even though I was certain this song was *not* coming from my dad.

Snake rumbled again. He stood beside Faith, her hand on his head. I could see him tremble, could hear his throaty warning, but he didn't charge, he wasn't even looking at the new guy. His attention was focused on Hal.

Turq emerged from the hotel room with Carlos in his arms, and suddenly, we learned a lot more.

The big guy had lied.

He *was* armed.

Before I could utter a word, he swiveled into a crouch behind the stack of mattresses, a large-bore handgun growing off the end of his right arm. The sights on the weapon were pointed directly at Turq's head.

Without a sound, Snake streaked across the pile of mattresses, his jaws closing on the guy's wrist with a snap. The gun fell to the ground. I leapt toward it, kicking it aside, pulling Snake off at the same time. "He's our friend," I yelled. "His name's Turq!"

Faith hurried over and picked up the gun. She held it like she knew how.

Turq stood like a statue, still holding Carlos.

"Damn," Carlos said. "What'd I miss?"

The tension broken, I walked over to Hal, yanked the shotgun from his hands, and pointed it toward the ground. My heart felt like I'd run a marathon. I thought it might explode. The big guy sat on the ground examining his wrist. He had stumbled over the mattresses, taken off balance when Snake hit him.

"It's okay, Turq." I shoved the mattresses back together with my foot. "Put him here."

I held my hand out to the big guy, which seemed stupid after I did it, considering he had a good six inches height, and at least eighty pounds, on me. "Sorry about that," I said. "We get a little jumpy when guns come out."

He took my hand and pretended to let me help him up. "Name's Sam," he said. "Sam Edgerton. I really am one of the good guys." He grinned again. It seemed to be his natural expression. I think that's why I trusted him despite the song.

"Jack Lewis." I gave his hand a pump. "The dog is called Snake, he's deaf, but very protective." I inclined my head toward our friend. "And the Taker in the blue shirt is Turq. He's protective, too."

We watched as Turq placed Carlos on the mattresses and stepped back. His garnet eyes revealed nothing. It surprised me that he hadn't heard the arrival of the big guy before coming out with Carlos that way.

"I'm the useless one." Carlos extended his hand. "They just keep me around for entertainment."

Sam shook his hand, and I introduced the rest of the bunch to him as I laid the shotgun beside Carlos and blurted out to the entire assemblage how Turq, Carlos, Snake, and I had already proved to be a pretty intense fighting group. "We managed to wipe out a huge number of Takers in New Mexico. That's how Carlos was injured."

Once again, I heard myself seeming to spout a warning to someone. It occurred to me to wonder what my best friend, Cade, had been doing while all this commotion had been going on. But I couldn't dwell on it. From the corner of my eye, I could see him standing just behind and to the left of Hal. Something about that bothered me. But I couldn't figure out what it was exactly.

"Come on over," I told Sam. "Make yourself a hotdog."

I handed a second bag of chips to Carlos. "You hungry?" I asked Faith.

She nodded so I laid all the rest of the dogs on the grill. Snake got a couple of cold ones, and I also gave him a bowl of kibble from the trunk of the car. He preferred the hotdogs, but he ate the kibble too.

I sat in one of the desk chairs from the rooms and opened yet another bag of chips before unscrewing the top off a bottle of water. "Help yourself to another, Sam. Our ice is almost gone so whatever we don't eat will go to waste."

He glanced at Snake.

"Or him. Yeah." I laughed and patted my leg.

Snake trotted over, and I gave him the last bite of my third hotdog. "Can you still shake hands?" I asked.

I saw the confusion on Sam's face. I'd already told him Snake was deaf, but being a good sport, he stepped over and held his bruised hand down to Snake's level. I was impressed. It didn't even tremble.

Snake placed his paw in the man's palm but didn't meet his gaze. It made me think he remembered the time he'd put his trust in Thad, back at my house when this whole mess started.

"He's a good dog," I said. "I'd trust him with my life—"

Sam examined the puncture wounds in his hand. "I get that."

"I've got a bottle of peroxide in the Chrysler," I said. "We need to pour some on those." I chuckled without meaning to. "Good thing he didn't bite down, isn't it?"

Sam laughed, too. "I'd say it's a good thing he wasn't going for my throat."

"Uh, yeah. You should see what he does to a Taker—"

Sam glanced at Turq. In a quiet voice he said, "Is that what you call them?"

I nodded. "Them? Yeah, I mean they pretty much took every-thing, didn't they?"

"Yes, they did," Sam said. "Them, or whoever is controlling them."

I let my gaze find Turq. "Except for him. He saved me and Snake, both. Carlos, too, come to think of it. He's one of us—"

"He's the quiet one," Carlos said.

We all laughed.

Faith took her hotdog and chips and made herself a spot on the mattresses beside Carlos. Snake edged his way through us until his shoulder touched her knee. "Has he got a bowl. For water?"

"In the trunk. I'll get it." When I returned with Snake's bowl, Faith filled it with water. After he drank his fill, he leaned against her, and she laid her hand on his head like before. I handed Sam the brown bottle of peroxide and he poured it on his hand without comment. I figured he already knew to wash it with soap and water, too.

CHAPTER EIGHT

Jack

I threw a few twigs on the charcoal and opened a bag of giant marshmallows I'd found in the trunk. "Dessert," I said as I stuck one on a long stick and browned it up. Then I tossed a couple—untoasted—to Snake. He scooted forward to catch them, but he didn't get far from Faith's knee. "Looks like you've got a bestie, there." I tossed him another and held my roasting stick toward her.

Faith smiled, pulled the marshmallow off, and tasted it delicately. "I needed a best friend." She licked her fingertips. "I've been alone for a while now."

I tilted back in my chair. "How'd you get by?" I thought of all I'd been through. "I wouldn't be here if not for these guys." My gaze fell on Carlos, Turq, and Snake.

She shrugged. "Mostly I just hid and walked and walked and hid." She nibbled the sticky treat. "I lost twenty pounds from all the walking."

"Damn," Cade said. "I'm like Jack. If not for Hal here, I'd be as dead as a bug on a windshield."

Hal didn't comment. I hoped he wasn't going to hold a grudge about the shotgun. I decided I wouldn't.

Faith shrugged. "I got lucky. The people I was with were killed in a wreck, well, one of them didn't die in the wreck—" Her mouth fell slack for a split-second. "But the other two did." I watched her throat muscles struggle to swallow the rest of the marshmallow.

"Anyhow, after that I made my way back to Lewiston, but my mom was dead." She took a deep breath and straightened her spine, adjusting her armor. "And the town was deserted, like here, so I just started walking."

She shrugged as if walking all over Texas was no big deal. "Part of the time I rode a bicycle, but it got a flat a while back and I haven't found another. I saw one in front of the school, but it was locked up, and I couldn't get it." Once again, she laughed self-deprecatingly.

I gave her control of my marshmallow stick, and she leaned over, grabbed one from the bag, and roasted another for herself. Then she continued, "I walked the soles off these old Skechers after my bike got a flat, so I thought I'd try to find a bike store after I found some new shoes." She watched her marshmallow carefully. "I didn't find any though. Shoes, I mean."

Such a simple thing. Shoes. I'd grown so used to just taking everything I needed, because I had Turq and Snake and Carlos to help me, I never thought how it would be to travel alone. And on foot.

I smiled across the fire at this girl who had already stolen a piece of my heart, and I waited on an old Janis Joplin tune to start up in my head. But no song came, just the plop of Faith's marshmallow falling into the fire.

We both lunged for it, laughing. It was too late for that one, but she immediately grabbed another and poked it onto the tip of the charred stick.

The night deepened to black, all at once, the way it always does on the plains, but the little grill fire put out a surprising amount of heat and light. In the distance, the last sliver of sunset ghosted the horizon. Overhead, the stars began to show themselves as tiny white sparks. For a few moments, the world was downright cozy. Without the light of towns and cities, the Milky Way was nothing short of awe-inspiring.

I threw a few more twigs into the fire to make it crackle.

"I'm surprised you came this direction," Cade called across the fire. "Hal and I were thinking of going north where there's more water. Or maybe east."

"Yeah." I glanced at Faith's pretty face, sorry to be interrupted. "This flat land is dry most of the time."

"Kansas was dry, too," she laughed. "I wound up there by accident."

My heart paused in my chest. "I thought you came from Lewiston, Texas."

Faith licked her lips, and the tips of her fingers. "Oh, I did," her voice was low, almost a whisper. "But I went to Kansas, New Mexico. It's a tiny place, not too far away—"

"—little place in the middle of nowhere. I know." I studied her face again, to see if this was real, or if I'd hit my head and was hallucinating. Everything seemed on the up and up. "Near the town of Kansas there's a huge, ancient house built by an old gangster named—"

"Bitty Sloan." Faith's eyes grew wide in the firelight. "How did you know?"

"That's where Thad and I went when we left here." My head felt foggy, like waking from a dream. "I kept hearing Kansas songs in my head, I thought it was because of my dad, but now—I'm not so sure." I stared at her as I spoke. "I don't know how we missed seeing you. We were there for a while." I let my eyes wander toward the coming-on stars, thinking, trying to make sense of what she'd said. "I mean, we stayed there for *weeks*. Until a new bunch of Takers came through."

"What are y'all whispering about over there?" Cade asked.

Sam looked at him. He'd been listening quietly the whole time.

"We're just talking music," I said. "You know how my dad loved his classic rock—which reminds me, does anyone know a country song called "Closer to Heaven?"

"One of my old grandad's favorites," Sam said. "By a singer named Rodney Crowell. Grandad usually liked old country music, but this newer one spoke to him somehow." He hummed the beginning of the song and I felt something settle into my bones. Something rough, like sandpaper.

My eyes must have reflected my confusion because Sam said, "What? Is that not the one you meant?"

I spoke the few words I'd been hearing.

"Yep, that's it." His hand—the one holding the hotdog—journeyed on to his mouth, his camo t-shirt stretching to accommodate the movement of his biceps and shoulders.

"I've been hearing that song in my head since you arrived," I said. "Strange, huh?"

He shrugged.

"I guess your grandad also wore Old Spice after shave and smelled like beer, right?"

Sam stopped chewing. "Damn, son. Did you know the old man?" He looked me over. "No, he's been gone a while. You couldn't possibly."

"I didn't," I said. "But for some reason it seems as if I can see him." I tapped the side of my head. "In here." I focused my sight inward for a moment. "Tall, white hair, military short, flat on top." I thought for a moment longer. "He's grizzled." I ducked my head, embarrassed. "Don't think I've ever said that word before, not in my whole life, but it fits. He's a grizzled old Marine who could kick every one of our asses with one hand tied behind his back." I smiled without even knowing why. "He ran a bar. That's why he always smelled like beer."

I cleared my throat and walked to the Chrysler for more water. I didn't look at Cade, I knew he was probably thinking I'd lost my mind. He's the only one who knew how I used to wake in the mornings with a song playing in my head—and how those songs often helped me make simple decisions in my life—he'd called me a dork when I told him about it way back when.

After that, I hadn't told anyone else.

But since the rip, things had become much more vivid. At first all the songs had related to my dad in some way. They'd saved us during the firenado, showing me what to do, and I'd thought I was channeling Dad. This thing today? It was completely new. Even to me.

Could I be adapting the same way the Takers had begun to adapt?

And what about Faith going all the way to Kansas, New Mexico, the same little place where we'd made our stand against the horde?

It was almost too much to take in.

I walked back to the grill. All the sticks and twigs had burned away, but the charcoal still glowed brightly. Sam stood with one foot on the seat of a straight-backed chair.

"—it was rough," he was saying. "I'd just moved back home to help my Granny run the bar. Hadn't been there but a couple of months. Then they came."

"How'd you survive?" I asked. "Were you down in a basement like we were?"

He was about to answer when Cade said, "It was awesome the way they came up out of those puddles, wasn't it? Like the world's best special effects."

He must've realized how that sounded. "I mean, it *wasn't* awesome when they started grabbing people and eating them." He chewed at a place on his thumb near the cuticle, something else I'd never seen him do before. "Did you notice they never ate the dead, only the living?"

Turq focused his gaze on Cade, then on me, as if interested in our opinion on the matter.

I glanced at Carlos. "Yeah. We've got some theories about that."

CHAPTER NINE

Ambush

Carlos' fingers went to his throat, and I knew he was touching the image of the crucifix that had been flash-fired there during the firenado.

"We, uh, we think maybe they eat the living in hopes of ingesting their souls," I said.

Cade howled with laughter. "Jackie, that is the craziest thing—"

"I think you're right." Faith's voice was quiet. "Those words floating under their skin, the what-did-you-call-them, their sin words?"

I nodded.

"They're all about murder, torture, lust and greed—"

"Deadly sins," Sam said. "Ten Commandment Sins."

Carlos propped himself up a little straighter. "Exactly what I said."

Cade stopped laughing, but Hal made a derisive noise. "Hell," he said. "They're just ET monsters, fell in from outer space or whatever. Maybe blasted at us by the mothership hovering around out there. You know, from another planet."

He glanced at Turq, but there was no response. He remained stoic. One word floated across his bald head, barely visible in the firelight.

Remorse.

The word was *remorse.* God help me, I wanted to hug him, just go over, wrap my arms around him and squeeze. *I wondered what his words would say if I did?*

Without giving myself a chance to back out, I stood, but Snake stood, too, blocking my way. His hackles rose and a deep growl rumbled through his chest.

We all stopped talking. Stopped moving. The silence engulfed us like quicksand. I stared hard into the night. Twilight had crept away while we chatted, and now we were completely on the other side.

From the corner of my eye, I saw Sam reach behind his back. His hand emerged holding a gun. I didn't know if Faith had given his back, or if this was a different one. He grasped it with both hands, taking aim at a target no one could see.

In the silence, I heard Carlos pump the shotgun. I laid a hand on Snake's head to keep him from rushing into the stand of trees. His whole body vibrated like a tuning fork.

"Who's there?" Faith called out.

I swiveled toward her, ready to chastise her or clamp a hand over her mouth—*something*.

She just shrugged. "We lit a fire," she said. "Like a signal."

I turned back toward the rustling sound. She was right, of course. "Who are you?" I called louder. "Show yourself or we'll shoot."

Turq stepped forward putting himself between the shallow tree line and us.

"No—" I said, but it was too late.

The first bullet hit Turq and spun him around, his clear word-fluid spurting, letters and liquid running down his arm.

I yanked off my t-shirt and threw it at him. "Wrap it with this!"

He caught it one handed and whipped it around his bicep, pulling it tight and tying it with his silver teeth. With his other hand, he grabbed the bolt action rifle from the shooter who appeared to be having difficulty with the old mechanism. Turq smashed the butt of the gun into the guy's neck, then flung it aside.

The shooter lay on the ground, neck broken.

A second bullet whizzed past my knee, and I realized someone had taken aim at Snake. I steadied my revolver and aimed at a running form that appeared to be headed toward the Chrysler.

Sam's bullet got him before I even squeezed the trigger. We both ran toward the target, but it wasn't a him after all. It was a woman. Rough, face-tatted, wearing filthy old camo and sporting a one-sided clipcut. The bullet had entered under her arm.

"Heart shot," Sam muttered.

Wow, I thought. She was hauling butt when he drew down on her in the darkness, but I didn't have time to wonder at such impressive skill, Snake had someone on the ground, near the mattresses.

"Hold him, boy!" Carlos yelled, aiming the shotgun down toward the form writhing on the asphalt.

"Noooo," Faith screamed. "You'll hit the dog!" She flung herself over Snake's back and smashed him on top of the person he had taken down.

Turq saw what was happening. In three large strides, he crossed from the edge of the brush to the mattresses. He picked Faith up and tossed her toward me. I caught her on a stumbling spin, then he pushed Snake aside, raised his giant, toeless foot and stomped down on the would-be-killer's head. It split open like an uncooked egg. Brain matter flew.

Faith fell to her knees, retching.

Sam hurried over to make certain the broken-neck guy wasn't getting up again and then he located and picked up the rifle that had shot Turq.

"Get ready for the black stuff," I yelled. "We can't let it get Turq!" Even as I said it, I knew we couldn't stop it if it came.

But no rip fluttered open.

No black rain fell.

Turq patted his arm bandage.

I was dumbfounded. "You think we stopped the leakage in time?" Could it really be that easy?

He patted his bald head and the word remorse floated back to the surface.

"Maybe you've been redeemed," I murmured. "And you never have to go back to Purgatory." Of course, he didn't answer, couldn't answer, I suppose, but I saw him tug his makeshift bandage tighter, just in case.

"Weren't there four of them?" Sam asked.

We all swiveled our heads, looking. We had regrouped around the glowing barbecue-grill-beacon.

"I think so," I said. "I caught a glimpse of a big knife—"

"Machete," Sam said. "I saw it, too. I'll bet they want our vehicles, probably smelled our food."

"And they went right after Turq and Snake first." I laid my palm on the dog's heaving sides. "He may be the only dog left."

Faith said, "They ambushed us, didn't even wait to see if we were friendly." She hugged Snake's stout neck. "We would have given them food, right?"

Everyone was saved from answering when Hal and Cade came strolling around the rear of the motel, a silent teen between them.

A quick, evil, thought spat itself into my mind. Cade and Hal, unscathed, bringing back an armed—now unarmed—prisoner. How'd they catch the guy, with nary a scratch on either of them? Mom's voice chimed into my head. "Well, isn't that *ironicle?*"

Yes, it is, Mom. And I will keep that in mind. She never had been one of Cade's biggest fans. She'd tolerated him, though. Tolerated him with kindness.

Hal held up a large machete. His other hand gripped the wiry teen's upper arm. The kid's clothes were in tatters, like Turq's turquoise shirt.

Cade had both his hands grasping the kid's other arm. "Looky here," he crowed. "Look what we caught."

Sam pulled a pair of handcuffs off the back of his belt and stepped up to meet them. "Turn him around," he said. The boy struggled, but Sam snapped the cuffs on him. "Why'd y'all try to kill us?" he demanded.

The kid worked his skinny shoulders around and around as if testing the cuffs. From his actions, it appeared this was not his first time in restraints.

He finally stopped squirming and looked up at Sam. "Why not? You got cars, food, you even got one of them things." He jerked his head toward Turq. "What'd you do, reprogram it?"

I looked at Turq once again, to gauge his reaction. His only response was to tighten up the shirt wrapped around his wounded arm. Reprogram. Did the kid know something we didn't? "Who are you? Why'd you say that?"

He flung his head to the side and peered at me from beneath strings of hair that might once have been brown. Even from across the grill area, I could see that his small eyes were mean and red.

I looked a little closer at his face. "What're you on?"

He glanced away, and I knew I'd hit the nail on the head. Drugstores were all open now. What couldn't be found could be manufactured. Carlos and I talked about it every time we had to locate a CVS or Walgreen's in search of something to deal with his burns.

"He's a druggie alright," Sam said.

The kid yanked his elbow out of Cade's grasp and tried to run, but Snake had him by the calf before he made three steps.

"Stupid, too," Cade said. "What'll we do with him?"

I pulled Snake back.

"I say we kill him." Hal's face was impassive. "Like he was going to do to us."

Maybe I was wrong. Maybe they hadn't disarmed him without a scratch.

Faith shook her head. "We can't kill him just like that—"

"I've got zip ties in my Jeep," Sam said. And we all realized we hadn't even seen a Jeep yet. "We'll hobble him, feed him, torture his ass until he tells us if there are any more of them out there—"

The teen began to scrabble away again.

The hair on my scalp prickled, and I led Snake over to Faith and Carlos. After a moment, he stood and made his way to Turq, sniffing his leg, then standing on his hind paws to get a whiff of the wound covered by my t-shirt bandage.

When he did that, it made me realize I was shirtless. I peeked at Faith to see what she thought of my skinny frame, but she wasn't looking at me. She was watching Snake. I wished he could tell us what he thought about our friend's gunshot wound.

"Is the bullet still in your arm?" I asked Turq.

He flexed his bicep. In the starlight, I could see words floating down into his forearm.

I stepped forward. The only word I could read was *Heaven*. What the heck did that mean? The "Closer to Heaven" song made itself known, but I couldn't examine it too deeply. Cade was speaking. I did, however, wonder why no song had given me warning about these killers.

"—probably go ahead and drug him tonight, you know, knock him out, and when we leave tomorrow, just turn him loose. We'll be hours away before he even wakes up."

"That's a thought," I said. "I mean, I'm not big on torture." I looked at Hal. "Or murder—"

"Self-defense," Hal said.

I ignored him. "Why don't we just hobble him, he's already cuffed, and maybe we should gag him, too. In case others are lurking nearby."

Cade held up half a dozen pill bottles. "Or we could use some of these to knock him out."

That got my attention. "Yours? Or his?"

"Took 'em out of his pocket." He held the labels close to his face. "Let's see … Hydrocodone, a few Tylenol III, some plain old Tramadol, and what do we have here?" He produced a plastic baggie. "Could these be the magic Fentanyl lollipops I've heard about?" A chuckle rose from his throat. "With those cargo pockets, the boy is a walking pharmacy."

Visions of Marla and Kevin flashed through my head. I reached for a bottle. "Carlos could use some of these. If y'all don't mind."

Hal took control of the Fentanyl and one of the other bottles, his face still showing no emotion.

"I trade 'em for food," the kid said. "We all did." He pointed his chin at the place where they had burst out of the trees.

"Are there more of you?" I didn't expect him to answer, but he surprised me.

"It was just us. We found stuff and traded stuff—"

Hal snorted. "And killed people." He turned and walked away. "*Found stuff* my ass."

The kid clamped his mouth shut and hunched his shoulders together as if to ward off physical blows. I wished Hal had clamped his own mouth shut. I wanted to hear more about the gang we'd just wiped out. "Are you sure there aren't any more out there?"

The boy ignored me.

I started toward the fire. "He can have whatever's left on the grill. He looks half-starved. Then I guess we can tie his feet together with the zip ties like Sam said." I didn't want to. I didn't want a prisoner, but what else could we do? Didn't want to kill him, though I would if I had to.

I took a couple of hotdogs and stuffed them inside leftover buns. "After he's been fed, if he doesn't tell us where he's been and what he's seen, then we can decide what to do with him." I glanced around the parking lot and tree line. "I'm afraid there might be others like him hiding out in town, maybe that's why there aren't any other survivors—"

Faith and Carlos murmured agreement. Sam moved the kid's hands around in front of him so he could eat, then told us to watch him carefully while he jogged back to get his Jeep. "I hope they didn't find it," he muttered, disappearing into the gloom.

We all glanced back at the kid, but he wasn't listening. His mouth was stuffed full of food.

Within minutes Sam drove a big Jeep right up to the fire. The kid had just finished inhaling the hotdogs and chugging down a bottle of water.

Sam brought over a box of supplies and zip tied the boy's ankles together. Then he did his hands as well. The pair of handcuffs went back on his belt.

Turq had begun scraping up the bodies of our would-be assassins and moving them behind the motel to the place where the others rested. I went to help him, then Sam and Faith joined in, too. Only Hal and Cade—and Carlos, who couldn't really walk without assistance—ignored the grisly chore.

We were almost finished when we heard Carlos shout, "No!" And then we heard the *Ka-boom* of the shotgun.

I reached Carlos first. "Are you okay? Where's the kid?"

Hal and Cade arrived together. I could smell marijuana smoke. "Damn," Cade said. "What happened, bro?"

Carlos lay back on the mattresses. "He had a knife. Tried to take the shotgun."

"So, you shot him?" Hal's voice was edged with glee.

I looked at Hal's grinning face. My hands balled themselves into fists. "I can't believe y'all left him alone with Carlos."

Hal didn't respond. I think if he had, I might have gone all Snakeman on him. Perhaps Carlos felt it, too.

"I don't think I hit him," Carlos said. "I dozed off. We thought he was tight. It happened so fast."

"My fault." Sam picked up the pieces of the thick plastic zip ties. They'd clearly been cut. "I didn't even search him. Assumed he had only the machete. Now we've got a lunatic running around out there with a knife. Probably a switchblade since it sliced through this industrial plastic like it was butter." He showed us the pieces.

"I'll take first watch," Carlos said. "I feel like it's *my* fault he got away."

"I'll stay up, too," Faith said. "No way I can sleep now."

I shook my head. "It isn't your fault, Carlos." I somehow prevented myself from glancing at Hal and Cade. "None of us thought to search him. We aren't used to dealing with humans. We're lucky he didn't kill you—"

We all regrouped around the glowing coals.

Sam stuck a long stem of grass into the coals until it caught, then brought out a small brown cigar and touched the burning grass to the end of it. He inhaled deeply. *An after-dinner ritual,* I assumed.

Faith lit up a cigarette and the two fragrances blended with the odors of cooked meat and gunfire. The smell made me wish I'd never found those hotdogs in that farmhouse. It also made me wonder, again, just who had kept that generator running. And why there was no other sign of them.

A soft breeze whuffled around our feet. No one seemed to feel the need for sleep now. Not with the kid running around out there, armed.

"Tell us more about your granny," Faith said to Sam when we were all reassembled. "You were just about to tell us about that bar—"

Sam inclined his head toward the back of the motel. "Those desperadoes reminded me of how it all began. I was on my way to pick up Granny." He clamped the cigar in the corner of his mouth. "And I stopped at a rest area before the cut off to the national forest …"

CHAPTER TEN

Sam's story

Faith put out her cigarette and scooted a little closer to the small grill. "Was it you and your wife? Or just you?"

Sam twirled the solid gold band on his ring finger. "Danielle was killed in a car accident coming home from work one night before all this." He waited for us to process that. "The light turned green, the driver of the SUV coming the other way was texting. Hit her broad side. I didn't even get to say goodbye."

He swigged from a bottle of water. "We'd been married less than three years, and then in the blink of an eye, I found myself staring at her still face in a hospital trauma room."

No one seemed to know what to say.

Sam reached into his box of supplies, pulled out a speckled blue metal coffee pot, filled it with a bottle of water, then opened a red plastic tub of Folger's coffee. "I didn't open her eyes," he said. "But I should've." His spoon rattled against the metal coffee basket as he filled it with Folger's. "I had nightmares in which we buried her alive. If I'd opened her lids, I would have seen the lack of light. Would've known for certain." He took the end of the cigar from his lips and dropped it down in the coals.

Faith broke the silence. "That's so sad. No kids?"

He shook his head and set the coffee pot over the hottest part of the still-red coals in the grill. "I guess that's a good thing, right? Otherwise, I'd be dragging them through this nightmare."

He sat down and put his foot up on the empty chair again.

"You'll think I'm crazy when I tell you this next part." He looked across the fire at me. "Maybe not you, Jack. Not after what you told me about my grandad." His voice trailed off. "For a solid week I felt her around me. She even called my cell phone one night. Her name and picture appeared on my screen like always. I *smashed* my thumb down on the ANSWER button, but no one was there. It was just a blank. Nothing."

He gazed up at the unbelievable stars as he spoke. "I ran to the desk where I'd put her phone after the cops gave it back to me. The screen was cracked in a snowflake pattern, but I could still call it and get her voice mail. I'd done it a dozen times since the night she died. Made certain to keep it charged."

I thought of the cell phones I'd taken from the file drawer at school.

Sam leaned forward to check the coffee. "And then she called me back." His hand nudged the enameled pot closer to the center of the grill. "When that call came, I snatched up her phone and mine. But it was the same thing." He shook his head. "I pressed recent calls on her phone, but there were no outgoing calls." He shrugged. "The only thing on her call history were all the incoming calls. From me."

A speckled blue cup appeared in his hand. He filled it and sipped before he spoke again. "I remember collapsing into her desk chair, head in my hands. She hadn't called me. Not from her phone. I felt like I was cracking up." He drained his coffee cup and refilled it.

I wondered if the hot liquid scalded his tongue.

"I decided I needed to get away for a while," he said. "Give up trying to sleep in our bed. Stop standing at the breakfast bar every morning with my cereal bowl in one hand because I didn't want to sit down at the table and look across at her empty chair." He glanced around at us, at our faces. "I called my gran. My only living relative."

Even in the darkness we could see the smile that crossed his face when he spoke of his grandmother. It was almost funny if you thought about it, this huge guy, calling his granny for comfort.

"Thrilled her," he said, motioning toward the coffee pot and box of utensils to indicate we should help ourselves. "She'd been trying to run the bar by herself since Grandad passed the year before."

"What did she say," Faith asked.

"She knew something was wrong, of course. You know how moms and grannies are. We made plans to go fishing. I stuffed an old backpack with a few t-shirts, locked up the house, and hit the road."

Cade had picked up a charred stick and was using the black end to doodle on the concrete around the base of the grill. Hal appeared to be asleep.

"Then what happened?" Faith prodded.

Sam laughed at her curiosity. "It was a couple hundred miles before I reached the rest stop." His voice was smooth in the firelight. "I only saw one vehicle in the semi-circle drive-through, a faded red Bronco snugged up to the curb.

"The rest stop was one of those older ones, steel wagon wheels holding up concrete picnic tables. This one had a large plexiglass map on the wall highlighting nearby points of interest.

"A sloppy looking trio of boys stood near the map smoking and scratching. They couldn't seem to keep their grimy hands off their crotches. I figured they had crabs. When they saw me, one of them bent over the water fountain and pretended to drink.

"I gave them a wide berth and went on into the john, did my thing, and stood washing my hands at the sink. That's when I heard the commotion. A woman's voice said, 'Give me that!'

"In response I heard the high-pitched giggle of a teen-aged boy. 'That's mine!' The woman insisted. A deeper voice said. 'Shut up old woman.'

"I got to the doorway just in time to see the biggest kid—he looked to be about eighteen, maybe even twenty, or maybe that was only twenty years' worth of grease in his clown-red hair, delving into Granny's handbag. The giggler held her from behind, his hands hooked into the crooks of her elbows like grubby claws. 'You can have the cash,' she said. 'Just give me my pills and my car keys.'

"Greasy, the one digging in the purse, grinned and held up a set of keys on a twinkly fob. He smiled a near-toothless smile and clicked the smart key. A Toyota Highlander blipped its horn and flashed its lights. 'Boys,' he said. 'Looks like we got ourselves a new ride.'

"He dangled the keys at Granny. 'Don't worry, old woman. We'll take good care of it.' He dangled the keys again. 'Won't we, J-dog?'

"The kid holding her squeezed her elbows together behind her back. 'You're hurting me,' she said. 'Just give me my pills.'

"The third teen, a stocky Latino who looked like he could bench press a horse, held out his crudely tattooed hand. 'Les'see if the old broad gots anything else we need.'

"Greasy ignored the hand and dumped the contents of the purse on the bench near the map display. Three amber pill bottles rolled off onto the concrete. 'Get 'em,' Greasy said. He flipped his hair out of his eyes and opened her wallet, probably hoping for cash and credit cards.

"The big kid leaned over to retrieve the bottles, and that's when he spied me in the doorway. I didn't know if these punks had any weapons, but I had to assume they did. The kid stuck the pills in his huge pockets and backed away from the bench. 'Looks like we got company.'

"I said. 'You just saw me go in there, numb nuts. You boys need to lay off the dope—it seems to have fried your brains.'

"The skinny one dragged Granny backward until she was pressed against him like a shield. I held up my hands. 'Don't worry, I'm unarmed. Just let the lady go, and I won't hurt you.'

"Greasy flicked a glance at his boys and sniggered. 'He won't hurt us. That's freakin' hilarious, dude. You some kinda comedian or something?' He reached into the waistband of his saggy jeans and pulled out a pistol. 'Take the old bitch to her car.' He motioned toward the Highlander with the gun. The skinny kid didn't hesitate.

"I kept expecting a trucker or some day-tripper to come whipping into the drive, but none did. I was glad. I wouldn't have to worry about bystanders. It looked like this one would be all on me.

"When Greasy pointed the nose of his weapon toward the SUV, I stepped out of the doorway, and yelled, 'Hey!'

"The red-haired idiot turned toward me just as the edge of my boot caught his wrist. The gun went flying into a mound of pink and yellow lantana bordering the walkway.

"Before he could react, I followed my foot with my hands and then he was on the ground in front of me, all four fingers of his gun hand bent backward about ninety degrees. He didn't have time to whimper before I whirled him around and smashed my knee into his spine.

"I may have kneed him a little harder than I intended. He went down face first onto the sidewalk. One of his front teeth flew out of his mouth and landed a short distance away.

"Skinny had Gran almost to the Highlander. He didn't seem to realize Greasy still had the key. The Latino bear with the ugly prison tattoo seemed to be the brightest. He was busy digging around in the lantana in search of the gun.

"I stepped toward him with my hands raised as if to strike. While he watched my hands, I smashed his left knee from the side with the same boot that had released the gun from Greasy's fingers. The bear went down like a sack of shit.

"By this time the skinny kid appeared on the verge of a meltdown. He couldn't seem to decide whether to ditch Granny and make a run for it or try to use her for protection. In a decision I'm sure he soon regretted; he chose the latter. 'Just give me the woman and I'll let you pick up what's left of your friends and go.'

"His voice jittered. 'I'll break her neck, mofo. I'll kill her if you don't stop right there.' He'd given up on the Highlander and was headed for the rust-red Bronco with the busted back window.

"I continued toward them at a leisurely pace. My gaze connected with that of my gran. I was not surprised to see a bit of defiance left in the old girl. That was all I needed.

"When the kid glanced around to see how close they were to the Bronco, I winked at Granny and charged them at full speed. Without hesitation, she flung her weight forward, bending at the waist, breaking his hold on her elbows, and giving me just enough room to drive my fist into his throat.

"He grabbed for his neck with both hands, gasping, choking, windpipe crushed, all the air knocked out of him. I followed him to his knees and gave him a couple of swift short punches to the head to knock him out.

"That's when I heard the click of the gun.

"Normally, I would've made sure the big guys were completely out of the picture first, but it was the skinny one who'd had grips on my gran.

"I turned slowly around. The Bear stood there with the gun trained on the widest target available—me. Granny stood nearby; her lips clamped together in a hard line. I shrugged and held my hands up in a gesture of surrender. 'You win, buddy. What do you want? My wallet, my Jeep, what?'

"His finger twitched, shockingly close to the trigger. I could tell his knee was destroyed. He leaned a bit, a damaged ship on a sandbar. It made him even more dangerous. He didn't know what he wanted or what he should do next. Obviously, I had to decide for him. 'My Jeep's fully stocked for two weeks of camping. Here, let me get the key.'

"I made sure he understood I wasn't going for a weapon when I stuck my hand in my pocket. At least, not a conventional weapon. I'd subscribed to the theory behind MCMAP for years. My grandad, the old Marine, made a believer of me when I watched him whip a couple of bad guys in the bar with nothing but a wet bar towel and a cue ball. The bad guys were in their mid-forties—drunk bikers, or maybe they were oilfield roughnecks—my gramps had been nearing seventy.

"Bear nodded toward the woman. 'Give 'em to the *abuela*. You'll drive.' She glanced at the Jeep. 'I can't drive a stick. I don't even know how to start it.'

"The Bear rolled his eyes. I could see he was rethinking getting out of bed that morning. I shrugged and tossed the key fob toward him. He let it land near his feet without making a grab for it. 'You,' he jerked his head toward the place it had landed. His bad leg was slightly bent, all his weight on the good leg, the one I hadn't kicked. He jerked his head toward the key again. 'Pick it up, *pendejo*.'

"I ambled over, made a show of crouching, never taking my eyes from his face. I wanted to take him off that good leg, but he seemed ready for that. He kept the bore of that Smith and Wesson trained on my face. The way his hand shook worried me a little.

"'Steady there,' I said. 'I'm not gonna eat ya.' I scrabbled my fingertips in the dust near him, pretending I couldn't quite get a hold of it. 'C'mon *puta*—'

"It took a split-second to double up my fist and punch him in the crotch. Good thing I'm ambidextrous. Down he went again, but not before he squeezed the trigger. The bullet whined past my ear and ricocheted off the pavement near Granny's feet. I grabbed the gun and smacked The Bear on top of the head with the butt of it. 'Stupid ass.' I directed the words at him, but in my head, they were meant for myself. That was too close. He never should have gotten that gun. I screwed up. Just like not double-checking that kid for a knife tonight. Gettin' old I guess."

He waited for one of us to contradict him. But no one did so he continued. "I walked over and put my arm around my gran. 'You okay?' I asked. 'I'm all right, sugar,' she replied. 'I knew you'd take care of me.'

"I gave her a brief hug. 'That was too close for comfort. Next time we're meeting in a restaurant, not a rest stop.' She laughed and said, 'Sammy, you crack me up.'"

Our group sat in silence for a moment, then Faith said, "I'm glad you're on our side—but what about when *they* came?"

Hal awoke, made some noise about needing to pee, then ambled over to the Challenger and lit up a small pipe.

I started to caution him to watch for the kid with the knife, but he was older than me by several years. I figured he should know.

CHAPTER ELEVEN

Still Sam

Sam nodded. "I'm getting there—"

"Go on," Carlos said. "I wanna hear what happened to the *pendejos*." He looked at Faith and mouthed *sorry* for the language.

She just smiled.

Sam took up his story again.

"I retrieved the Highlander's keys from Greasy's limp, outstretched hand. He was out cold on the sidewalk. I wiped the keys off and handed them to Granny. 'You okay to drive?'

"She nodded and bent down over the creep to make sure he was still breathing. 'What do we do about these?'

"I looked over the trio—Greasy on his toothless mouth, the Bear coiled in the shape of a comma, out cold, hands gripping his injured crabnest, and the kid across the drive, nearer the Bronco, half on and half off the curb, out cold as well, but also still breathing. 'Thin skulled little bastards, aren't they? They'll be alright.' I stuck the gun—unloaded—in the waistband of my pants and took my granny by the arm. 'You sure you're okay?'

"She rubbed her elbows. 'I'm fine. Take more than that little pipsqueak to get the best of this old gal.' She laughed the way she always did when it came to adversity. 'At least when my grandson's around.'"

"Damn," Carlos, said. "Your Granny sounds as tough as mine."

Sam nodded. "She was something all right." He rubbed his jaw. "After I let the air out of the Bronco's tires so they couldn't follow us, we went on to the campsite. Spent a couple days fishing and reminiscing, then Gran said she couldn't be away from the bar any longer. That's when we decided I needed to just move back in and help her run the place for a while."

I nodded in the darkness. It was easy to imagine him chucking drunks out of batwing doors on their ears. "Where was the bar?" I asked. "Did y'all make it back there before the rip?"

Sam turned his chair around backward and straddled it. The coals lit our little iron grill from the bottom up. "The Borderline Bar," he said. "Right there on Hwy 380 where it meets 62. Right on the Texas–New Mexico line." He shook his head, just a little. "We had two good months. Enough time to show us what life could be. We'd both lost our better halves."

A look crossed his face. My mom would've called it *wistful*.

"So, you got to reconnect with your grandmother before all hell broke loose."

Sam poked at the coals again.

"Is that when they came?" Faith prompted.

He nodded. "We were doing okay right up through May. I felt better than I had since Dani died." He stuck the stick back into the coals, rolling it over and over, charring it as he spoke.

His actions seemed to fascinate Turq. The Taker tilted his head so his eyes could follow the movement.

Sam stopped rolling the thin branch between his thumb and fingers and watched Turq's face. It took a few seconds for the creature to realize the stick had stopped moving.

His garnet eyes turned toward Sam, and I'd swear everyone at the campfire felt the weight of those insect-like orbs. I wished I could read his floating words, but he was too far away. In the semi-darkness, it was impossible. It didn't matter. I didn't always understand what they meant, anyway.

"It seemed like any other day," Sam said. "Slow for a Friday, but business was beginning to pick up the way it always did toward quittin' time. Lotta folks—oilfield workers, mostly—stopping by on their way home."

He stuck the stick back in the coals as if the motion helped him think.

At first, I'd wanted him to hurry and tell his story, but his deep, cowboy voice had grown on me. It relaxed me in a way I hadn't felt since the firenado. As if here was someone we could trust, someone who might help us figure things out.

I thought of how I still hadn't been to see my house. Thought of how my laptop had been sitting on my plaid bedspread like any old morning when all this started. I'd thought my whole life was tied up in that laptop. My schoolwork, my games, all that music, all those movies. Now it was probably nothing but a hunk of melted junk. Maybe I needed to go back and check it out. Start facing things, instead of just running. Maybe I needed what Mom would've called *closure.*

I realized I'd zoned out for a moment when I heard Sam talking again.

"Gran worked in the kitchen," he said. "We served chicken wings and nachos, peanuts and pretzels. Not much, just small-time bar food." He closed his eyes for a moment, reliving the good smell of the kitchen, perhaps. "I had a couple customers at the drive-up window, and one at the bar nursing a beer."

In the upward glow of the grill, I thought I saw his jaw muscles tense as he spoke about the images in his mind.

"Had my head stuck out the drive-up window, checking a driver's license, when I saw the sky ripple." He twirled the stick, then continued. "'Big storm coming?' I asked the customer." The guy drove an old pickup, the bed of it home to a giant aluminum water can chained to a beat-up toolbox. 'Must be,' the guy said. 'Funny color, ain't it?'

"I remember really looking at the sky as I handed him his 12-pack and change. 'It does look odd. I hope you get home before all hell breaks loose.' He thanked me and went on his way. Headed straight into the greenish looking clouds on the Texas side of the line."

Faith leaned forward, listening, as Sam continued, "The next car was a young woman wanting a premade Daiquiri. I told her we didn't do that. 'Come on in, and I'll make you one to drink at the bar.' She shook her head and drove away."

He prodded the coals with his stick. "I saw that girl a while later when I scrambled back up from the supply cellar. I thought we'd had an earthquake. The whole place shook. The sound … well, you all know about the sound." His hand went to his ear. "A support beam fell on my head, a glancing blow, but I must've been unconscious for a few minutes."

He poured himself another cup of coffee into the blue speckled cup.

"Her car sat at the edge of the highway with the driver's door open. She hung from a tree, insides on the outside, dripping into the dust." He passed a hand across his eyes. "I've seen war. I'm a Marine like my grandad. But I'd never seen the things I saw that day." His voice grew softer. "At least they didn't get Gran. I found her face down outside the door, one hand clutching her chest, the other pressed to her ear."

"Must've been her heart." I remembered the pill bottles the thugs had tried to take from her at the rest stop. "She was lucky, like my mom. At least they didn't get flayed."

Turq shuffled his feet in the darkness. It was a slight sound, but we all seemed attuned to those now.

I glanced over at him as a stray shaft of moonlight reflected off his gray skin. The word *sorrow* stole across his shoulder.

Sam continued. "The sound had been so loud; I couldn't figure out what was going on. Then I saw *them* marching away, down the highway. There weren't any more people at the bar." He shrugged. "The rain had already stopped. The puddles were just puddles."

I opened my mouth to protest, but he held up one hand.

"I had been home from Afghanistan for years, but these creatures took me right back. They seemed like some strange platoon, killing, then marching on."

"Wha'd you do, man?" Carlos asked.

Sam said, "I wrapped my Gran in her favorite blue and white quilt, and then I buried her."

The breeze shifted and the smoky sweet odor of cannabis wafted across our little group. I looked across the coals at Faith. I could see in her eyes she had her own story to tell.

"How about you, Faith? Where you were when the world fell in?"

CHAPTER TWELVE

Faith's Story

She didn't hesitate. "The night of the rip I was out with my friend, Shay, and a couple of guys she knew. We went to this bar an hour and a half from Lewiston. The Borderline Bar."

Sam looked around slowly. "Are you kidding me for some reason?"

Faith shook her head. "Shay's friend, Masen, did something in the parking lot. Right there under that big elm tree. Bought something or sold something, I don't know what, and then we went through the drive-through and got some beer." She stopped talking and took a big drink of water.

"What'd the driver look like?" Sam asked. "Maybe I'd remember—"

"Heavy was the driver. I rode shotgun. You weren't at the window. I remember a sweet-faced lady with fluffy white hair and a dark blue shirt."

Sam stared hard at Faith. "That was Gran. She watched the window while I went down to the cellar."

"The weather had turned," Faith continued. "Started pouring rain, a real gully-washer my mom would've said, so we drove on over the line into New Mexico to this cave Heavy knew about. Blue Cave he called it. He kept looking at the weird sky. Saying it looked like hail."

She stopped talking, and I was afraid she wouldn't start again, but she did.

"He loved his car. It was a fully restored 1969 Camaro. He didn't want it to get beat up." She paused. "Anyhow, the cave was up this mountain trail, the dirt road already muddy. The thunder boomed like shotguns back and forth across the hills. The rain *poured*. I thought Heavy would wreck us for sure."

I leaned forward, enthralled. I could almost hear the thunder, see the lightning flash through the heavy rain.

Faith lit a new cigarette before she said, "Masen was in the back seat with Shay. He was kind of the leader—a bully if you want to know the truth—he told Heavy to drive on into the cave the way they always did." She smoothed Snake's soft spot as she spoke. "I was getting really scared."

The way her head was tilted, her long hair shadowed her face. I tried to send her courage across the fire. I know that sounds stupid, but it's true.

She took a breath and continued. "The cave turned out to be just a little further up the road. We all had to get out and hold branches aside so Heavy could drive in."

"Right inside?" Cade asked. "Man, I'd like to see this place."

Faith nodded. "It was just a big open space. Not too dark since it wasn't even sunset."

"The whole car? Right inside?"

She nodded, again, a slight smile on her lips. "The whole car. With lots of room to spare." She rubbed Snake's ears gently. He pressed his head against her knee. "Have you never been to Carlsbad Caverns?"

She glanced at Cade. I didn't think she wasn't chastising him, but she got her point across.

"What? Oh, yeah. Sure. Who hasn't?" He chuckled. "I see what you mean. A whole fleet of cars could fit in there."

"Anyhow," she said. "We'd barely got out of the car when the sky ripped open. We didn't know what it was at first. Just that unbelievable tuba sound, like Jack said."

She glanced at me and did the half-smile thing again. I smiled back and immediately felt like the world's biggest idiot. Who smiles and flirts during the apocalypse? I waited for Cade to call me on it—embarrass me the way he'd always done, but Faith didn't give him a chance.

"We all dove back into the car and covered our ears. Heavy

restarted the engine and Metallica blasted our eardrums on top of the grinding tuba sounds."

"I know that cave," Sam said. "Kids always partied there. Lots of graffiti. Explored it myself a time or two. Not far away is a little town called Stutter Creek. I've had sandwiches at the café there." He sipped his coffee. "I'll bet the Camaro's engine helped drown out the tuba a little, too. Didn't it? In that enclosed space?"

Faith nodded. "Maybe so, at least my eardrums didn't burst. It didn't last that long now that I think about it. But at the time, it seemed forever." She shivered. "We didn't stay in the cave after the noise quit." Her shoulders went up a little. "Masen said it was a tornado that must've passed nearby. He was eager to get back on the road and see the damage. I think he hoped we would see something, you know, *bad*." Her lips twisted into a grimace of disgust before she continued.

"We were so far out in the country, there were no other people around. Masen seemed very let down about that. He kept saying, 'why aren't the trees broken? Why is there no damage?'"

I saw her right-hand float down to grip the loose skin around Snake's neck.

"We all saw the funny marks in the sky—the fluttery looking places—we even saw the slime coating the trees, dripping from the highline wires, but Shay and the guys were getting drunker and drunker, higher and higher. They kept saying it was just clouds and thick rain. *Thick rain*." She shook her head. "They thought that was so funny, every time they said it—*thick rain*. They'd been smoking and drinking nonstop since we got in the car." She closed her eyes. "I'd taken a toke or two as well, just to fit in, you know?" Her voice caught up in her throat, stopping her tale again.

"Anyhow, we didn't see any of *them* until we got back on the highway." Her gaze flicked toward Turq.

"Go on," I murmured. "What happened next?"

"We practically flew back toward Lewiston. Heavy drove like a maniac."

"Did you go back on 380?" Sam asked.

Faith nodded. "We'd seen a couple of stalled cars by then, almost rear ended them, and everyone started arguing and yelling. I just wanted to get out and walk, but of course it was miles and miles from home." She paused again, as if judging how much to tell. "And then Masen went nuts on us."

"How do you mean?" Sam asked.

Faith tossed her hair over one shoulder. "It seemed like he couldn't calm down. Like the sounds and the weird weather had flipped some switch in him."

I nodded. "Adrenalin, maybe."

"Fear," Sam said.

Faith looked at the ground. "Drugs, probably. Something he got from the guy in the parking lot. He was a bully before the rip, but afterward, he became a monster. Just seemed like he wanted to go and inflict some damage on someone."

The night lay upon us like a well-worn blanket. We all waited on her to continue. When she did, her voice had changed to that of a storyteller.

"The faster Heavy drove, the less we talked. I just held on, praying for a miracle to get home safely. Then we came up out of a dip, and there were several cars wrecked in the middle of the highway. A real tangle of metal and glass. We could see people behind the wheel, but Masen said they were all dead. He wouldn't let Heavy stop to check on them."

Faith ducked her head. "I got so upset, screaming, crying, wanting to go back and check, but we just flew on past as if the cars weren't even full of people. As if they weren't covered in ooze—"

"Damn." The word escaped my lips before I could stop it. "Sorry, I just—"

"It's okay," she said. "I couldn't believe it, either. If Shay hadn't been wasted maybe she would have taken my side and tried to make the guys stop."

"When did y'all encounter the Takers?" I asked.

She lowered her voice to little more than a whisper. "When we got nearer to town. Masen got louder and uglier, telling me to shut up, scaring me even more." Her fingers held tightly to Snake's collar. "And then we saw a hitchhiker."

"Masen yelled, 'You wanna stop so bad, girly?' His face looked like murder. He hung it over the back of the seat at me like a weapon. 'Pull over, Heavy. This chick wants to learn how to roll someone.'

"Heavy didn't say a word, just swung the car toward the shoulder of the highway. We slid up behind the odd-looking hitchhiker in a tattered jacket. Our headlights glanced off a bald head with tattoos that seemed to appear and disappear—"

"Oh, hell," I said. Every one of us knew what was wearing that jacket. And it wasn't just a hitchhiker.

Faith nodded. "I didn't know exactly what Masen meant to do, but I knew it wasn't good. I kept saying 'just let me out, let me go *home*.' But they all ignored me."

She took another drag on her Marlboro, and then continued, "I nudged Shay with my elbow. We'd both wound up in the back seat when we left the cave, but Shay just scooted further into the corner and popped open another beer."

Reaching into her back pocket, Faith pulled out a small notebook. From another pocket she took a mini flashlight. "I wrote it all down," she said. "It's how I pass my time."

I wanted to ask where she'd found the working mini-light, but I figured it could wait until later.

She began to read. "Masen flung the car door open, and Metallica propelled him toward the hitchhiker like a cannonball." Her reading voice ratcheted up a notch. "Heavy put the gearshift in neutral and ate the roach he and Masen had been smoking. I remember how Shay's eyes glittered in the backseat moonlight. The rain had stopped, but the air felt like warm soup." She paused, maybe to control the tremor in her voice.

"Is this the first time you've read this out loud?" I asked.

Faith nodded. "I have only encountered a few people so far."

I nodded. But it was hard to imagine her hiding and running for all these weeks. Alone.

She moved her finger under the last line she'd read. "I could feel my heart quivering in my chest as I watched Masen rush up behind the hitcher." She swallowed. "From out of nowhere, a knife appeared. I didn't even know Masen had it. The guy hit the ground and clear fluid began to leak out of him as Masen stabbed and stabbed and stabbed—"

She stopped talking, and I noticed Turq's entire face now turned toward her.

"I saw black letters wiggling on the ground. They seemed to be part of that clear fluid—"

I touched her shoulder, and she almost jumped out of her skin. "We've all seen it. The clear blood, the black words."

She nodded.

"Did the black stuff come?" I asked.

Faith looked at me with eyes as big as the rising moon. "Yes," she whispered. "It came in a downpour. A deluge. Heavy hit the gas and Masen jumped in as we roared away. But I turned around and watched. The black stuff fell from one of those skinned places in the sky—it fell like dark rain, then it just *engulfed the hitchhiker-thing.*"

She half-turned toward Turq, then yanked her gaze back toward her book. "It covered him up, and he disappeared like he'd been consumed. Then the dark liquid burst into a million bugs—locusts, I think—and flew buzzing back into that hole in the sky." Her little flashlight clicked off. "I thought it was the stuff we'd smoked. It seemed so real and so unreal at the same time."

I nodded, unable to picture Faith high or drunk. "The hitcher must've been one of the good ones, like Turq."

"How do you know?" she asked.

"The fact that it was alone and had on some sort of clothing." I stepped over to the ice chest, got a bottle of water, and nodded toward Turq. "That's why I wanted to wrap his wound so quickly when the bullet grazed him." I handed her the dripping bottle of water. "The word-fluid must be full of pheromones. It brings the liquid-locusts every time."

Turq's hand went to the t-shirt still tied around his upper arm.

Faith twisted the lid off the water and gulped as if the telling had wrung all the moisture from her.

I wanted to say, *it looks like the Takers aren't the only monsters loose in this world,* but of course no one needed to hear that. It would be stating the obvious. Our history was jam-packed with monsters.

The difference was they didn't usually fall down upon our heads through holes in the sky. I dried my hand on my jeans and sat back down. "What happened to your friends?"

Faith drew her knees up to her chest and clicked the mini light on. She snuffed out her cigarette, and I saw her hand reach for Snake again. "They all died," she said. "Heavy was doing about ninety when a different hitchhiker stepped out in front of us." Her voice took on that dreamy, storyteller tone again. "By then I knew they weren't really hitchers at all."

"What happened?" Cade asked. "Did y'all hit it?"

"The fender clipped the thing and twirled it across the hood. We went from ninety to nothing in a terrible, shuddering slide." She moved her cracked glasses up a little, clicked the flashlight back on. "I flew past Masen's shoulder and struck the windshield just as a huge bald head smashed into it from outside. Van Gogh's *Starry Night* exploded in my brain as we somehow hit the thing a second time."

She stopped, gulped a drink of water, then looked back down at her notebook. "I lost track of Masen altogether as we careened off the highway into the bar ditch. All I remember is how the nose of the Camaro dug into the earth, spraying up a red fan of dirt that hung in the air like a curtain between life and death."

"*Day*-um," Cade said. "You sound like you're reading from a real book—"

Faith closed her eyes. "I wanted to be a writer. Back in the world."

"Go on," I said. I didn't tell her I had a journal, too. Didn't write regularly or pretty like she did, but without the internet, we had to do something. My problem was I kept losing them. The notebooks.

Faith took a deep breath and began to read again. "Someone's skull smashed into my face." Her fingertips sought her eyebrow as if feeling an old wound. "When I came to, the car had flipped upside down. On its roof."

A few coals still glowed down in the grill, but they no longer gave off much light. The night was eerily still and quiet.

"The stereo had cut off, but I could hear the sound of the red dirt raining down upon the metal undercarriage of the car." In a quieter voice, she said, "When that stopped, a horrible silence filled the air."

We waited.

"It took a moment for me to understand all that had happened," she said. "Then I realized I was wedged between the upside-down dash and the roof. I tried to pull myself out without turning my head while visions of wheelchairs danced through my mind like sugar-plums on Christmas Eve." A smile entered her voice, and I imagined how she'd spent hours perfecting that Christmas Eve phrase.

"I didn't want to be paralyzed," she said. "But I knew I had to get out of the car. In the movies, cars always explode after a wreck. I could smell the pungent odor of gasoline." She sat forward, feet flat on the ground, and I noticed Snake lean into her legs as if to steady her.

"The impact had popped out both windshields. The openings were just a fraction of their true size. I worked my way out of the space beneath the dash little by little. I didn't see the others—human or hitcher—anywhere."

She took a sip. Then went on. "The broken shaft of the steering wheel pointed downward, only a piece of the wheel still attached to the column. The driver's side window seemed a little less jagged than the passenger side, so I crawled across the ceiling of the car feeling everywhere for my glasses. Miraculously, I found them with my knee. Probably how the lens got cracked." She tapped it with her fingernail.

"Anyhow, I thrust my head out the driver's window. Heavy's hand stuck out from under the car right below my face. I watched as it swelled and purpled. The skin across the knuckles split open. Blood oozed, trickled down between his fingers."

She took a breath, and I expected her to light another cigarette, but she gathered her courage and began to read again.

"The sound of labored breathing pushed inside my head. Heavy was still alive. I tried to speak, but dust clogged my throat. I ran my tongue out. My lips were coated with coppery grit. 'Heavy?' My voice came out all raspy. Like an old gate hinge.

"'Faith?' Shay's voice came from somewhere behind me. The moon shone through the raw opening where the back windshield should've been. Even filtered through the haze of red dust, it lit up the interior of the car like a weak flashlight, but Shay wasn't inside. Neither was Masen. I scanned the area as well as I could.

"My palms were on the ground near Heavy's hand, the rest of my body still inside the car. As I struggled to get out, a massive gray form blocked the moonlight. Words skittered across its broad chest, beneath its see-through skin. Latin-looking words I could not understand—"

"Oh, man, Faith." The way she spoke put me right there with her. "That brings everything back."

She glanced at me, but continued with her story, needing to get it out, the same way Sam did. "I yanked myself out of that window," she said. "My knee squashed down on Heavy's swollen, bleeding hand, and I didn't even care.

"'Faith, where *are* you?' Shay called me again, fainter than before. I staggered to my feet and almost fell over Masen dragging himself away. One of his lower legs appeared to be hanging on by *tendons*. I remembered how his knife had flashed in the moonlight as he stabbed and stabbed and stabbed. And then I saw Shay face-down in the ditch, her body broken, hips facing up instead of down.

"A *shushing* sound wove its way into my brain, and for some reason that got me going. I took off at a stumbling run, my back muscles shrieking for me to stop. But I didn't stop. I could do nothing for Shay or Heavy, and I didn't care if Masen lived or died. His long, lanky form continued to struggle along in the bar ditch like a half-squashed bug, the mangled leg leaving drag marks in the dirt.

"In a panic I lurched up the side of the ditch toward the highway. When I glanced back, a slanted beam of moonlight picked out the massive gray shape. It was headed straight for Masen.

I looked away, but just like passing a wreck on the side of the road, I had to look back. The shape's long arms reached for Masen as if across time and space. To my horror, it grasped the bully by the head, slung his six-foot-plus frame over its shoulder, and strode directly toward a stand of stunted mesquite trees."

She squeezed her eyes shut as if to clear the memory. Her fingers clutched the sides of the spiral notebook into curls.

"Even at a distance," she said, "I could hear Masen struggling to breathe. I still wondered if the weed we'd smoked had been dusted with something to cause such horrific hallucinations, but I couldn't stop to make certain. The shushing sound was growing louder.

"I made it up the slope of the ditch to the highway and there, in the distance, I could see them, the whole gray mass, marching toward me, their red eyes glittering, bare feet scraping the asphalt, words of murder and torture swimming beneath their skin like evil promises—and I ran, stumbling toward a hiding place on the other side of the four-lane."

Around the grill, we all let out a collective sigh.

"Is that how you got away?" I asked.

She nodded, eyes awash in unshed tears. "They were so busy with my friends they never found me hiding in the stubbly cotton field."

I looked at her face. Did she even realize how she spoke, how she wrote, like a poet?

"Did they stick all your buddies on the mesquites?" Cade asked.

I wanted to smack him in the back of the head the way his dad always did when he said stupid stuff, but he was on the other side of the grill.

Faith nodded. "One of them flipped the Camaro off Heavy like it was nothing." She looked at the ground. "That was the last thing I saw before I lay down between the rows of old cotton." She closed her journal. Smoothed her hair. Adjusted her glasses. "I hid out in that fallow field, and I've been hiding ever since."

I opened my mouth to tell her we'd all been hiding in one way or another, but Sam tossed his coffee dregs on the coals and made them sizzle.

I stood. "I'm going to bring the Chrysler closer to the first room."

"I'll walk with you," Faith said.

We strolled the short distance to the Chrysler, the moon barely lighting our path.

"I want to stay in the room with you and Snake if it's okay, and maybe Sam, but please don't leave me alone with those other guys." Her eyes were wide.

"No problem. What about Turq? He usually goes where I go."

She smiled. "He's okay."

That sealed it for me. After that admission, I knew we were on the same wavelength. As we walked back to the fire together, George Harrison's love song, "Something," resurfaced in my head. But oddly enough, no other song. Not even a warning song about the knife-wielding kid running around. Nothing. I couldn't understand it.

CHAPTER THIRTEEN

Skin

Hal appeared, swigging the last of his water. "Think I'll just cozy the Dodge up to the door, too. Especially with that little sneak running around. Wouldn't put it past him to try and hotwire this puppy." He threw his plastic bottle on the ground, climbed in the driver's seat, started it up, and rolled it right up to the door of the furthest room.

Cade trotted over. His dark hair eclipsed his eyes. "See y'all in the a.m.," he said. "I guess we'll head on to Abilene with you."

"It's okay with me." I slugged him on the shoulder. "I still can't believe you're alive."

Cade laughed ruefully. "I can't believe any of this. To me it feels like we stepped into a video game."

"I hear that, bro."

He slugged me back and walked on toward the Dodge—and Hal.

That bothered me. Cade and I went back years. Should I tell him I *want* him to stay with us? That would be stupid. There wouldn't be room. Snake and Faith on one bed, me on the other. Carlos on watch, Turq back and forth.

But he could always share the bed with me. We'd done it dozens of times. Dozens. Why the sudden allegiance to Hal? Was it because of Faith? Was it jealousy?

A new song began to stutter through my head. "Ti-i-i-ime Is on My Side." Rolling Stones. Stone*age*, for sure. Okay, okay, I get it. Take my time. He feels like this guy saved his life. Maybe he's leery of Turq, not Faith.

Time.

Got it.

And if he'd rather be with Hal, so what? I've got a crew here. They saved my life, too.

"Jack?" Faith shook my arm a little.

She stood right beside me, her face inches from mine. Her scent, oranges mixed with rain. How could anyone smell that fresh after all we'd been through?

"Yeah?"

She laughed. "I said, do you think we can use the bathrooms here?"

I had to stifle my own laugh. "Sorry, I was thinking about Cade. We've been friends since we were in third grade, you know?" I stuffed down the rest of the explanation. She didn't need to hear all that mumbo jumbo. "I don't see why not," I answered. "We probably won't be back this way again." And even though I'm the one who said it, that statement, that thought, punched me in the gut like a prize fighter. After all, this was my hometown. *My* Eden.

For hours afterward, right through my turn on watch, one of Mom and Dad's old Seals & Crofts' songs, "We May Never Pass this Way Again," slid through my head, tickling my brain cells with longing. I wondered if I had summoned the song with my earlier thinking. Didn't matter. I knew what I needed to do. I needed to go back. To see that my home really *was* gone, burned to the ground. Needed to see it for myself. Free myself from it.

At our room near the office, Faith took a small candle from her backpack, lit it with a blue Bic, and went into the bathroom. I never thought to carry candles. I carried lighters for making fires, and my crank-handle flashlight for everything else. I knew there were good batteries somewhere, and flashlights that would use them, but so far, we hadn't been lucky enough to find them.

In the back of my mind a new idea surfaced. What else did

Faith do that might benefit us? Maybe she had other good ideas that had helped keep her alive.

I lay on the full-size bed, Snake beside me, and thought about all the ways the lot of us were different, and the same, roped together by this adversity. It made me think of fish in a fishbowl. All our differences on display now that there were so few of us.

Dozing, I dreamed about black sludge and colorful vegetables. One thing terrified me, the other intrigued me. I'd never liked vegetables, but I'd had the trunk of the Chrysler full of them when the dark rain fell on the burning Takers and nearly swept us over the cliff at the buffalo jump.

In the midst of my dream, voices woke me. Whispers in the dark.

My hand went for the pistol beneath my pillow.

"S'okay, Jack. It's just me."

I sat up, comforted by Carlos' slight accent. Turq laid him beside me on the bed, reaching over me with his long, long arms. *Damn.* The strength that must've have taken.

Carlos lowered the small Maglite he'd been holding. "It's okay," he said again. "Faith went out to watch, but I don't want her out there alone."

I sat up. "Snake with her?"

Carlos nodded, eyelids already closing like window shades being lowered by a careful hand. "Take this." He pushed the shotgun at me.

As if on cue, a deep growl arose from just outside the open door, followed by a sudden volley of snarls and barks.

I ran outside. Sam was already there. Snake stood, quivering, at the edge of the wooded area.

"Was it him?" I asked.

Sam nodded. "Pretty sure."

"Damn," I said. "He didn't go very far, did he?"

Sam glanced at Faith. "You all right, girl?"

She nodded. The moon hung directly overhead now; its splintery light coating her hair in silver. "He just startled me and Snake, that's all. I think he thought it was safe when he saw Carlos and Turq go inside."

"The changing of the guard." Sam laughed. "He had no idea

Snake was watching. Idiot." He tucked his handgun in the back of his pants.

"I don't know why he would come back if he was free—"

"Drugs make you stupid," Faith said. "Almost everyone I've encountered has been wasted on something." She had her hand on Snake's head again. Her touch appeared to calm him.

"Self-medicating, I guess." I told them about Marla, Kevin's girlfriend back at my house, and how she'd been so terrified she couldn't function. "She's the one who caused everything to come apart that night. Trying to take all the drugs in my mom's medicine cabinet before I even knew what had happened to my mom." My heart pumped harder just thinking of her. "A different kind of Taker, Marla. And it cost her boyfriend his life."

I noticed Faith putting something in her cross-body bag. She seemed prepared for nearly anything. "Do you carry anything to protect yourself?"

She showed me a small automatic handgun. A .25 caliber maybe. I couldn't tell for sure. "I would like to have a shotgun like Carlos. But I haven't found one yet."

"We'll find one for you." I thought of the many guns we'd had before the firenado. I didn't even remember what had become of them.

"Guns and vegetables," I said.

Faith laughed.

Sam raised an eyebrow.

"I don't know," I said. "Just thinking out loud." I let my Dynamo go off and went out to the cold grill to bring the chairs back onto the sidewalk in front of the doors.

Sam grabbed a couple more chairs, which surprised me. We already had three chairs, one for each human, so I assumed he brought the other for Turq.

But as usual, Turq did not sit. Simply stood quietly, a short distance from us, and upwind, I noticed, as if our human scents were something to be avoided.

Faith and I sat with our chairs far enough apart that Snake could take his place between us. When my hand went toward the soft spot on his broad, flat head, Faith's hand was already there. Her skin was warm. My touch lingered for a second, just long enough for her to laugh and pull back slightly.

It didn't bother me. She didn't jerk her hand away. Besides, I got the feeling she only moved it because Sam was there. I wanted to find out for certain, but something else had caught my attention. Something disturbing.

Turq stood a few feet away, and even though his garnet eyes looked straight ahead, seeming to watch the entire area all at once, the blunt fingertips of his right hand had strayed to his left arm, where he'd caught the bullet earlier, and they were deftly pulling away tiny strips of gray skin.

I could see the puckered wound, exposed. It reminded me of something I used to do when I had a scab. Mom would swat my hand. *Leave that alone, Jack. Let it heal.* But little boys always peeled away their scabs, didn't they? Little girls, too, I'll bet. I guess monsters are the same.

I stood and walked over. He didn't seem to realize what his fingers were doing. "What's up, buddy?" I asked.

He turned his eyes toward me, and I reached toward his wound. "Does it itch?" I could see that he was only pulling away the thinnest outer layer, not enough to cause more leakage, thank God. It reminded me of the way we used to paint our palms with glue then peel it off when it dried.

I leaned closer to examine the wound. It looked fine to me, but everywhere he had peeled back the skin, the underneath was shiny and moist, on the *verge* of leaking.

"Um, Turq, ol' buddy," I hesitated, unsure how to proceed. "Maybe you shouldn't pull off anymore skin." I looked up at his eyes. "We don't want your words to spill out and make the black stuff come down, right?"

Even though he'd carried me around, even though we'd been living and riding together for days and weeks, this was the first time I'd ever tried to tell him what to do. Or in this case, what *not* to do.

Letters began to surface. It reminded me of the way song lyrics surfaced in my mind, slowly, sometimes incomplete, searching for daylight, or maybe moonlight.

But for the first time since I'd "known" him, Turq's letters did not form coherent words. They simply appeared briefly, then sank back down into oblivion, invisible until the next one or two appeared and disappeared.

"Hey," I said. "You okay?"

His eyes rotated down to view his own hand. His fingers stopped, and he paralleled his palm and did the back-and-forth tilt in the air.

The hair at the back of my neck stood at attention. I realized exactly how much I had grown to depend on this big gray thing. How much I'd grown to care for him. I reached out to touch his wounded arm, but he shrugged his shoulder back just enough that I would have had to lean forward, throwing myself off balance.

I let my hand down, slowly. "It's all right," I said. "Just tell me if I can do anything, okay?"

Turq inclined his head once.

I took that for a nod.

CHAPTER FOURTEEN

Eden Pirate

The rest of the night passed peacefully. I talked Faith into going back inside to sleep for a few hours, then she came out near sunrise and said she'd slept enough. All through the night, Sam came and went. None of us ever mentioned asking Cade or Hal to take watch, but since Turq doesn't sleep, he was there all along.

Once or twice I thought I heard *shushing* sounds, but then they would fade away. I worried more about them than I did the kid with the knife.

Toward daylight, before Faith came back out, "Can't Find My Way Home" resurfaced in my sleepy brain. *I'm going*, I told my subconscious. *When everyone gets up again, I'm going to drive back by the house, I promise.*

With that thought, a barrage of old classic rock songs tumbled through my head. They started with Harry Chapin's "The Cat's in the Cradle," about a dad who missed his son's childhood because he worked all the time and culminated in my old standby "Carry on Wayward Son." In between, there were bits and pieces of others I couldn't always name.

I plopped down onto one of the chairs and massaged my temples, surprised at the onslaught. The music hadn't gripped me this way since the standoff at the buffalo jump. *It's gotta be Dad. He must be alive. He must be. My music wouldn't keep goading me this way if not.* Or maybe I caused it all by telling myself how the music had stopped. "Don't bring down the juju gods," my friend Dee used

98

to say. That meant never say something wasn't going to happen because then it would.

Faith yawned, wishing for coffee. "Where's a Starbucks when you need one?" she quipped.

I tried to smile, but the tunes wouldn't let me converse, especially "Teach Your Children." When the song started out about living on the road, living by a code, I nearly flipped out. It could have been a letter from my dad, it seemed so clear.

"What's wrong?" she asked. "Headache?"

"Little bit of noise this morning—going crazy, I think."

She walked behind me and laid a hand on each of my shoulders. "I used to do this when my mom had a bad headache."

Her fingers began to knead the muscles on top of my shoulders, then her thumbs dug into the hollows beside my shoulder blades. I rolled my head around, eyes closing automatically. "Feels good," I mumbled. "I didn't realize the—"

"Tension?" she said. "That's exactly what my mom would say." She laughed a little, as if she'd embarrassed herself.

I was about to tell her about the music in my head when I saw Cade headed our way. "Hey, Bro." I let the word hang in the air.

Faith's fingers stopped, and then started up again. It felt a little odd, having her massage me with him looking on.

"Hey, Jackie? You still get the songs like you used to?"

Well, there ya go. No secrets with him around. "Yeah," I said. "More than ever." I cleared my throat, touched my fingertips to one of Faith's kneading hands. She stepped back and sat in the other chair nearby. Turq shuffled his feet.

Cade sat in the third chair, lowered his voice to a stage whisper, "Seriously, does that thing ever get tired or hungry?" He jerked his thumb over his shoulder toward Turq. "I haven't seen him sit down once or even take a drink of water."

"I know." I looked at my big gray friend in his tattered turquoise shirt. "I stopped trying to figure him out. Just had to accept him. After he saved my life, I really had no choice, especially after the mess in New Mexico."

I rubbed my temple. Where were all these songs *coming* from?

Snake appeared like a furry shadow and sat beside my knee, as if he could feel my pain.

Cade's voice changed from smart-ass back to normal friend. "The songs didn't used to hurt, did they, Jack?"

"No," I said. "But since the rip, some of them are like knives."

"Is that why your eye does that thing?"

I looked at him. "What thing?"

"You know that pirate thing, like you've only got one good eye."

My hand went to my face, but I couldn't feel anything different. I stood and started toward the room where Carlos lay sleeping, decided I didn't want to disturb him, went over to the Chrysler, and leaned down to check my face in the side mirror.

Sure enough. My right eye was squinty, the other one appearing large in comparison. *Popeye,* I thought. *The Sailor Man. Geez, how long's this been going on? No wonder my head hurts, squinting that way all the time. Or is it the other way around and my eye is squinting because my head hurts?*

"Guess I'll invest in an eyepatch." I tried to make my tone light, joking. But I couldn't keep my gaze from straying to Faith, to see her reaction. Here I'd been thinking she was into me when she probably just felt sorry for me. No wonder she'd offered to rub my neck. I looked like a fool. I felt like a fool.

"Wanna borrow my glasses?" she joked. "Maybe your good eye can see out of my one good lens."

Her morbid humor took me by surprise, and I laughed out loud.

"We make a good team," she said.

"The blind leading the blind?" When I said that, the Blind Faith song resurfaced in my skull, and for the first time, I wished I could share it with someone. With Faith. See what she thought about my crazy brain. About Blind Faith. What a coincidence.

She smiled softly. "Yeah, blind leading the blind."

Something passed between us, across that little sitting area, something that had to be ESP. I suddenly thought maybe she *didn't* care about my funny eye—just like I didn't care about her funky glasses. As far as that goes, I didn't even care about her looks. All I noticed was the way she moved and her soft, dark eyes that drank me in like a straw. And I figured she must be pretty tough to still be alive. I admired that.

But even before I'd seen her, when I heard her voice that day in the locker room, I'd been hooked. The sound of her voice went directly into my brain just like one of my songs.

"Hey, Brown Eyed Girl ..."

She looked at me from her lawn chair, one eyebrow raised, just a bit, barely visible over the rim of her specs.

"Thanks for the neck rub." I rolled my head back a little. "Feels better. It does."

Faith laughed. "Magic fingers." She waved them in the air like spider legs.

I opened my squinty eye and tried to make it focus more clearly. Something about the way she said "magic fingers" stirred feelings in my body that had nothing to do with my neck. I walked around the back of my lawn chair, hoping no one noticed.

Cade did, of course. He had a sixth sense about stuff like that. *Horn-mones*, he called these feelings. *Teenage horn-mones.* I tried to ignore the smirk on his face. To tell the truth, I wanted to smash it off—with my fist.

Thankfully, Sam came out. "We got a plan, boys?"

I was glad he intended to go with us to Abilene. "I'm going to drive past my old house before we go," I said. "Just so I'll know." I glanced over at Cade. "It won't take long."

He nodded. "I—yeah. Just prepare yourself, dude. I mean, it's all gone."

Faith said, "I'll ride with you." We started to the car under the watchful eye of Sam and Turq.

Sam raised one hand. "I'll go, too, check for supplies in town."

"My thoughts exactly. Might as well look, there are two large grocery stores in town—"

Cade shook his head. "They've been stripped," he said.

"What about the smaller ones? Grady's and White's Main Street Market?"

"Yeah, them, too." He shrugged. "Guess that's what we get for being right on the Interstate."

Hal snickered. He'd strolled up quietly, observing. Not participating.

I thought of the gang from last night. "Must be a lot of rovers."

In a nonchalant tone, Faith said, "Looks like we *are* going to have to learn to grow our own food. Like we talked about."

I nodded. "And don't forget hunting rabbit, prairie dog, gopher."

"Fishing's still good," Sam said. "I guess the slime was absorbed after a while. Or dissipated somehow. It did kill a lot of fish, but not all of them." He laughed a little. "Haven't seen a lot of lakes or rivers around here, though. Just a lot of pecans." He cracked a couple of nuts together in his palm and carefully pulled out the meat. "Good ones, too. Which surprises me since they got slimed along with everything else."

"We have a couple pecan trees in our yard—"

"Had," Cade interjected.

"Had," I repeated. "The new pecans don't ripen until late fall. Around Thanksgiving. Those must be from last year. Guess the hard shell protected them."

Turq bent over and picked up a few nuts from beneath the big tree near the office. He examined them before crushing them together in his palm.

Sam walked over and stuck a few shelled ones in the creature's hand. "Maybe don't squeeze them quite so hard," he said.

Turq looked them over, then looked at the hard shells in his other hand. He seemed to be trying to figure out the relationship. Finally, he turned up both palms and let them all fall to the ground.

I headed to the car, still amazed at his inexplicable lack of need for food or drink. Everyone knows any life force must have fuel. So, where's he getting his?

Carlos appeared in the doorway, holding on to the jamb to keep himself upright. "We leaving?"

I nodded. "Looks like you're ready."

"Always." He staggered out a couple steps, grasping at the backs of the chairs for stability.

I turned, but before I could get to him, Turq scooped him up and headed to the car.

Cade stretched and yawned. "We need to look for some gasoline. How about we meet y'all down at the old Pancake Place diner. You know, Jack, right at the entrance to the Interstate."

"You sure?"

Hal nodded his agreement. "Lot's of old cars we haven't tapped yet."

I started the Chrysler as Turq put Carlos in the backseat.

"He could stretch out in my backseat," Sam offered.

I looked at Carlos.

"S'okay with me," he said.

We all knew he'd been uncomfortable the day before with Faith and Snake in the back seat of the Chrysler.

"I'm the newcomer," Faith said in a quiet voice. "I can ride with Sam if it will make Carlos more comfortable."

"Nah," Carlos said. "We'll try this." He grinned. "Just pile up a few of those blankets, will you?"

Sam did.

Turq set our burned friend inside on top of them. I saw Carlos touch the image of the crucifix on his throat as a grimace of pain shadowed his face. It still amazed me to watch Turq with him. Caring was the word that came to mind. He cared for Carlos, no doubt about it.

"Ready?" I asked.

Faith opened the back door for Snake, then she hesitated and climbed in after him. I thought she wanted to ride shotgun but so far that had been Turq's domain. Oh, well. One change at a time.

"See y'all at the Pancake Place," I said to Cade.

He looked at me over his shoulder. Gave me a thumbs up. In the back of my mind, I figured he was calling me Old Mother Hen. It used to be one of his nicknames for me, because he said I always had to be in control of every situation. And that was true. But only because that's the best way to be sure of the outcome.

By the time we turned out of the motel parking lot, last night's moon was a ghostly white coin high in the pale of the sky. Puff clouds dotted the far reaches, and a small breeze breathed the hint of cooler weather into our open windows.

A mantle of sadness settled over me as I drove through the downtown area, past Mom's library where her body still—I assumed—lay in state in the Comparative Religions room.

The Chrysler seemed to slow of its own accord. Should I try to go in and get her? Bury her in the cemetery or even in the park? What would she look like now? If it was really bad, could I live with that image? I hadn't let myself think about it before now, but in a way, she was already buried. The entire library had been turned into a mausoleum.

Maybe I'll leave well enough alone.

I drove on past the Dairy Queen with its busted windows and parking lot full of busted cars. We coasted through the silent streets, watching for any sign of movement, a dog, or a cat, even a squirrel. But all we saw were a couple of mice scurrying around the outside of the Piggly Wiggly.

"Looks like a great town," Faith murmured.

"It was," I said. "Eden, Texas. Kind of appropriate, right? If they were looking for pure, unsullied souls." I glanced over at Turq to see if he would confirm or deny my theory, but he didn't. Couldn't, I guess. "I think they're as clueless as we are when it comes to why we're all here." I laughed at my sudden burst of philosophical musing. But then I recalled a memory of the Takers in St. Stephen's church the day after the rip.

Which gave me a comical sort of image of a big gray Taker-boss with his finger jabbing toward a spinning globe of Earth. "Eden," the big gray said when his fingertip made contact. "The garden!"

I shook my head, but the image stuck like glue.

The garden. And all those Takers in the church.

I wondered what became of them. They had all donned clothing, too. I assume they were also Turqs. Just like the one Faith said her friend, Masen, had stabbed. Walking along the road.

The "Woodstock" song flared in my head. That iconic beat and Neil Young's guitar—odd that I knew that old song so well. Almost as if Dad played it so often because he knew something like this was coming. "We are stardust, we are—"

I shook my head before "golden" slipped out.

Nah. He just loved the old hippie stuff. He would say so himself if he were here.

Maybe I should drive by St. Stephen's. Just to make sure the other Turqs were gone. But would our Turq want to stay there, join them?

I'd have to ask Cade again if he'd seen them. Surely, he'd know if an entire congregation of church-going Takers were still in town. I might ask him out of earshot of Hal. But what would we do if they *were* there?

I had no more time to ponder. We were turning onto my street. My house and the ones on each side of it were burned to the ground just like Cade said. The whole middle of the block area was nothing but a big black smudge where they used to be.

Snake whined. His old home was on the corner of the next block. I wondered if I should let him out. If his previous owner was in that house, he would be nothing but a mummy or a skeleton. *Do animals need closure?*

I stopped the car in the middle of the street and stepped out.

Cade was right. There was nothing left but ash, a few scorched bricks where Mom's beloved fireplace once stood, charred kitchen appliances—stove, fridge, microwave, dishwasher—and blackened sinks and toilets. All those things that once seemed like necessities. *Ashes to ashes,* I thought again.

In what used to be the den I saw a huge lump of plastic that might have been Dad's old desk top computer, and here and there tiny remnants of furniture, a bit of fabric or a leg that might have been part of the dining table, but that was all.

Except for the skull.

CHAPTER FIFTEEN

Home

I should have been expecting it. Thad said he was the only one who had survived the fire because after I left, he'd found my Dad's Scotch and got stinking drunk. He said the women had made him leave and when he found the Chrysler and came back for them, the house was engulfed. He assumed it had started from the candles they'd lit.

It made sense, in a way.

I leaned over to examine the charred skull. There wasn't much left. The fire had obviously burned unchecked.

Turq stayed in the car, but Faith got out and came up beside me. "Who is that?" she asked.

"I think it was Marla's boyfriend, Kevin. Thad accidentally shot him while trying to save Marla from a Taker. He bled out on the dining room table." I looked at the bit of table leg nearby. "Snake and I took off that night. I left Thad and three women here. Two of them worked for Thad, and the other one was Marla."

I thought back to her last words about how she was going to kill me because it was my fault Kevin was dead. "I never saw any of them again except for Thad. He found Snake and me on the other side of town. He was driving the Chrysler." I stood and looked around the room for other human remains.

"How awful." Faith murmured.

"Yeah." I nodded. "On top of the Takers and all that, this was too much for me, you know? All I could think about was finding my parents." I glanced around the ruins of my life. "Seems like there should be other bodies here if they were in the house when it burned. Mo, Lara, Marla—"

"Maybe they all got out, and Thad just assumed they were here."

"Maybe. He did say he was drinking." Something caught my eye. It was followed by some small sound. When I glanced up, Turq had moved into the yard as if coming to get me. Snake was nowhere to be seen.

"Oh, hell," I said. "Do you hear them coming?"

Faith had been crouched over the skull. She stood slowly; one hand cupped to her ear. Her eyes widened behind her lenses.

Turq turned to face the intersection.

Sam sat in his Jeep, but as I watched, his head also swiveled toward the sound.

Hundreds of bare feet on sandy pavement, *shushing* effortlessly, in natural cadence, each one a near-perfect replica of all the others. It occurred to me they could be powered by some sort of internal battery. Something I'd never heard of. Something alien or futuristic.

They turned the corner en masse. None of this bunch wore clothing, but they did seem to be on a mission. Not for us, though. This group seemed military, precise, a formation marching in the early morning.

I gave Faith a tiny push toward the car. "Run," I said.

Hundreds of garnet eyes glittered in the sunlight.

Faith made it to the Chrysler in record time, grabbed the door-handle, and slid inside. Turq opened the back door without missing a beat. Snake banged into his leg when he shot past him to leap into the seat. That surprised me. Until now, every time he'd seen a Taker, other than Turq, he had gone into attack mode. Maybe he wised up after they broke his leg back in Kansas.

Sam drove up beside us and popped the passenger door open from inside the Jeep. "C'mon!" he commanded.

Turq slammed my back door and got in with Sam. He didn't hesitate, just climbed in. I heard the *cha-chunk* of Carlos' shotgun from the backseat.

Sam motioned for me to lead. He didn't know where we were going.

Shooting a glance over my shoulder, I told Faith to hold on, then I pressed the accelerator. I'd been driving only a few months—since the rip—but I knew this car well enough to know it had a good engine if you treated it with a little respect. I didn't tromp the gas, I pressed it gently but firmly.

In moments, we were blocks away from the marching horde.

In the rearview, I could see them, a square block of moist gray bodies. Unfinished faces, blank and smooth, bright garnet eyes dazzling in the strong sunlight—they looked like an army of giant toys. Except for the squiggly black letters forming and reforming death words beneath their translucent skin.

If you'd never seen them eat someone alive, yank out their entrails and stuff them into their gaping, silver-toothed maws, you'd think they really were toys. Large, fleshy, robot toys under remote control.

"What are they doing?" Faith asked.

"Just what I wondered. Did they even know we were there? I mean, they didn't try to rush us, or anything—"

From the corner of my eye, I caught another glimpse of movement. "What's that?" I jerked my head toward the house to our right.

Faith half-turned to get a better look. "It's one of them," she said. "It's wearing clothes. Seems to be hiding—oh!"

"What is it?" My eyes sought the rearview as we sped past.

"They've got him!" she said. "A couple of them appeared out of nowhere—oh, my God, they're tearing him to *pieces*." She covered her eyes with her hands. "Why would they—"

The screech of brakes brought my attention back to the mirror. Faith turned around again, her hands grasping the seat back, craning her neck to see over the headrest.

Snake leapt at the back glass.

Sam had slammed on his brakes.

"It's Turq," Faith yelled. "He's getting out of the Jeep, going to help that one."

"Oh, hell." I pressed the brake and swung the Chrysler into a wide U turn in the middle of the next intersection.

"Drive toward them." Faith pulled her small gun.

I drove toward the shimmering mass beyond the Jeep. Turq

strode toward the trio on the opposite shoulder of the road. The clothed Taker was beyond hope.

"Stop the car!" Faith yelled.

I coasted to a stop. We were on the edge of town, nearly to the Pancake Place.

She stepped out, her small frame not much taller than the car, automatic clutched in both hands, and took aim at the group.

"Now!" I cried.

She pressed the trigger and the gun *pop pop popped* until all the rounds were gone. By the time the last one had cleared the barrel, the nose of the gun was pointed high above the horde.

Faith dropped her hand to her side. She had managed to hit at least three in the front line. They broke formation, leaking fluid and strings of black letters.

A sky hole rippled.

The mass of Takers parted like the red sea, leaving the wounded in puddles of dripping liquid, just like when they'd been *born*.

Carlos yelled across the way, offered Faith his shotgun, and she grinned and took it, handing him her handgun in return.

She didn't even aim, just fired the shotgun at the scattering horde, bringing down two more. She broke open the gun and handed it back to Carlos.

"You're right," she yelled. "That *works*." I assumed she was referring to my tale about shooting them so the black rain would come, the way we'd done back at Bitty Sloan's house in New Mexico.

We watched as letters squiggled on the pavement, and then the inky sludge began to fall. Turq had already made it back to the Jeep.

Confusion reigned.

Through the gap in the shoulder-to-shoulder pack, I caught a glimpse of something odd. It looked like long dark hair.

Cade's hair.

CHAPTER SIXTEEN

Traitor

Jack!" Carlos yelled. "They've got your friend!"

I shook my head, staring through the gap from my slightly better vantage point. "I don't know if they've got him, or if he's *with* them."

The gap had closed so we couldn't be certain.

A bullet whizzed past Faith and pinged off the Chrysler, but the sludge was falling fast and thick now. It *splopped* to the pavement and rushed toward the Takers in dark, shiny rivulets.

"Who's shooting at us?" she yelled

I gunned the engine. "Maybe it's Hal. I *never* trusted him."

The Takers Faith had shot were quickly obscured and consumed. The rest of the pack gave them a wide berth, so the sludge-rain didn't get them by mistake.

When all the injured ones had been covered, the mess burst apart into buzzing black locusts and flew back into the still-wavering sky hole.

That's when I got a good look at Cade and Hal and their new friend, the teen from last night. With the knife. Only now, he had a gun. There were other humans visible, too. Some looked like women.

My gut churned. "Traitors!" I hit the steering wheel with the heel of my hand. "Nothing but *traitors*." I couldn't seem to say anything else. The wall of gray closed back up around them.

"It kind of makes sense," Faith said. "I mean, we've got a nice Taker, they've got all the bad ones."

I didn't have a reply to that. But I did have another question.

"Where were all these Takers last night when we were having our little cook out?"

"Do you think your friends were trying to sucker us in, somehow?" Faith asked. "I mean, they found that kid, then they probably let him go, maybe to go back and tell the others. Then he came back when he thought I was alone on watch—" She also seemed to be trying to figure things out in her mind.

"I saw it, but I can't believe it." I kept my eyes glued to the rearview, my fingers clamped around the steering wheel. I took a solid breath, trying to force myself to refocus. "We've got to move on. Get to Abilene. Then Colorado. I mean, that was Cade back there. *Cade.*"

Faith laid a hand on my forearm. "I'm sorry. I can't believe it, either. Just like I can't believe what they did to that other Taker like Turq."

"He always had a weak spot," I said.

She looked at me with a question in her eyes.

"Cade," I mean. "I guess he fell in with Hal and that other kid, maybe that whole bunch who rushed us at the motel, because they were the only ones around."

"Yeah," she said. "I noticed they were the only ones not fighting back last night."

"I thought of that, too." My guts felt sick. Puking sick. "Help me watch for cars that might have gasoline," I glanced at our fuel gauge. "You know, earlier models, easy to siphon."

Faith nodded. "I'm glad I found you guys, or you found me. Seems like things are changing again. But with you, I feel like we'll be okay."

I forced my fingers to loosen their grip on the steering wheel. That was almost the same thing I thought about Sam. "Learning as we go," I said. I looked in the rearview. Sam was motioning for me to pull over.

"What the hell?" he yelled when he pulled up alongside.

"I don't know," I yelled back. "They turned on us—they didn't look like prisoners or anything, right?"

He shook his head. "Not from my vantage point." He inclined his head toward Turq. "His words."

I leaned out my window, Sam had the Jeep right beside me, which put Turq next to my side of the car. I could see words tumbling beneath his skin. *FIGHT. CHANGE. PROTECT. CHANGE. PEACE.* Those were the few I caught as they appeared and then disappeared.

Snake whined, his head stuck between the front bucket seats, front paws on the console like always. He peered around me; square snout pointed at Turq. He seemed to be testing the air. Maybe some new odor emanated from the Taker. Or a pheromone. I'd thought that before, but before now I would've said pheromones only applied to insects. This constituted a whole new ballgame.

"Don't worry, Turq." I recalled how the horde had shredded the other clothed Taker. "We're in this together."

He held out his fist and the word *FRIEND* floated down his forearm into his knuckles.

I bumped his fist with mine. "I wish you could tell me what we should do. I mean, fight?"

His chin dipped a bit and then he pointed toward the highway in front of us. "Yeah," I said. "I agree." I leaned around him and told Sam we were looking for old vehicles to easily siphon.

Sam laughed. "I've got a punch, a flat-can, and a half dozen containers. As long as it isn't diesel, any vehicle will do."

I was impressed. "Carlos," I yelled into the Jeep's backseat. "Why didn't we think of that? I've seen the flat catch-cans for draining fluids under cars. Jeez."

"Hell, I should have. I've sucked more gas than you can imagine—back in my youth, of course."

I laughed.

It felt good.

Carlos muttered, "But I never thought of just punching a hole in the fuel tank."

"Learning as we go," Faith chimed in.

Snake whined again. He didn't seem to share our ridiculous good humor.

We took the ramp to the interstate and before long, Sam pulled over at one of the few pileups we'd seen in no-man's land. Between

Eden and Abilene there were farms and ranches and miles and miles of oilfields. The highways were never congested unless you counted the big rigs, and they all ran on diesel. Most of them simply sat beside the highway as if the drivers had managed to get them off the road before they died.

I remembered the one rig that had saved my life when I was with Thad. The driver had been old school, with a glove box full of paper maps. I thought about him a lot. We'd seen his corpse in a stunted mesquite not far from his truck. He'd probably been a road warrior all his life. It was his map that had pointed us to Kansas, New Mexico, and the historic Bitty Sloan House.

I pulled in behind Sam's Jeep and got out to watch as he crawled under a Ford F-150 and tapped the fuel tank with a hammer and punch. The truck was tall enough he was able to fit beneath it with room to spare. "Best-selling light truck on the market for several years," Sam said. "I just wish the fuel tanks were polyethylene like those on the Chevy. A breeze to punch. Maybe we'll get lucky next time."

I watched him carefully. "I've got to hit Auto Mart or Ace Hardware the next time we come to a town. I've been going about this the hard way."

Sam stopped the flow of gas with a large bolt he'd also had in his toolbox while I quickly emptied the flat can into one of the regular containers. "I've got half a dozen of these," he said. "With your help, we'll fill them in no time." He nodded at the bolt as he removed it from the hole. "We hit the jackpot. This guy must've just left the gas station." He spared a quick glance at me. "If you've got any empty containers, bring 'em on over. This is a big tank."

I hurried to the car and removed our two empties from the luggage rack. "We've got to get a little trailer to pull, or something." I handed him our containers. "I hate carrying extra fuel on top of the car, but Carlos convinced me it was dangerous to keep the cans in the trunk. Our food and water take up most of that space anyway."

"I hear that," Sam said. "My back seat is food; the cargo area is fuel—it's well ventilated with the open windows—and the roof is where I keep my tent." He glanced from under the truck, his eyes scanning the road behind us. "Better get that fuel in your tank, son. I feel like a sitting duck out here."

I hefted the red plastic gas can. "Thank you," I said. Then I hurried over and added the fuel to the Chrysler using the little funnel from the trunk. I never failed to thank the makers of the car each time I used that manufacturer-included funnel to gas up the vehicle. There's no way they could have known how important that little implement would become.

On the other hand, I would have cheerfully slapped the person who had the brilliant idea to hide the tiny gas cap release button near the bottom of the driver's door. It had taken me ten minutes to find it the first time I needed to refuel. Not fun when you're watching for monsters over your shoulder the whole time.

Sam filled all our empty containers, walked my other one back to me, and then poured as much as possible into his Jeep.

We both heard the roar of the Challenger's hemi at the same time.

I looked at him, and he looked at me. "I say we shoot first, ask questions later. I know he was your friend—"

"Survival of the fittest," I said.

Sam nodded and began to remove something from his cargo area. "Give me a hand," he yelled into the Jeep.

Turq got out and together they unrolled two spike strips.

"Bring some dirt, Jack," he called. "Sprinkle 'em down to knock off the shine."

I glanced up at the sun and turned to rummage in the trunk again. The cases of bottled water sat in shallow cardboard boxes. I yanked one loose, ran to the shoulder of the road, and filled it with good red dirt. Faith saw what we were doing and hurried to help. In moments, the strips were laid out and lightly covered with earth.

I looked at Sam as I dusted my hands on my jeans. "You just happened to have these in your Jeep?" The spikes reminded me of the Taker's teeth.

Sam laughed out loud. "Digging through cop shops is my new hobby. I know where they keep the good stuff."

"Got any flash-bang in there?"

"As a matter of fact—" He pointed to a bulging canvas backpack propped in the corner. "I've got the real thing. The only problem is getting close enough to use them. Tear gas as well."

"Wow," Faith said.

We ran back to our vehicles. "I'd like to wait around, see if the strips work."

Faith nodded. "They might just drive around them—"

"—if they see them in time. Maybe we dulled the shine enough. I hope so." But in the back of my mind a song bloomed. "Have you ever heard an old song by a man named Bill Withers?"

"Lean on Me," Faith said. "A song about standing by your friend when he is weak, and you are strong. Oh, man. Why do you ask?"

I told her it was one of the songs in my head. "I don't know what it means. Should I stay and make certain Cade isn't being held against his will? I mean, he's my oldest friend. Maybe they've brainwashed him or something."

Faith tapped her chin with the tip of her forefinger. "You did say he had a weak spot. I take it you think he's just a follower."

I nodded. "I never thought so before the rip, but then we've never been tested like this before."

"I know what you mean. My friend Shay turned out to be way different than I thought, too." She flipped her hair back. "I think it saved my life though, her screwing me around the way she did. I didn't want to go with Heavy and Masen in the first place. She set it all up. I got sort of tricked into it."

I was immediately reminded of the way Cade tried to humiliate me in the gym that day and ended up saving my life, too. "Maybe I should do something," I said. "We've been friends since we were little." I thought about all the stuff we'd been through. "But I don't know how I could get him away from them."

"We could hide out until tonight, the way they did last night." Faith's willingness to help, even though she didn't know Cade, made me want to reach over and touch her.

But Snake began to rumble. And we both knew what that meant. "They're coming."

Faith shaded her eyes with the flat of her hand. "Yeah, they're coming." She put her hand down. "The Challenger is leading them, not coming very fast, though. I don't think they want to get too far ahead of the pack."

"They'll probably see the strips, then." I glanced at our handiwork. "That line of red dirt is a little conspicuous, isn't it?" I couldn't help laughing. We'd assumed they would be charging after us at top speed. "I wonder what they have in mind?"

"Maybe Cade is trying to run interference for you?"

"Lean On Me" continued to play through my brain as I thought about the ambush from the night before. "Maybe. And maybe he wasn't part of the bunch that tried to kill us last night, but I know that kid is with them now. What could that mean?"

"Shoot first, remember?" Sam called as he drove up beside us.

"Do we make a stand, or outrun them?"

"We can make a stand right here in the open or go on to your aunt's place and make our stand there," Sam said. "I don't like the way they are marching along so confidently. What do they know that we don't?"

I wondered the same thing. "Maybe they're just confident they've got us outnumbered. Plus, they assume they know all our weapons because we didn't try to hide anything from them at the motel."

Sam nodded. "Whatever we decide, we'd better do it quickly. They seem to be picking up speed."

My music changed to "Carry on Wayward Son," the song that always told me to stop procrastinating and get on with the business at hand. "I've got several boxes of shells for the shotgun."

Carlos held up his hand. I passed four boxes across the gap between the cars. Turq took them and gave them to our friend. *There's that word again.*

Faith and Carlos exchanged guns and each of them reloaded. "Locked and loaded," Faith said.

"We're ready." I nodded. "I say we end it now. I don't like having to look over my shoulder—"

"My *man*," Sam said. He swung the Jeep into a U-turn and stopped. I could see him lining grenades up on the dash. Turq held one in his hand as well.

I took a deep breath and focused on the song in my head.

The big Jeep began to roll slowly. It was headed directly toward the Challenger. They both seemed to be picking up speed. I wasn't sure about my role, so I just paced along, ready to do whatever was needed.

All at once, I heard Sam's handgun. *Boom, boom, boom.* He seemed to be shooting over the car and into the crowd.

Of course—he'll want to bring down the black stuff.

The Challenger accelerated even more. It was difficult to see the faces of the occupants because of the glare of sunlight across the windshield.

"What is Sam doing?" Faith cried.

"Trying to bring down the dark rain," I said.

"He needs to turn around now!" Her voice had grown shrill. "It's like that old movie where they drive at each other—"

"Yeah, like they're playing chicken, like in *Footloose.*"

Faith nodded. Her left hand gripped the dash, her right hand gripped her gun. I didn't know if she intended to rise out of the window or shoot right through it. I just hoped Snake wouldn't get a wild hair and try to leap out.

All at once we heard the front tires of the Challenger meet the sharp spikes we'd covered with dirt. Sam had created such a diversion the driver hadn't noticed them.

The speeding car swerved back and forth across the lanes as the driver—we assumed it was Hal—attempted to control the steering. Both front tires were blown. If it had been one tire, the driver might have regained control, but not with both gone, not with the back tires smoking as he stomped the brakes.

The Challenger careened off the highway into the bar ditch, rolling over and over, coming to rest on its top. One body hung halfway out of the driver's side window, another had soared through the air and landed in front of the car.

"Oh, my, God." Faith's eyes were wide, terrified. "It's like the wreck I was in with Shay."

"It's okay," I said. "*We're* okay." I tried to see if there was any movement at the car, anyone getting up, or getting out. "Are they alive?" I asked. "Can you tell?"

Snake was revving up in the back seat.

Faith gulped several breaths of air. "That's Hal, hanging out the window. He looks—his neck looks broken," she said. "Like my friend, Shay, was broken." She craned her head around as we made another sweeping U. "The one inside the car might be moving. I can't really tell. Oh, no. The Takers are headed toward them. Someone is climbing out of the car. I think it's that kid, but I don't kn—"

Carry on! The music blasted me. I wanted to see if Cade made it out alive, or if he was even in there, but the horde was almost on us. Almost on them.

Sam blew past me, and I saw his arm come out the window, heard the boom of his big handgun again. He shot as many as he could no matter where they were.

Even as the things began to fall, Sam slowed and showed the horde the side of the Jeep. The tip of the shotgun came out and Carlos joined in.

Kaboom!

He scattered the ones nearest the Jeep. The sky scars opened. The rain fell in torrents.

Sam hit the gas and shrieked a U-turn on two wheels.

I hesitated a few more seconds, just long enough to see a second figure—a female figure—crawling out of the wreckage.

"That could be me." Faith's voice came out a hard whisper. "That's probably how I looked, pulling myself out of the wreck that night. I'll never forget looking down and seeing Heavy's hand swelling, turning purple—"

She said more, but I'd stopped listening.

When the female figure stood upright, I recognized her. The jut of her bony hip, the cascade of her stringy dishwater hair.

"That's Marla." I watched her in my mirror. "Kevin's girlfriend. The one who wants to kill me." Of course, she'd be the one to survive. But what about Cade? Where was he? Was he the one lying in front of the car, or was he even there at all?

I didn't have time to investigate. The song in my head had grown to a crescendo, and the dark rain had begun to coalesce across the horde like a hungry river. I hit the gas and followed Sam into the sunlight.

CHAPTER SEVENTEEN

Aunt Edna

A few miles down the road, the Jeep pulled over. There had been a major wreck right below a massive sky-scar. I looked up, wondering for the thousandth time just what was going on up there beyond that innocuous blue.

"Sorry, Jack." Sam unfolded his six-and-a-half-foot frame from the driver's seat. "Thought it best to hit and run."

"Just what I had in mind, too." I tried to pretend he didn't intimidate me with his size. Last night, in the firelight, he hadn't seemed quite so large. "You and Carlos did a great job. And those metal spikes—"

"Worked even better than we hoped, didn't they?" The big man grinned. "I just wish we hadn't been forced to leave the strips behind."

I nodded as I glanced inside the Jeep. Carlos lay still, one hand over his eyes. "You okay, buddy?"

"I'm all right." He uncovered his eyes. "I'm sorry if that was your friend in that car. I—uh, I said I little prayer for them, for the dying, just, you know, in case." The crucifix on his throat glowed whitely.

I reached in the open window and grasped his hand. I didn't trust my voice to reply. Didn't want to look wussy in front of Faith. She'd gotten out of the Chrysler and now stood, looking back down the Interstate. "I wonder if they're still on the march."

We all glanced back, but there was nothing to see. My head music had faded to a faint soundtrack, back to "Lean on Me." But we'd already put at least fifteen or twenty miles between us and them. And the sky-holes had sealed up neatly when the locusts flew back up with their bounty.

Sam looked at the multitude of cars and pickups tangled together in front of us. "This is a pretty good pile-up," he said. Some had burned, others were pristine—and empty. The empties were the ones that gave me the jitters because I knew their drivers had likely been yanked out by their heads. Yanked out right through the open doors and windows.

"Yeah," I looked up at the sky scar. "There was probably a downfall right here for some reason. Should we tap some of these tanks? I've got one empty can. And who knows when we'll have another chance to fill it."

"Good idea," Sam said. He got his tools, and we filled my empty container and put it back on the luggage rack while Carlos managed to open the back door of the Jeep and work his way to where his legs hung out the opening.

Turq saw him and plucked him out, then stood, waiting for direction.

Carlos pointed toward a hidden place on the other side of the pile of cars. "Over there is a good bathroom, I think."

We all looked away. It had to be humiliating to be carried to the side of the road to take a whiz. Once again I recalled the vibrant hotshot biker we'd found roaring along on his Harley back in New Mexico.

Faith headed toward the car furthest from the wreck. "I wonder if it would be worthwhile to check out the trunks on some of these vehicles?" She stuck her head in the empty Honda Accord, plucked the keys from the ignition, and then hesitated.

Grinning a little, she plopped down in the driver's seat, flung her long hair over her shoulder, stuck the key back into the ignition, and gave it a hard twist. Nothing happened. She did it again, just to be sure. "Oh, well," she still had the half-grin on her face. "Doesn't hurt to try, right?"

I laughed. Had she seen me do the same thing earlier? I watched as she gave the interior of the car a quick search, found nothing of importance, and then went to open the trunk. "Nothing in here either," she called. "I was hoping for something we needed. I don't know what."

I knew how she felt. The idea of running out of food and water was a constant worry. Especially out here, miles from nowhere. Nothing ahead of us, nothing but monsters behind us.

We hurriedly searched the rest of the cars, those without occupants that is. But no one had anything we needed. It amazed me how light we all traveled back before our world fell apart. But back then there had always been a convenience store or a motel just ahead.

Except out here on the edge of the plains. Out here it was easy to drive a hundred miles between rest stops, more than that between towns. I remembered my dad once saying our little town of Eden was about halfway between Dallas and El Paso, and they were nearly six hundred miles apart.

We all resumed our places in our vehicles, and then we hit the road again. I wondered why Sam had never thrown a grenade at the horde of Takers, but maybe he hadn't deemed it necessary after the spike strips worked so well.

Another song came to me, playing softly in place of "Carry on Wayward Son." It was one of my mom's songs, by a woman named Julie Roberts. "I'd Sure Hate to Breakdown Here." For the longest time I thought it was sung by the actress Julia Roberts. Mom laughed at me when she told me the two women weren't one and the same. I hoped she never knew how I used to fantasize about Julia Roberts after seeing *Pretty Woman* on Netflix. Seems ridiculous now.

I asked Faith if she knew the song. "It's about breaking down miles from nowhere." I glanced at the wide sky scenery. "Like this place. But I think it's probably metaphorical, too—"

She said she couldn't recall it. "Sing it," she said. "Maybe I'll remember. My mom played the radio all the time in our house. Not Sirius, it was too expensive, just the local country station." A smile crossed her face. "She played the oldies station, too. Old rock and pop, you know."

I nodded, thinking of how our home had always had music playing, too. "Our folks. If they only knew how much they had influenced us after all."

Faith nodded. "Jack—"

I looked at her, thinking she would try to goad me into singing.

Instead, she glanced out the window, one finger lightly twirling a hank of her long reddish-gold hair. "I'm sorry about your friend."

Not knowing what to say, I looked out at the passing nothingness. Power lines still stood—useless. Cars were stalled here and there—useless. Random houses appeared in the distance from time to time—useless, unoccupied. I wasn't about to try and tell her thank you or anything else. Not at that moment, not with my throat blocked by that hard lump of *something*.

At least the slime from the initial rip is gone, I thought. Even the crackly glaze it left behind had crinkled up and blown away in the summer wind. It must've served its purpose, though, destroying everything like some sort of toxic birth fluid.

"Do you dream, Jack?"

I laughed. "Yeah. I dream about opening the fridge in my kitchen back home and seeing that miraculous white light come on." I glanced at her face. "I'm not kidding." I tapped my fingers on the wheel. "Of course, I dream about other stuff, too, but that stupid light is a recurring one."

I couldn't tell her I dreamed about girls. A lot. Her, specifically. I couldn't admit I also have nightmares in which the Takers overrun us in the night, as we're sleeping, wiping us out. Wiping out all humanity—and the last dog.

"Me, too," Faith said. "I used to have nightmares. Dreamed I was completely alone and always would be." She reached back and tickled Snake's floppy jaw. "I haven't been dreaming that one lately, though. Not now that I've found you and the Snakeman."

I smiled at the way she said she'd found us when it was clearly Snake who had tracked her down that day. "Maybe we'll be all right for a while. Once we get to Abilene."

Faith smiled back. "Maybe we will."

We took turns driving. I napped in the shotgun seat while she drove. She was careful. As I'd known she would be.

Every time we passed the cut off for one of the tiny towns like Stanton or Coahoma, she would murmur, "I wonder if anyone is there."

I wondered, too. "Maybe once we settle in Abilene, if we do, we can come back and explore them. Look for survivors like us." I also wanted to look for other pets. I figured some had escaped and were living under houses, or under porches. Somewhere.

Faith nodded. "Sorry I woke you. Go back to sleep."

"Let me know when you get tired of driving."

"I will," she said. "But I won't. Get tired, I mean. I love this car. I was hoping to get a car of my own soon."

"I hear that." My memory flashed back to the red Mustang." I closed my eyes, determined not to think about it still sitting in the sun in the high school parking lot.

The next time I woke, I could hear Faith humming under her breath, very softly. Snake slept in the back seat, content for once. I checked the rearview to see if Sam was still with us.

"He's there," Faith said. "And we're almost to Abilene."

"Wow." I rubbed my face. "I slept."

She laughed. "I don't know who snores louder, you or Snakeman."

I felt my cheeks grow warm.

"I'm only kidding," she said. "You both needed rest. Obviously." She tapped cigarette ash out the window and then threw the butt out, too.

I almost said something about wildfire, but what she'd said sounded so adult it made me stop and think that she knew what she was doing. It also made me think how we'd quickly moved up a few years on the age line. Right up to our parents' ages. Or so it seemed. I felt like I had a doppelgänger, and it was *me*.

After directing her where to turn, I said, "We don't go into the city. It's about twenty miles south after we take this cutoff."

As she slowed, approaching the turn, she said, "You know, I'm pretty sure I've seen a couple of foxes near the road."

That woke me. "For real?"

She nodded. "One could have been a coyote, but the other was red. Definitely a fox."

"Of course," I said. "Foxes sleep underground, coyotes too, I guess. At least when they have pups."

Faith made the turn, and Sam followed without question.

Young trees crowded the road, and the bar ditches were completely grown over with wild sawgrass. It was easy to imagine all kinds of wildlife skulking around, just out of sight. "Looks like the county mowers are falling down on the job," I joked.

"Mother Nature's reclaiming the land," Faith murmured.

Her voice gave me a little chill. It reminded me of how she'd sounded reading from her journal by the fire.

"Here's the last turn." I motioned toward the upcoming intersection. "See the sign for the farm-to-market road?"

She nodded.

"A couple more miles and then we'll see the driveway on the left. It curves down to the house through a stand of live oak."

We drove slowly, eyes peeled for Takers, but everything was quiet. Once, I thought I heard a bird, but it must've been my imagination. The only birds I'd seen were the little dog owls that nest in abandoned prairie dog burrows. But I'd only ever seen them out in open fields, not in forested areas like this.

"Did you encounter many wrecks while I slept?"

Faith nodded. "A lot. But the interstate is so wide I barely even had to slow to get around them."

"That's good."

We skirted a small pickup half-on and half-off the pavement.

"There's the house." I pointed through the trees. "You can see the metal roof reflecting the sunlight."

"I see it," Faith said, and then we both saw something else.

I felt sucker punched. "Ahh, damn," my words whooshed out.

Aunt Edna had been flayed. The only thing left was her partially clothed skeleton hanging like a windchime in a big oak tree near the porch. "She didn't even make it to the silo. Fat lot of good that did."

"Are you sure it's her?" Faith's voice was soft, hopeful. "I mean, we're still a way off—" She slowed to cross the cattle guard that would mean we were officially on Edna's land.

"It's her." I tapped my chest. "I feel it in here, and here." I tapped my temple, where John Denver had begun singing "Rocky Mountain High."

Aunt Edna had grown up in Colorado. She'd always joked that a Rocky Mountain High was the only way to go. I'd assumed I was hearing that song because of my grandparents who still lived in Colorado. I'd forgotten they were her *parents*.

"Besides," I murmured, "see that faded work shirt fluttering around her? She always wore that when she went to feed her stock. *Keeps the sun off,* she said. *And the barbed wire, too.*" I cleared my throat.

"I hate you have to see her like that," Faith said. "Reminds me of my mother. She was strung up on her own clothesline pole out in our backyard."

"Oh, my God—"

"Yeah," she glanced away, "I always teased her for hanging her clothes out there instead of drying them in the dryer." She swallowed hard. "She said she just loved the way they smelled after being in the sunshine."

"My gran always said that, too. About the scent, I mean." I hesitated, not wanting to take away from what she'd just told me. But she pressed on.

"Your gran, the one in Colorado?"

John Denver sang a little louder. "Yeah. I want to go there next." Then it occurred to me. "Hey, what about your grands, and your dad?" I'd only heard her mention her mom.

"My dad did the disappearing act years ago when Mom tried to get child support. My Granny died of cancer, and Grampa got dementia and went to live in a nursing home in Georgia. To be near his sister. He didn't last long, though. Died a couple years ago. His sister, too."

"You just had the one set of grandparents? Like me?"

She nodded, and a tear plopped onto her leg. "Yep. I'm really an orphan, Jack. That's the bad thing about all of this. I mean, losing my mom was the absolute worst, but next to that the worst part is … I'm alone. Completely."

I laid my hand on her knee, palm up, open. "Not anymore."

Faith placed her hand in mine. I won't say it fit like a glove, but it fit like it was made for me. Like two halves of a walnut shell put back together. A deep sigh escaped her chest. "Do you mean that?" She ducked her head just enough that her hair fell across her forehead, across her glasses.

It seemed a defensive gesture in a way. I couldn't believe I'd been so bold. This girl. She just invited me. As if we were meant. The guitar music from "Something" played over the top of "Rocky Mountain High."

"Jack, I—" But she didn't get to finish that thought because Sam bumped over the cattle guard and pulled in behind us. I'd begun to think he was lost.

We drove slowly on up to the farmhouse.

"Your aunt?" Sam asked, getting out of the Jeep. I noticed how the vehicle sprang up on its axle when he emerged.

"Yes." I glanced at her, hanging there. "But I guess we'd better go in and check out the house, anyway."

Faith touched my shoulder, keeping her face averted from the big tree. "Is it really necessary?" Her gaze flicked toward the bones.

"You don't have to come. It won't take long, but I have to see if my dad has been here."

"Oh," she said. "That's right. I'm not thinking straight. The way the breeze twirls the loose bones of her arms and legs … the way the sunlight plays along the cheekbones and accentuates the dark eye sockets …" Her eyes sought the skeletal remains as she started toward them.

CHAPTER EIGHTEEN

Carry on

Faith!" I gave her hand a little shake. "Snap out of it."

She turned toward me, and I'd swear her eyes belonged to someone else. Behind her lenses, they were no longer brown. Now, somehow, they were gold. Like the light coming through a raincloud. "Jack?" She squeezed my hand. "I'm sorry. What—what did I say?"

"You seemed to be in some sort of trance. It was downright spooky. You were talking like a poet again, only this time it was eerie."

Faith closed her eyes. "I'll stay in the car with Carlos. I've got my gun if I need it."

"Don't hesitate to use it—or just yell—"

She nodded. "I feel exposed, sitting out here in the daylight. I'm used to shadows and hiding ... *like a spirit in the night*." Her grin told me she knew what she was saying. As if she'd read my mind. Did she know it was also an old Springsteen song?

From the backseat of the Jeep, Carlos raised his head and his shotgun. "We'll be fine. Go, see if your dad's been here."

"I thought you were asleep," I said.

Carlos laughed. "Not since the cattle guard."

I could almost feel his pain. But he always told me not to worry. He had been through the fire with me. Literally. We were bonded. We knew each other's souls.

"Thanks, man. C'mon, Snake." I opened the back door of the

Chrysler, and he stepped out. I couldn't understand why his behavior had changed so drastically over the last couple of days.

I did my best to avoid looking at Aunt Edna, but then it occurred to me that I should probably bury her. She had a barn full of equipment that would do the job. I took the three shallow porch steps to the open front door.

"Dad hasn't been here, has he Snake?" My fingertips touched his flat head. "He wouldn't be able to go off and leave her hanging there like that if he had. No way." *Unless he was being pursued at the time.*

"Can't Find My Way Home" came on softly, edging out "Something" and "Rocky Mountain High." Thoughts of Dad almost always brought it on. Unless I needed to go, then it was "Carry on Wayward Son."

"Hold up," Sam called. "We'll go in together." He glanced at my aunt's skeleton, swaying in the slight breeze.

I eyed the bare ground. "Guess I'll be looking for a shovel. Looks rocky here."

"We'll get it," Sam said. "No problem."

Turq got out. The Jeep sprang up even more.

"How'd he do?" I felt like a parent, asking the teacher how his child had fared on the field trip.

Sam held up his hand and did the slight back and forth motion Turq was known to do. "Easy peasy. Doesn't say much."

I smiled despite Aunt Edna's corpse hanging there. Then I felt guilty for smiling. "First Cade, and now this …" I didn't mean to say it aloud, but it came out anyway.

Sam's jaw muscles tightened. "Tough," he said.

We stepped through the door, me in the lead. Inside—heartbreaking. Two dead cats, and Urchin, the black lab mix she'd rescued from the middle of the highway one dark night. On the table, the remains of what appeared to be a chicken pot pie just out of the oven.

"Oh, hell." Hot tears built up in the back of my nose. "This really sucks." I don't know why these remains seemed worse than my aunt outside in the tree, but they did.

Sam kept the screen from slamming shut behind us. "This is bad."

I couldn't speak anymore, but in my head, I was thinking how much worse it would have been if Aunt Edna hadn't had all her windows open.

Sam clasped my shoulder with his big hand. "Sorry, son."

"Yeah." I turned and went back outside. The atmosphere inside was too much.

"I'm going to go ahead and look through the rooms," Sam said. "Make sure there's no one else."

I knew what he meant. He was going to make sure there were no more bodies.

"Carry on!" jumped into my head. It was so loud it stopped me in my tracks. Dad had already left me one note, that day at the high school. It made sense he would leave me another if he'd made it this far.

I grabbed the screen door before it could flap closed behind Sam. *You can do this*, I told myself. *You* have *to*.

The music began to subside when I went back into the house. "Rocky Mountain High" and "Can't Find My Way Home" still played on a loop, softly, round and round my skull, beneath "Carry on Wayward Son."

Through the kitchen and down the hall toward the bathroom, shades of Marla flitted across my mind.

I half expected her—or someone like her—to pop out of one of the bedrooms or closets. The gloom was as thick as the dust on the tables.

The back of my neck felt naked, exposed. I wanted to walk sideways down the hallway, like a crab, try to see every doorway at once. I almost wished Turq hadn't stayed outside.

I pulled my pistol and held it beside my leg, cautioning myself not to shoot Sam if he suddenly appeared.

But he didn't. And nothing else jumped out, either.

I tucked the gun back into its holster and walked into the living room, and there it was. The sign I'd been looking for. Not a note, but a photo. Hanging on the wall as if it had always been there.

But it had not. I'd never seen it before.

It was an old color photo of Aunt Edna and my dad when they were kids. They were standing side by side, arms around each other, big smiles lighting their young faces, each grasping the handle of an Easter basket with fake green and pink grass poking over the top. They were obviously wearing their Sunday best.

All the blood left my head. I felt as if I might "let a faint" as my aunt used to joke. *Don't you let a faint, now, Jack,* she'd say. *It's just a little blood. Nothing major. Don't be a city kid.* I was always snagging my skin on old nails or thorn bushes when we came to visit. *This is a farm,* she'd say. *Gotta watch your step all the time.*

I had always adored visiting her here. Feeding the two cows and coop full of chickens, wading and swimming in the creek when there'd been enough rain. Riding her old Appaloosa, Freckles. Those visits were often the highlights of my summer. So how come I'd never seen this photo? I touched the glass with my fingertip. Dusty. I pulled it off the wall and pressed it to my chest without thinking.

It was my dad. As a kid. With his kid sister. *Damn. Damn. Damn.* The hot tears flowed.

Sam cleared his throat. "I'm going out to the barn for a shovel."

"Yeah," I said. "Thanks. That's where it will be. I used it to shovel out the manure every time I came to visit."

He laughed. Probably not sure if I was serious, but I was. I had never minded. Not at all. I hoped there were two shovels. That would be faster.

I pulled the back off the frame, withdrew the old picture, and slid it into my back pocket. I intended to put it in the glovebox when I got back to the car.

Turns out, there were two shovels and a pickaxe. Between the three of us—Sam, Turq, and me—we had Aunt Edna and her pets planted in the field in nothing flat. We put them in the tall grass between the house and the barn, facing the sunrise because that's what she always loved. "God, if you are really there," I murmured. "Please make sure my aunt is reunited with her loved ones in Heaven." I said those words aloud, but in my mind, I continued with, "And that goes for my mom, too." I wasn't ready to give up on my dad, not yet.

"I wish we could bury Freckles and the cows," I said. "But I know it isn't feasible." Finding them had been awful, though. It reminded me of the barn at the horse farm near the Bitty Sloan house. "C'mon," I told the others. "Let's go to the silo and see what's there."

We went back to the house, and I stepped inside and grabbed the keys off the hook beside the door. They'd hung there for years on a big leather fob made in the image of a horse's head. I couldn't believe Aunt Edna hadn't been carrying it. When the noise started, it seemed she should have grabbed it and headed to shelter. Isn't that what she'd had in mind, all those years of stockpiling survival stuff? Maybe she was outside when they came. Couldn't get back for the keys.

"Follow me," I told the others. "We'll drive over. If we find food and things we can use, we'll want to load it up." I looked at Aunt Edna's pickup parked under the carport. No doubt the engine had been rendered useless when the rip occurred, but as always, when I saw a seemingly perfect vehicle sitting somewhere, I had to check it.

What I did know, after I climbed into the cab and stuck the key in the ignition, was that it wouldn't start. I gave the key a twist and the truck didn't respond at all. Just like the others I'd tried before, the vehicle acted like it had never heard the word *battery*, much less had one under the hood.

I exited the cab and shrugged at the crew waiting patiently. There were so many things we didn't know about this mess—just like the Covid-19 pandemic back in the day. We'd muddled through on that one with the help of scientists and vaccines. I wondered if we could muddle through this now, without the help of anyone. It was easy to recall how one Covid variation after another had hit us like waves. Wave upon wave as Pat Green once sang.

"Soon it'll just be like another version of the flu," Dad had said. "We'll get our annual Covid shot along with our flu shot."

"And it will keep on morphing, every year, just like the flu virus does," Mom had agreed.

And they were right. As far as I could remember. That's exactly what happened. But some people still got sick and died from it, every year. Dad said some died from the flu, too. Always had, just not as many.

We all got back in our vehicles with Turq automatically going shotgun with Sam again. Faith smiled. "I'm getting to where I like that guy."

"Who, Sam?" I pushed the Chrysler's start button.

She laughed and glanced at the Jeep. "Him, too. But I meant Turq."

Snake whined and pressed his head in between us from the backseat.

"He is something, isn't he?" Carlos and I spoke at the same time, then laughed.

"I'm glad you're riding with us again, amigo."

Carlos grinned at me in the rearview. "I like to spread my awesomeness around as much as possible."

I gave him a backward high five and then pulled the old photo from my pocket.

Faith moved her knees when I opened the glove box, but she didn't say a word about the photo.

She didn't have to.

CHAPTER NINETEEN

The Silo

I drove straight down the rural road to the silo cutoff. Although it was on my aunt's land, it was a good distance from the house. The road was nearly deserted. We didn't encounter anything other than a couple of dead cars. There were drivers in them, though. One had an entire family wrapped up in its innards—as my Grampa would've said—but we were used to that already. "Dust In the Wind," another Kansas song, played through my head.

The silo gate still wore its heavy chain and padlock.

Sam stepped out of the Jeep behind us with a giant set of bolt cutters. I guess it was his *Taker* key.

In the back of my mind, I worried about the day we would run out of things to take. Before that happened, we really might have to think of settling down beside a river someplace. Grow and catch our own food. Find a good sod house or cabin. Like the horse barn I'd explored in search of medicine back in New Mexico. It had been built into the side of a hill.

But prior to any of that I had to find my dad and my grandparents. Or at least find out what happened to them. I also wanted to do one more thing. I wanted to learn why Cade had turned. Why he wouldn't just fall in with us the way he should have.

Sam held up the bolt cutters, and I held up the key ring. He laughed as I sorted through the keys for one that matched the padlock.

I noticed Turq watching us closely. It made me wonder if he could've just snapped the lock. I recalled the day the unclothed

Taker had me by the arm, and Turq grabbed me while at the same time elbowing the other one in the head. That sucker went down like a ton of bricks, and I thought I was dead meat, but instead, I was saved. Saved by a giant gray creature with garnet eyes and silver teeth and wearing a breezy turquoise shirt.

Finally, I found the right key, opened the lock, and let the chain fall to the gravel. Sam gave each side of the double gates a shove. They flew backward and clanged against the silver-painted iron posts cemented into the earth. The sun flickered off the bright metal fence and gates. Aunt Edna would've had my hide if she'd seen us open the gates so carelessly.

We got back in our vehicles and drove up the crunchy gravel road to the Quonset hut set in the middle of the overgrown field.

Wildflowers dotted the rough pasture, and the entire scene could've been a landscape painting, all green and golden grasses and blue skies.

Past the corrugated metal hut, a pair of immense rust-colored doors were set flush into a circular concrete pad. Those doors always amazed me. It was hard to imagine them slowly opening.

I steered the nose of the Chrysler up to the silver pipe rail beside the hut.

"Well, here we are."

Carlos sat up from his nest in the back seat and opened the door so Snake could hop out. Then he twisted around and hung his legs out, too.

Snake made a beeline for the single entrance door set into a narrow concrete upright a good forty to fifty feet away.

Faith got out and made her way to the giant, rusty, missile doors set into the concrete pad. "How do we get these open? They must weigh a ton."

I strolled to where she stood. "About ninety tons, I think." I stuck my hands in my pockets. "But we don't go in here. These are the doors that would open up if the missile was brought up to launch."

Her look of astonishment made me smile. "You mean one of those huge things would come up through here? I saw photos in our history class. ICBM. Cold war stuff, right?"

"Yeah. Inter-Continental Ballistic Missile. Atlas F, my aunt said. Lots of them were scattered around the country. All aimed at Russia, I think. I believe we still have some in Montana and North Dakota."

Faith nodded. "So how do we get inside if not through here?"

"Follow the Snake." The big dog was doing his best to get inside the single upright door that sat between the missile access and the Quonset hut.

Faith looked at the odd door set into the narrow concrete shelter. "That reminds me of a painting by Dali or someone."

"The Persistence of Memory," I said. "Melted clocks hanging in trees—nearly as odd as a single door standing in a field—"

"Yes! I love that painting. I can't believe you know the name of it."

The joy on her face made me feel light. "Pays to hang around libraries," I murmured, but after I said it, my lightness dimmed a little. An image of Mom's body stacked against the wall with the rest of the staff tempered my every thought of her and her workplace.

Sam came to where we were standing. "Hell of a deal," he said. "I knew the old silos were scattered around, but this is the first one I've visited."

"Hey!" Carlos yelled. He'd managed to get out and was now leaning against the car, one hand shading his eyes.

I felt terrible leaving him there, again. I'd been too eager to join Faith. "I'm coming, buddy," I called. But Turq beat me to the punch. He strode over and put one arm around the injured man's shoulders. We knew he was about to pick him up like a child, the way he always did, but Carlos had other ideas.

"Just hold out your arm like a crutch—oh, what am I saying? You don't know a crutch from that big hole in the ground, do you?"

He finally got his wishes across, and they made their way toward us. It was plain Carlos wanted to be more independent.

"Come on," I said. "Let me show you the below ground room where she kept supplies. You guys are going to freak when you see it."

Turq grew tired of the slow pace, picked Carlos up, and carried him to the odd-looking door where Snake still sniffed and pawed. He stood Carlos in the shade of the small overhang and was about to pry the door open when I finally got his attention. "Key!" I said, searching through them again.

Turq backed away.

I unlocked the padlock and pulled the door open.

Eerie darkness greeted us. I cranked the handle on my Dynamo.

Sam loped back to his Jeep and reappeared with an extra-bright camp lantern. "This might be easier," he said. "Doesn't need cranking."

So outfitted, I nodded at Turq to bring Carlos.

"Oh, I don't think so," my friend said, changing his mind on the spot. "If I could motor on my own it'd be one thing, but I don't think I want to be carried all the way down there." He peered over my shoulder at the steps disappearing into the void. A metal handrail made the trek a little safer, but our light only reached so far. He looked at me. "What if something happened to Turq? I couldn't get back up."

"We won't go all the way down," I said. "Just to the first level."

"How deep is it?" Faith whispered.

I shrugged. "This one only goes down two levels, but Aunt Edna stored her supplies on the first floor. As far as I know, she never got through the second level blast doors or to the tunnel leading across to the silo either. That's where the missile was stored. It's at least 185 feet straight down. This part was the control center." I ducked my head and started across the rough concrete entryway toward the dark steps."

Faith followed and looked over the rail. "So, we go down these steps to the first level?"

"Yeah." I cranked and shined my Dynamo around the narrow stair well. Blackness inched back, reluctantly.

Sam held his lantern higher. It helped—a lot.

Faith took a deep breath. "This is spooky." She stopped and looked back over her shoulder. "Will Carlos be okay?"

He waved her worries aside as Turq offered an arm to help him back to the Chrysler. "Don't worry 'bout me. I'll probably take a nap." His voice trailed away as he went toward the car. "Anyway, I've got the shotgun."

I didn't like leaving him alone. But he was right. The stairs were too steep for him to be carried.

"Okay," I started down the steps. "Here we go."

Snake went first, Faith came after me, then Sam.

"This stairwell leads to what Aunt Edna called the ready room. I never thought to ask why she called it that, all I remember is that it also had a kitchen and mess area for the five-man missile crew. I think they called them *missileers*."

Even with the lantern behind me, the darkness below ate up the light. I shined the Dynamo down the steps as I spoke. "When we get to the bottom, we'll make a turn and go down another set of steps. Then we'll come to the blast doors." I took a few more steps down. "Hold on to the rail. Some of these feel a little slippery."

The temperature grew cooler the deeper we went. It was so quiet our breathing sounded artificial, like one of those machines in the hospital. Snake's claws were light on the cement steps. I imagined him tiptoeing the way he always did. My Dynamo had a high pitch. The faster I squeezed, the higher it squealed.

In moments we'd cleared the first set of steps and turned to go down the second set. My skin felt clammy. Maybe from fear. "Watch out," I shined my light around. "Looks like a shiny spot on this landing."

"Hey," Faith said. "You don't think they could've got in down here, do you?"

I shook my head, making myself believe it. "I don't see how. I mean, we just unlocked the gate and the door. On the other hand, be careful. I can't believe it's so slippery here."

"The secret life of slime," Faith said. "I saw it on PBS one time. Can't help but think about it now … the way those weird hagfish produce slime to defend themselves. It said one fish can produce enough slime to fill a five-gallon bucket within minutes of feeling threatened." She stopped walking. "Oh, my God. They also said the military was experimenting with hagfish slime because it was so strong it could even be used in missile defense."

"And now we're living the apocalypse because the entire world was drenched in it. Slime, I mean." The words slipped out of my thoughts. Oddly enough, I'd heard of hagfish, too. I'd just never made any connection.

"Do I hear water dripping," Faith asked.

"I don't hear anything," Sam said. "But it smells like mud ever since we turned the corner." He held his lantern higher. We examined the small area. Nothing seemed amiss.

"I really don't know how it could be wet."

Sam tilted the lantern toward the floor.

I looked at my Dynamo. "I sure like that big light."

Sam laughed. "I live for useful gadgets." He tapped the top of the lantern. "This one also has a solar panel on top. For camping."

I heard a sound from behind us, sort of a scrape.

My heart lurched into the back of my throat.

But it was only Turq, telling us in his own way to stop talking and *go*. I didn't even know he'd rejoined us.

Sam's good light threw our silhouettes against the concrete walls. It reminded me of the shadows of Takers crawling the halls in the Eden library. They'd almost caught me there.

I stepped down into the second stairwell.

We navigated the last few steps in silence and entered the containment area with lights held high. A turn to the left and back to the right and the set of blast doors became visible.

Sam pressed his lantern forward. "Those things are huge."

"Six thousand pounds. Steel wrapped around a concrete core." I handed Faith my flashlight. "Watch this." I grabbed the arms of the giant wheel on the front of the door, spun it a full turn, and pulled. The huge door moved as smoothly as if it had been built yesterday instead of six decades earlier.

Turq must've thought it wasn't opening quite fast enough. He stepped up beside me, stuck his nailless fingers into the gap, and pulled it even wider.

"Jeez Louise," Faith said. "Look at that."

I laughed. "Impressive, huh?"

She played my small light over the door's curved surface. Her voice echoed the awe I'd felt the first time I saw it. "It's massive. But why is it curved like that?"

"That's in case of a nuclear attack," Sam said. "You know, we were only going to fire at the Russians if they fired at us first. Anyhow, the idea was that the outward curvature of the door would help it withstand the vacuum effect of the blast."

"And that white door? The one that looks like an iron trellis?"

"That's the debris door," I said. "It's designed to keep anything from blowing past the blast door into the control room."

"Nuclear war," she murmured. "Like Hiroshima and Nagasaki. Death and destruction …"

I nodded. "Thank God it never came to these. Things would be way worse than they are now."

As soon as the words were out of my mouth, I wanted them back. How much worse could it be? We had all lost our homes and families, and we lived in constant fear of monsters that wanted to rip us apart.

"I know what you mean," Faith said. "The Takers are horrible. But at least we can breathe the air. And we'll probably be able to grow more food someday. The water isn't contaminated, either. At least I don't think so. Not since the slime disappeared."

Sam chimed in, breaking through our depressing musings. "Those missile guys had an amazing job though, didn't they?" He didn't wait for answer. "Can you imagine twirling the wheel to open that door and go to work every day? I'm a Marine, but seeing this makes me think I might've enjoyed a job like this. Even if it was Air Force." He grinned.

"Aunt Edna said the men were handpicked and trained."

"Were there any women?" Faith asked.

"I don't know for sure. But you know it was back in the sixties."

She shrugged. "It's still amazing. But it feels so odd, all this preparation for nuclear war and instead we got killing sound, slime, and robot-monsters. Sorry, Turq."

Sam leaned around us and lit up the interior of the perfectly round room. "Eureka!" he said. "Looks like your aunt had it all." He held the lantern even higher so we could all see inside.

In the center of the room a steel column—painted white—supported this floor and the one below. The column was massive, like an upside-down funnel, the wide end on top, supporting the ceiling, and the cylindrical tube section running straight down through a cut-out in the floor to the level below.

Both steel floors were attached to this upside-down funnel with mammoth, heavy-duty springs. That way the floors could move up and down and side to side in case of an incoming missile strike. The floors did not touch the walls, instead, an iron safety rail ran around the edge like a fence, leaving a several inch gap between wall and floor.

The same safety rail went around the center column itself. Above the column was an escape hatch. In case of emergency, one of the *missileers* would pull the lever thereby releasing a load of sand which would pour down and reveal an exit tunnel leading to the surface. "When we go back up," I said, "you can see the escape hatch about sixty feet away. It's been permanently capped now, though."

"Where would they have escaped to?" Faith asked. "Wouldn't the air be toxic from a nuclear strike?"

Sam said, "Maybe it was in case they were trapped in here by fire or some sort of breach." He shrugged. "Not everyone was on board with our missile defense system, you know."

"Maybe we'd better double check that hatch-cap when we go back up." I glanced upward. "I doubt a Taker would have trouble opening it from outside."

"Wow." Faith stepped into the room. "Look at all this *food*."

Where room partitions once stood—to divide different sections such as the kitchen and mess areas, perhaps—now there were rows upon rows of stout metal shelves radiating out from the center like the spokes on a wheel.

Each shelf held boxes and bags of vacuum sealed foods made specifically for fallout shelters. A quick glance showed us everything from pancakes to beef stew. The picture on the packages labeled *spaghetti dinner* made my mouth water. Aunt Edna may not have been a *prepper*, but she must have been on a first name basis with them.

"Jackpot." I glanced around. "I guess it's a good thing my aunt was a little eccentric." All at once I got a snippet of "Amazing

Grace"—*how sweet the sound*. I mentally patted myself on the back for burying her with her fur babies before we came down here.

"Look," Faith said, "She left us paper towels, toilet paper—" she let out a whoop. "And even clean pillows and blankets vacuum-sealed in plastic."

Sam pried open a metal storage container. "Flour and yeast and all the stuff for making fresh bread." He grinned. "I'd love fresh, hot, bread with butter melting on top. Don't suppose there *is* any butter or milk? Those are two things I really miss."

I held up a carton. "Dried milk. Just add water."

Sam shrugged and moved over to the wall where dozens of cases of water were stacked. "This is seriously amazing. I even see MREs over there. I wonder where she got those."

We all made our way around the circle, admiring the extravagance. There were a few cots set up in one section, along with two radios and several flashlights and lanterns. On one shelf colorful bolts of fabric lay like forgotten artwork. Underneath the shelf I saw a clear plastic container marked "sewing kit."

"My aunt must've known something. It appears she went into overdrive recently. I've never seen most of this." I pointed to a military style footlocker. "I wonder what's in there. Must be important." When we opened it, the thing was full of batteries.

Even Snake seemed impressed, especially when he sniffed out the sacks of kibble in another storage container. There were cans of dog food as well.

"She loved her pets," I murmured, thinking again of Urchin and the cats. "I'll bet there's kitty food, too." I swiped at my eyes with the tail of my shirt, hoping Faith didn't notice. We'd been through a lot, but I still didn't want to come off as someone who couldn't cope. I remembered a poster I'd seen in the school counselor's office one morning.

IT'S OKAY TO VISIT CRAZY TOWN,
JUST DON'T UNPACK YOUR BAGS AND STAY

I thought about that a lot after I found myself on my own.

In the back of my mind, "Teach Your Children" began to play. It was the Crosby, Stills & Nash song about living by a code. I figured this one might be generated by my own emotions. "Man, what I wouldn't give to have my aunt here with us now," I said. "She knew everything about *everything*."

"I'll bet she would be glad to know we'll be using this stuff." Faith's voice was soft. The concrete walls almost absorbed her words before they reached my ears.

"You're right. She would." I began to pick up the shrink-wrapped flats of bottled water. "She kept talking about a new water system last time I was here. I guess that won't ever happen now. But this is better for us anyway. It's portable."

"Portable and potable!" Faith said.

I laughed. "Yep. Definitely potable. Just like that category on Jeopardy. Potent Potables. Thank you, Aunt Edna." In my head, I said a quick thanks to God. God and Aunt Edna. I almost laughed aloud. It sounded like a Willie Nelson song.

Turq held his arms out like a shelf, and I loaded him up. "Just stack it beside the car," I said. "Aunt Edna had a stock trailer. I should've looked for it down at the barn. We could take a lot of this stuff with us." Finding her the way we did kind of threw me off. I needed to get my head back in the game.

Sam carried cases of food and drink up, too. We didn't load him up like we did Turq, but he hauled his share.

Faith and I also carried stuff. I made certain to stock up on dog food, and she latched on to the powdered milk and cereal.

On our next trip down, Faith said, "It's spooky back here." She'd just come from behind the shelf stacked with vacuum packed pillows and blankets. She'd only been carrying a backpack when we found her. Didn't even have a tent. To her, this must look like the mall. Too bad there were no shoes.

A sudden sound drew our attention to the stairs going down to the next level. "What was that?"

Faith grabbed my arm. "Did it come from above or below?"

"Down—"

I looked around to account for everyone, and that's when Snake popped up above the steps like a canine jack-in-the-box.

Faith leaned down and hugged his neck. "Snakeman, you scared the devil out of me." She drew her hand away and looked at her palm. "He's kind of wet," she said. "Muddy."

I called him over, ran my hands down his coat. "Sure is." I looked at the downward stairs. "He's obviously been down there, nosing around. But if it's that wet and muddy …"

Faith's eyes met mine.

"Maybe there's been a cave in. I read where the government sometimes pumped mud into the tunnels running across to the silo. So vagrants wouldn't be able to go across. But I don't know if it was done here."

"I think it's time to go," she whispered. "All of a sudden, it doesn't feel so safe."

I nodded. "Grab what you want—"

Sam and Turq reappeared from up top, and we told them what was going on.

Sam didn't say a word, just grabbed more water, turned, and headed back up the stairs to the sunlight. Turq did the same, but Sam kept glancing back. "I'd really like to go down there," he said. "See what's left of the control center."

I ignored him. To be trapped down there by Takers would be the worst thing that could happen. We wouldn't stand a chance.

Back in the parking area, we looked at our stacks of supplies. We'd barely made a dent in Aunt Edna's survival stores.

"I'm going to lock the door, then we can go get the trailer and load most of this in it." I snapped the padlock in place. For a moment I leaned my ear against the metal surface. It was warm from the sun. Would've been searing hot if it hadn't been standing open in the partial shade.

Was that a sound from the other side? I couldn't tell, but I assumed it was my imagination. If Takers were there, a metal door wouldn't stop them. Even if it was steel. The hair on my arms rose as if from static electricity.

I shook my head and hurried over to the group.

CHAPTER TWENTY

The Hut

I say we divide everything as evenly as possible between the vehicles," Sam said. "The rest can go in the trailer. But it's your call, Jack. It's really your stuff."

"Thanks, Sam. Everyone get what you want, then I will go for the trailer."

Carlos seemed impressed with our haul. "Hey, Jack."

I stopped sorting and waited.

"This might be a good place to stay for a while, you know?"

I looked out toward the scrubby mesquite and live oak trees. "Yeah, I thought so, too. There's a pond back in there. We could check that out." I motioned toward the Quonset hut. "There's a tunnel connecting that hut to the silo and to this space, too. And there should be an ATV around somewhere." I had a sudden stupid vision of Takers on 4-Wheelers.

Carlos laughed. "See what I mean? It's got everything."

I laughed a little. "I'm afraid there's been some sort of cave-in or something. Snake went down and came back up wet and muddy. Besides, I've got to make a trip to Colorado before winter. I don't want to get caught up there when the snow flies unless we intend to stay."

I gazed around the area. "I have to check on my grandparents. See if my dad's been there. Or is there."

Carlos nodded. "I'm going with you, but afterward maybe we'll come back here." He chuckled. "Maybe I won't be so crippled by then, and we will clean it all up. Then, we'll go down to Mexico. See about my family."

"Sounds like a plan. Just as soon as you're able." The memory of Carlos sitting in the floor holding a teddy bear to his chest gripped me. That was the day we had found the farmhouse with the empty crib, and he'd told me what happened to his own wife and child in Yellow Bend.

Sam chimed in. "You say there's an all-terrain vehicle here somewhere?"

"Yeah. Aunt Edna was a whiz with engines. She rebuilt the old one, and the last I heard, it was still running. You know, before all this."

"I'd like to see that thing. I like to tinker with engines, too." He pulled a bandana from his hip pocket and swiped it across his face. The Texas sun rode high now. "I wish I could've met your aunt. She sounds like my kind of people."

He walked over to the shade where he opened and drained a bottle of water, and I thought, *Yeah, she would've taken to you, too.*

We finished divvying up the rest of the food, water, and supplies. I'd been pleasantly surprised to find Tylenol and Ibuprofen along with complete first aid kits ready to go. We all took a kit except for Sam. He had his own.

"It just occurred to me that I don't have a trailer hitch on the Chrysler, but if you're willing to pull it with your Jeep, we can go back to the barn and get it now."

Sam nodded. "I'll go and take Turq with me. I don't like the idea of you and I both going off and leaving Faith and Carlos—"

"Thank you," Faith said.

And that was the end of that discussion.

Sam and Turq were gone and back almost before the three of us finished our snacks of canned corn, Vienna sausages, and Saltine crackers. Snake wolfed down a can of Alpo. "We are so spoiled." I held up the small tin of corn toward Sam when he drove up with the enclosed horse trailer.

We made short work of loading everything. I glanced into the Chrysler's trunk. "We've got plenty of room now." When I said those words aloud, I realized I was entrusting almost all our supplies to Sam, a guy we'd known only a couple of days. Was that wise? He could drive off into the sunset with our trailer, and we'd have no recourse except to shoot him. And I'd seen his stockpile of ammunition.

I put my fears aside when an old James Taylor song, "You've Got a Friend," edged into my thoughts. When it was followed by Bob Marley's "Three Little Birds," I knew we were on the right track. Everything will be all right. Just like Bob said.

Turq was our workhorse. As he stacked his cargo into the compact space of the trailer, new words became visible beneath his skin. *Trust* floated across the back of his neck; *Friend* appeared under the skin of his scalp. The third word, *Heaven*, gave me goosebumps. That one had appeared before. It floated out from the torn edge of his short-sleeved shirt and down into his wrist. It made me wonder what other words were beneath the fabric. Words I might never see.

I also wondered if he knew why the words were there. If so, he didn't seem able to tell me. Could he feel them moving around?

We needed some way to *really* communicate.

After loading the trailer, it was a short walk to the Quonset hut.

"I don't know why this is called a hut," Faith said. "It looks big, to me. I think of a hut as something small and primitive." She pulled her hair around over one shoulder and wiped her hand across the back of her neck. "It looks like someone took a gigantic tin can, sliced it in half lengthwise, and then set it back down."

"My dad said that's why the military used them, because they could be moved pretty much in one piece." I wanted to say more, about how it was just one big room with a little bathroom tucked into one end—but for some reason Blind Faith and Kansas began a battle of the bands in my skull again. "Can't Find My Way Home" competed with "Carry on Wayward Son." They pushed out James Taylor and Bob Marley as if they were trespassers.

My thoughts turned mushy, and I began to worry what we would find once we opened the hut's overhead door. Images of Aunt Edna and my old high school principal back in Eden, who had also been impaled on a tree branch, crawled into my head. The images pulsed with the beat of the music.

My stride lengthened.

Before I realized it, only Sam was keeping up. I didn't mean to leave the others behind, but the music told me something was wrong. I took a deep breath and held it, trying to keep my pounding heart from punching through my chest. As if in a bad movie, my fingers reached for the plain old handle on the plain old garage door built into the plain old hut I'd been visiting for years and years.

The music grew louder, drowning out the drone of the cicadas in the nearby live oaks. I watched my hand reaching, watched my fingers grasping, watched my grip tightening and pulling—

The door wouldn't budge.

Frustration made me give it a hard shake.

The heavy door rattled in its frame.

Then Turq was there. He placed Carlos on the ground, propped against the building, and reached for the handle to yank it up.

"Wait!" I called. "We don't want to destroy it." I could imagine him tearing the handle off completely.

My skull music jumped up a decibel, and I put one hand to my forehead to massage my thoughts into being. "Something is telling me my dad has been here, that he may even be inside." Dozens of possible scenarios flashed through my mind. *Dad in there asleep. Dad in there, flayed and rotting like Aunt Edna in the tree. Dad hurt and waiting on me to hurry up—*

Sam reached over and took my horsehead keys.

The noise in my head made it difficult to focus. A heavy-duty padlock was set into the doorframe on one side. Aunt Edna had hired a welder to put it there. To keep any riffraff out, she'd said.

In my haste, I'd forgotten all about it.

Sam located the correct key in a matter of seconds.

"Sorry," I murmured. Flashing spots of light peppered the edges of my vision as the music cranked itself to brain bleed level.

"You okay, son?" I thought it was Sam's voice, but I couldn't be certain. I imagined my pirate eye exploding under the onslaught of sound.

No matter. I burst underneath the door as soon as Sam shouldered it up.

Dad

I knew it.

I'd walked right onto a message scrawled across the concrete floor in thick, black marker.

Found my wife, dead, Eden Library.

Found my son's skull in our burned-out home.

Found my sister hanging in a tree.

Don't want to be the only one left.

Jackson Lewis – music teacher, Eden, Tx.

God help us all.

I fell to the floor on my knees, hands tracing the black marker words over and over. "It's a suicide note." The last time Dad and I were here, we'd repaired the wide metal catwalk for Aunt Edna. It spanned the width of the building. We'd been so proud of ourselves.

"That will be a big help," Aunt Edna had said. "This place is going to make a great garage for the engine repair shop I'm going to open."

She'd really cackled when she said that, so I figured she was joking, but with her, you couldn't be sure.

Faith put her hand on my shoulder. We looked up at the catwalk.

He'd climbed up carrying the rope. Probably knotted it carefully, so he wouldn't fall all the way to the concrete and break a leg—or his neck—and lie there, suffering. His body still swayed slightly from the draft we caused when we opened the overhead door.

"I don't understand," I said. "If he thought that was me in the fire, that skull, why didn't he bury me? Why didn't he bury Aunt Edna?" I didn't expect an answer, but I sensed Faith and Sam shooting silent glances at each other above my head.

"Maybe he didn't have time to bury your aunt," Faith said.

"Yeah," Sam agreed. "This message looks like it may have been here awhile. Maybe it wasn't even your dad—"

How could they be so *cruel?* Not my dad? "It says right there he saw the skull, found Edna. That's why he … why he …" I jerked my chin toward the ceiling, unwilling to look up and see him hanging there again.

"Jack," Faith's voice came soft as a feather. "It doesn't say that at all." She sat down beside me on the rough concrete. "This message says *GONE to CO*. It probably is your dad, but I don't know why he didn't sign—"

I stood and looked at the words again. In a way, they reminded me of Turq's words, the way they quivered and wiggled in my vision.

Turq stepped up and appeared to read the message. He looked at me, and I looked at him. *All* his words were *good* words, now. But they still swam beneath his translucent skin like strange fish. He looked at his arms, where the letters wavered and dove, surfaced and disappeared only to resurface somewhere else.

His tattered shirt made me suddenly ashamed. He deserved something for sticking with us. For saving us. I looked back at the huge message. The letters wiggled and disappeared, resurfaced from within the concrete as something else. Some other message. Different words altogether. I closed my eyes to refocus my vision.

Turq moved closer so that his strong arm was against me. Somehow, having him standing there, barely touching my skin, gave me the courage to look up again. Dad was not there. A long rope hung, frayed and useless, halfway to the floor. The catwalk we'd repaired dangled dangerously, the large bolts we'd installed now scattered across the cement like Tinker Toys.

I examined the real letters scrawled across the floor. They said exactly what Faith had read out loud. Three measly words. Not even signed.

But of course, it was my dad. His music had nearly scrambled my brains. "Dad," I whispered. "Where are you?"

The tunes had fallen to a dull roar. Now they cut off abruptly as the poorly repaired section of the catwalk creaked and groaned and tore completely loose from its mooring.

I watched in slow motion as the small section of iron mesh walkway fell from on high and struck the concrete with a *bang* hard enough to send up a shower of sparks.

We threw our hands up as protection but there was no need. It wasn't true fire any more than the vision I'd had was true.

Lowering my hands, I straightened out of my self-defensive crouch. "I saw my dad hanging there," I said. "When I walked in, the message said he'd found mom's body, that he'd seen the skull in the ash and assumed it was me. It said he'd found his sister in the tree—and that he didn't want to be alone."

"It's all right," Faith murmured. "It wasn't real. You saw what you were afraid of seeing. But at least it appears he *has* been here. *Gone to Colorado* is a pretty darn good message, isn't it?"

I closed my eyes. "But the music almost gave me a stroke," I said. "It was so loud—"

"I know," she replied. "I could hear it."

I jerked my head up. "How could you?"

"It was loud," she said simply. "But even so?" She dismissed our shared music with a wave of her hand. "How'd your dad get in and out of here? Think he had keys? And why *didn't* he bury your aunt?"

"Good questions. He could've had keys, I guess. But not burying her back at the house? If you knew my dad, you'd know that just wasn't like him at all." My tortured brain still wouldn't let me think clearly. Head felt like soup. The music was gone now, but for a few minutes, it had been *bad*.

Sam spoke up. "I've been involved in some shady military things in my time. Some mind control experiments used music. Technology let them blast images across the world as well. Invisible to some, vivid to others." He looked at the gap where the catwalk had been. "Technology may well be the Beast mentioned in the Bible."

"Slouching toward Bethlehem?" Faith asked. "Is that why it's all gone now, in the wake of the rip?"

Carlos had made his way inside. "Is technology all gone? Or is someone just fine tuning it?" He cut his eyes toward Turq. "Maybe my buddy here is nothing but a 3-D illusion. A hologram."

"I saw Dad." I tilted my chin up again. "Hanging. Up there. His face was black. His tongue swollen out of his mouth—"

Faith squeezed my shoulder.

"I'm sorry," I said. "It was just so real. And the letters on the floor? They changed just like the letters inside Turq's skin. They wiggled and swam and disappeared and reappeared." I closed my eyes.

Sam spoke again. "You're a conduit, boy. I heard about experiments with kids like you. I don't know why you have this thing—"

"Precognition? ESP?" Faith seemed to need to label it.

"—my Gran has it, too," I said. "Until now, it was just kind of ordinary. Like I'd get flashes of songs that would make me in a good mood when I woke up in the morning. Or a few words of lyric would tell me I needed to slow down and think or go back to the house for something I'd forgotten, minor everyday stuff I thought everyone experienced."

Frustration built up behind my eyes as I tried to explain it. I felt skinless. As naked as if I'd been flayed by one of *them*. I pressed the heels of my hands into my eye sockets to stop the hateful moisture. "I think I'm going crazy. Soon I'll be unpacking my stuff to stay."

"Son," Sam's voice was steady. "We need *your* brand of crazy. It may be the sanest thing we'll encounter today." He walked toward the back of the hut to check out the tiny bathroom.

Oddly enough, his words made me feel better. His words combined with Faith's hands and Turq's solid form beside me.

Snake wormed his way in, and Turq backed off a bit. My best four-legged friend now pressed himself against the fronts of my knees, and finally, my trembling abated, moved back inside my core where it always lived.

From across the room, Carlos said, "Jack, your crazy music and colors saved us at the buffalo jump. Never forget that."

I looked straight across the wide expanse. Our gaze met, and it felt as if he, above all the others, knew what I was going through.

Sam came out of the bathroom. "Nothing there." He opened a door that I thought was a closet. It led directly outside. "Well, hell," Sam said. "We didn't even need a key." He strode back to our little group. "I say we get on the road. Someone wants us in Colorado. I'd say we go."

CHAPTER TWENTY-ONE

Lost Highway

We made our way back to the vehicles in silence. "Should we look down in the actual silo?" Faith stared across the way at the rusty rectangular doors set flush into the concrete circle.

I shook my head. Ordinarily I would've said we couldn't get inside without a specially built crane, but I had a feeling Turq could get one open if he we asked him to. I just didn't think we should push our luck. "I feel like we ought to go on," I said. "Sam's right. Someone wants us in Colorado."

"Carry on Wayward Son" had resurfaced, though not as loud as before. Now it was accompanied by another song. One I didn't know but must've heard somewhere.

"Hey, Sam," I called across the lot. "You know old country music?"
He nodded.

"Did Hank Williams sing something about a highway?" I looked at him to see if what I said made sense.

Sam sang a few words to "Lost Highway." He said it was a classic from back in *his* grandparents' day.

"Yeah," I said. "That's it." I closed my eyes and massaged my right temple. "We need to hurry."

No one said a word, they simply resumed their usual places, and in moments we were on the road. We locked the gate behind us in case we ever did pass this way again—despite the song that sometimes pestered me, saying we wouldn't—and I did my level best not to bawl as we put Aunt Edna's place in our rearview mirror.

I inhaled, took some Tylenol at Faith's urging, and chugged most of a bottle of water.

The sun was bright, our vehicles ran well, and we drove most of the time with the windows down to enjoy the fresh air blowing across the plains. It helped the pain that had gripped my head. It helped a lot. I'm sure the Tylenol didn't hurt, either.

We went north into the Texas panhandle all the way to Amarillo. We encountered many pileups that forced us to go off road, and once, on US 287, Turq had to get out and move a couple of cars to make a hole wide enough for the Chrysler to fit through.

We could usually go around any pile up, Texas is mostly flat, but this time there'd been so much rain—hard for this desert rat to imagine—that the shoulders had washed out on both sides of the road. The steep drop-off into the bar ditch just wasn't passable for the low-slung Chrysler.

"It is kind of a lost highway," Sam muttered as we watched Turq push the wrecks off into the watery ditch.

"Yeah, I guess so. I wouldn't have thought of it that way. Maybe I'd better start looking for a Jeep like yours." Sam's big tires had handled the muddy ditch easily, even pulling the trailer. "Maybe even a tow truck." My eyes sought the horizon. "When we start to see mountains, that's when we'll find out about traffic pileups and lost highways."

"You're right, bud. It's going to get tougher to get around these things." He glanced back at the blackened corpses that hung out of one of the vehicles.

We both scanned the nearly treeless landscape. "Where do you think all the other bodies are?" I asked. "There aren't any trees to hang them from, and most cars appear to be empty, except for these few."

"I've wondered the same thing, Jack." He started back toward the Jeep. "Didn't you say some of the Turqs marched through and cleaned up?"

"Yeah, but that was in Eden."

Sam shrugged as Turq strolled back to the Jeep.

I got behind the Chrysler's steering wheel and wrapped my fingers around the console shifter.

"Let me know if you want help driving," Faith said.

I looked at her eager face. "You sure? I hated to ask you." I couldn't believe I was relinquishing control again. Maybe it was just another way to please her. I'd quickly come to realize I'd do pretty much anything to make Faith smile.

And smile, she did. She flew around the back of the car while I stepped out and strode around the front to the shotgun seat. I couldn't believe she liked driving as much as I did. One more thing we had in common.

Still smiling, Faith slipped the gear shift into drive, and in seconds we were squeezing through the gap with room to spare.

By the time we got close to Amarillo, sticking to the highway to avoid going through the few-and-far-between towns, the two of us were ready for a meal and a break. I motioned for Sam to drive up beside us.

Driving through the miles and miles of wind-whipped vastness that made up the plains was always eye opening—Texas ranches were huge—but now the area felt even bigger. Big and empty. We had outrun the only other humans we'd seen outside Eden.

I pushed the image of Cade to the back of my mind. No song accompanied his memory. That alone was stranger than fiction. Cade was important. He should have music. I should have music. I wanted music to tell me what to do if he caught up to us again. I wanted to believe he wasn't dead.

Sam pulled alongside the Chrysler, and I told him we were looking for a place to stop. "You kids ever been to Palo Duro Canyon?" he asked.

"I haven't," Faith said. "But I've seen pictures online."

I nodded. "It's Texas' kid-brother version of The Grand Canyon. We camped there a couple times when I was younger." I looked toward the east. "Are we nearing the cutoff?"

Sam nodded. "It might be a good place to spend the night. Cook up a can of Aunt Edna's Spam, fry a potato or two from your trunk." He grinned, and I realized nothing got past him.

I sent up another silent thanks to God and Aunt Edna. "My mouth is watering already."

"I seem to remember a cabin," Sam said. "Another one of those grills out front. Unbelievable view. We might be able to drive right up to it."

Look at him, I thought. *Unbelievable view.* He still seemed able to appreciate the world. "Sounds good to me. And I hear the day passes are cheap this time of year."

He threw his head back and laughed. "That's always a plus. We'll pretend we're a blended family on vacation."

Faith motioned for him to lead, and in minutes we were at the cutoff to the park.

After we entered the open entrance gates, we drove along the canyon rim looking out over magnificent rock formations and striated colorations. It felt like a step back in time. I wouldn't have been the least bit surprised to see a Comanche warrior sitting atop a spotted pony on the far opposite edge. But maybe that was just my recollection of the sculpture of the famous Comanche Chief, Quanah Parker. I'd seen it on one of our family trips.

"Watch for the Lighthouse rock formation," I told Faith as we drove deeper into the park. "I think you can see it from here."

While we were looking for it, Sam turned into a campground and carefully maneuvered the trailer into position near a rustic rock cabin overlooking the dropoff.

I couldn't believe it. As a kid, we'd stayed in this very spot. There were only a few cabins in the entire park, and most were so remote you had to hike to them. I wouldn't have hiked anywhere to stay the night. I'd gotten extremely spoiled to our getaway cars, and if we somehow lost our supplies, it could be devastating.

Earlier, the sun winking off all those moist gray skulls had convinced me we were on a parallel path with the Takers. In fact, while Faith drove, I'd napped. And dreamed. I'd dreamed I was riding on the back of a hawk, soaring over the immense landscape.

From the hawk's perspective, I'd seen our car and Sam's Jeep, tooling along the near deserted highway in a spotlight of emptiness. But all around us—just out of sight—hordes and hordes of Takers were marching stoically toward the mountains, toward Colorado.

The dream had been so vivid I'd shaken myself awake.

"Bad dream?" Faith had asked.

I'd nodded. "Gray as far as the eye could see."

"Yeah. I feel it," she'd said. "The entire army of monsters marching along behind us, and on every side. Just outside our field of vision."

Snake whined, and Carlos had sat up a little straighter. "This ESP junk must be catching," he'd said. "I feel as if they are surrounding us, too. Pressing us toward the place they want us to go."

Now, I stood on a boulder outside our cabin and surveyed the landscape. Just below us, a stand of cottonwood rose to create a tiny pocket forest. Fragrant juniper bushes bristled here and there, spots of green against the stripes of rusty red and yellow ochre that made up the steep canyon walls.

In the summer, the Texas sun doesn't go to bed until after nine o'clock. That meant we had plenty of daylight left to make our little campfire in the iron grill on the cabin's rock patio. "We'll keep it small," I said. "It shouldn't be visible in the daylight. Not like the one we had after dark."

Faith inhaled the fragrant air as I put together the fire. "I think I could stay here forever," she said. It was early evening, the heat from the day dissipating quickly as shadows dipped into the canyon.

Carlos lounged on one of the tri-fold camp chairs from Aunt Edna's supplies. He shaded his eyes and peered across the deep space. "I wonder if any deer or antelope have survived." He shook his head. "I guess that would be a miracle. Animals like that don't like caves, right?"

"Probably not," I said. "But miracles do happen. Remember the horse near Bitty Sloan's house?"

Carlos stroked his scarred chin. "Right." He glanced at me, squinting into the lowering sun. "Remember how that ended though?"

"I do now. I had put it out of my head." My inclination was to glance over at Faith, see how she reacted, but she stood at the edge of the patio, staring into the distance.

"I'd like to see the Grand Canyon someday," she said. "But if I never get that far, this will do." She turned to me and smiled. "This will do."

I smiled back. "I'm going for a short hike. This place brings back so many memories." I made my way down the slope away from the cabin toward the stand of trees. My intention had been to ask Faith to come with me, but at the last second, I'd lost my nerve.

Snake bounded away the other direction. He seemed to love the landscape, too.

CHAPTER TWENTY-TWO

Metamorphosis

At the bottom of the slope, my heart thudded to a stop. Turq stood in the small copse of cottonwood with his back to me. His physique never ceased to amaze me. Strong, tall, muscular, unfinished. His body appeared smooth and translucent, gray and shimmery, like the fluid that flowed out when he was cut or injured.

If not for his turquoise shirt, I would have thought he was one of *them*. Then I saw the word *CHANGE* float across the back of his skull.

I looked closer. Not so smooth. Maybe not so shiny. Small movements of his fingers again, pulling long dry strips of fragile gray skin. Skinning himself. Alive.

A sudden sense of music floating, not through my head, but through this oddly eerie stand of trees. "Sinnerman." A song by a woman named Nina Simone. Her voice, not her words. My dad had this song in his collection. Said it was old. From Africa. It was in his classroom collection. He used it for teaching about the origins of spirituals.

The song certainly fit my buddy Turq, carrying his sin words around inside himself until they somehow turned to words of redemption.

I watched as a pile of gray skin grew around his toeless feet like strips of shredded paper. He slid the tattered turquoise shirt off his shoulders, let it fall to the canyon floor. Fluid began to well up.

Began to leak. Droplets crawled down his forearm, dripped off his nailless fingertips, plopped into the nest of skin and fabric as if seeking a home.

Seekers.

The word appeared beneath the skin of his back. It glided upward, disappearing only to resurface under the skin of his skull.

For once, he didn't seem attuned to me, didn't seem to know I watched.

My eyes searched the happy, Bob Ross blots of blue sky visible between the overlapping leaves in the canopy. Nothing rippled. Nothing seemed to be coming in response to his injury.

Larger and larger strips of skin drifted down to curl at his feet. His hand sped up, became a blur, a machine. Like automation. Like inevitable. Like fate.

I turned away, guts roiling. Watching felt wrong. Nothing would be coming to interrupt his self-destruction. Perhaps it *was* inevitable.

Maybe his time is up. I thought of Carlos and Hal saying how they felt the Takers were somehow programmed, and that once *this wave* was over, the enemy—whomever or whatever they were—would send us *the next wave.*

If that's true, what would become of them? I craned my neck, glanced back at my friend. *This. This is what becomes.*

My grief bent me over, kicked me in the gut even as I made my way back up the trail.

I didn't want to lose my friend.

"All My Trials," another old spiritual, replaced "Sinnerman." This time the words *were* in my head. This time, they didn't leave. This time, there was no doubt the music came from my dad's collection. This time, Elvis was the singer.

Dad, I said, or maybe it was another whispered prayer, *what is this? Are you still alive? I don't know what's going on … I need you. I need to know …*

The response came in the form of an old hymn, "Farther Along." Not my dad's song but my granddad's. He would often belt it out as he drove back from town, both windows of his old pickup rolled down, breeze ruffling his thin white hair as he sang:

Farther along, we'll know all about it
Farther along, we'll understand why
Cheer up my brother, live in the sunshine
We'll understand it, all by and by

I loved that song. It said there's hope for understanding, farther along. But I didn't know if it truly came from my granddad or if it was just buried up in my subconscious like a salamander in mud.

I sang another verse, "Tempted and tried, we're oft made to wonder … why it should be thus, all the day long …"

Faith met me at the edge of the patio. "What's that your singing?"

"It's an old hymn, 'Farther Along,' one of my granddad's favorites." I shook my head. "I used to think it was '*Father* Along.' Seemed appropriate, either way."

"You're frowning," she said. "What's wrong?"

"Turq." I glanced back over my shoulder. "He's down there, in the woods. He's—*changing*." I heard the crack in my voice, couldn't help it. The words to the hymn reverberated in my mind. *Cheer up my brother, live in the sunshine, farther along we'll understand why.*

"How's he changing?" Faith asked. "I didn't even realize he wasn't with us."

Yeah, I hadn't seen him walk away, either. They could be so silent when they wanted.

"Jack?"

The fear in her voice matched what I felt deep inside. Turq had become my lifeline. My rock. My protector. *Like* a father. I could always depend on him to have my back. "He seems to be morphing or something. Shedding his skin."

Faith started down the slope.

I touched her arm. "I don't think we should."

"But … it's Turq."

"I feel the same way, it's just—"

In an instant, she was gone. She didn't shake off my hand in a rude manner, just sort of slipped out from under it. Then Snake was there, too, looking up at me as if to ask why I was letting the girl go down alone.

She followed the path just the way I had—thoughts of *down*

the rabbit hole crossed my mind—and in a second, I heard her gasp.

Only a step behind her, I saw her hand cover her mouth. Shock illuminated her features. "What is it?" she asked.

Snake stopped stiff legged. I thought he might attack, then he slowly nosed forward, sniffing the air before letting his square snout seek the ground.

A puddle of translucent slime glittered in the dappled light. The late sunshine falling through the leaves played upon it in surreal white dots. Black thread-like lines wiggled slightly. I couldn't tell if they really moved or if it was a trick of the light. "Metamorphosis," I said.

If I hadn't seen the Takers rain to earth and then watched them rise from their silvery puddles as if they were being born; and if I hadn't observed Turq peeling his own skin, *molting*, I might not have recognized this event for what it was.

"Turq?" I called softly. "Where are you?" I couldn't believe he'd peeled that much of himself in the short few minutes it had taken me to go up and come back down.

Faith looked at me like I'd lost my mind. She peered at the slime. "Wha—"

I put my index finger to my lips.

A whirring sound came from overhead, then stopped. "Farther Along" skimmed the surface of my brain.

I looked up.

On the thickest branch of an ancient cottonwood perched a figure unlike anything I'd ever seen. It was large, translucent, the size of a man, but winged. The slim body echoed the shape of a rifle slug, the wings wrapping around it, diaphanous and multiple. I immediately thought of dragonfly wings, but there seemed to be twice that many. When the light hit the thing just right, it disappeared. The only way I knew it was still there came from the sound of those wings whirring for balance.

I shaded my eyes. "I see you, old friend. I see that you've changed. Where are your words? Did you shed them, too?"

Wings whipped the air. Words littered the ground around me. I put out my hand to catch one like a dark snowflake.

Heaven, the word said.

Snake whined, turned his nose to the sky.

My mind reeled. "Are you an angel? Did you make it to Heaven? Are you going there now?"

Wings beat the air like thunder. The leaves on the trees shook and scattered. A whirlwind rose through the canopy, twisting and tearing and twirling debris and sunlight.

Then Turq was gone.

I smiled at Faith's expression of wonder.

My voice didn't even sound like my own. It was filled with awe. "Maybe he's going home."

We walked back to the cabin in silence. I knew I should be happy for my strange buddy, but a feeling of dread came over me. Could we make it without him? What about Carlos? We'd gotten so used to Turq simply picking him up, carrying him—what would we do now?

"I barely got here," Faith said. "But I had already come to depend on him to look out for us."

"I know. I can't believe it."

A crash brought us out of our shared reverie.

Snake zipped past us, toenails chewing up earth, body smashing small bushes and twigs, the smell of leafy mold permeated the air, and then he, too, was gone.

Faith and I looked at each other and took off running.

The campsite was trashed, the big ice chest empty, lid smashed at the hinges. The old grill had been *crushed*, as if made of aluminum instead of iron.

"Duck!" Sam yelled. "They're probably armed."

I yanked Faith to the ground behind the Chrysler.

She pointed across the way.

I glimpsed Snake's rear end through the slender trees, obviously on the trail of something, or someone. "What's going on?" I yelled.

"They found us," Sam called back. "I heard screaming. They grabbed Carlos." He stepped out from behind his Jeep, face strained, white. "I think they're gone. I couldn't get back, too far away, in the wood."

"We have to go after them." I could imagine the pain Carlos must be in, being dragged, slung around. "We've lost Turq, too. He morphed into a flying thing. You just had to see it." I grabbed my bandolier from the trunk of the car, fastening it around my chest to hold extra ammo.

Sam picked up Carlos' shotgun and took another handgun from the Jeep. When he raised his shirt to holster the pistol, I saw a killing blade on his belt, a black Ka-Bar with a serrated edge. He also added a machete in a leather sheath.

I saw all this from the corner of my eye as I grabbed my handgun and ammo. As I added my own mid-sized machete to my belt, I wondered why Carlos hadn't fired his shotgun.

Faith pulled a revolver from her new backpack. She also withdrew a can of pepper spray. "If they get too close," she said when she saw me eyeing it.

"Looks good." I motioned for Sam to lead the way. "Why can't we hear them? I'd think that many Takers could be heard from miles away."

"Single file," Sam said. "Probably not more than a hundred. Like a military unit. Unbelievably silent on a dirt trail. And Jack …"

I glanced up.

"Humans are with them. Just like we thought."

I didn't say anything. I knew what he meant. I knew *who* he meant.

Faith and I looked at each other again. Then we followed Sam's lead.

We walked single file, too. Crept is a better word. First Sam, then me, then Faith. I thought it extremely odd that I hadn't heard Snake again. "How many humans?" I asked at last.

Sam shrugged. "I saw the backs of a couple scruffy boys—one might've looked like your friend, Cade—and then there was a skinny girl with dirty blond hair. The others I didn't see very clearly. I was in a copse of live oak checking out what appeared to be a game trail." He held up a hand for us to stop.

We stood perfectly still, searching the silent area with our eyes. Shadowy movement in the distance told me we were not alone. Was this some new strategy? Before now they just marched over everything and strung up all the people.

I couldn't stand there any longer. I nudged Sam so that he would see the movement ahead. Nodding my head toward it, I indicated we should go on.

Sam hesitated. "Could be a trap," he whispered. "An ambush."

What did he know that I didn't? Takers didn't ambush. They didn't hide and wait—did they? I held off stepping around him.

Faith's breath was warm on the back of my neck. Disconcerting. Standing around waiting was not my strong suit. "Hey," I said. "Did I hear whining?"

Sam broke. We didn't run, but all at once we were moving. Fast. Moving and cocking our weapons. I hoped Faith wouldn't accidentally shoot me in the back.

We came upon Snake sitting at the base of a near petrified juniper. All that remained of the old tree was a couple of leafless branches and the broken trunk pointing at the sky.

Low whines emanated from Snake's chest. The skinned tree accentuated the blood dripping down the trunk. "Oh, my God. Carlos." I rushed forward and held his body up so Sam could take him off the broken branch.

Carlos moaned.

Snake whined and stood up to lick his friend's face.

Faith took off her sweater and wrapped it around Carlos as Sam laid him on the ground. "No," she murmured. "Please, God, no." She placed her two fingers to her lips, kissed the tips, then pressed them to the barely pulsing crucifix on Carlos' throat.

His head lolled to one side. "Jack," he mumbled.

I leaned down, my head pounding with the lyrics to "Farther Along," but my name was followed by nothing but red froth coating his lips. "Carlos, man," I whispered. "Stay with us." I shoved my hand into my pocket and pulled out his grandfather's turquoise stone.

It was blue and lumpy and cool, about the size of a quarter, and shot through with a broken line of gold. I pressed it into his palm.

"Jack," he whispered.

"I'm here, buddy." I curled his fingers around the stone and leaned closer to his face.

"Do you believe in God, Jack?"

I nodded, my tears drenching his face. "I do, Carlos. I promise, I do."

Sam let go of the wrist he'd been checking for a pulse. "He's gone. The branch must have damaged an artery."

"They didn't eat him." Faith sat back on her heels, tears washing through the dirt on her cheeks. "Why did they kill him and not eat him?"

I couldn't believe it had come so suddenly. I certainly didn't know how to answer Faith's question.

Snake sat by his friend's head and licked Carlos' face again. He seemed to be trying to revive him. I plopped backward onto the leafy trail and pulled the big dog to me. "After all this time," I murmured. "I thought we were in the clear."

"Maybe that's what we were supposed to think," Sam said.

I could barely hear his voice. The hymn in my head had given way to "Carry on Wayward Son." The one that had driven me to Kansas with my frenemy, Thad. The place where we'd found Carlos tooling down the road on his Harley, his shotgun peeking out the end of a rolled up Mexican blanket.

Now look at him, I thought. *Torn up, burned, skin and bones. How did I not notice how thin he'd gotten?* Righteous fury engulfed me. *Look what they did to my friend.*

"Jack?" Faith's voice was rough. She placed her hand on my forearm. "Are you okay?"

"No." I shook my head. "This is so wrong. We were getting back to normal. Turq had turned, others were turning, too. I was sure of it. I thought we'd all find a place—"

Snake twisted around and began to lick my face. His chest rumbled the way it always did when he wanted to communicate.

"We need to bury him," Sam said. "I'll go back to the Jeep for my shovel."

I looked at him and started digging with my hands. "No time for that. We need to go after them."

Sam hesitated, then grabbed a hand-sized shard of shale, ready to dig in.

Faith glanced up, tears in her eyes. Then she, too, grabbed a sharp piece of shale and began to scrape at the earth.

We took turns feeling for breath in our friend's chest as we dug. Faith even got down and put her cheek next to his lips, to see if anything escaped. We couldn't believe he was gone so suddenly. Like Turq.

Faith left her sweater—the same one she had found in my dad's closet at school—covering the horrible wound in his chest. "I saw this coming," she said. "I just didn't understand." She took a deep breath. "Carlos told me something yesterday. He said, 'Souls in Purgatory are hungry for the love and prayers of those who loved them in life.' He quoted scripture and verse, but I don't recall the numbers." She gave her head a little shake. "He went on to say that if his theory about robots from another government turned out to be false, then these creatures might be the evil souls trapped in Purgatory like your internet physicist said. And probably they never had anyone praying for them in this world, but maybe the good ones did have prayers."

"So, what? We need to pray? Look where it got him." I glanced at Carlos as "Farther Along" flared. Beneath it, Jerry Garcia's guitar started up on one of my dad's favorites. I'd never cared much for the song "Ripple" until I overheard Dad strumming his old Martin guitar and singing the lyrics under his breath one day. I'd looked them up on YouTube. The poetry blew me away. Now, it seemed as if it could be the poetry of this whole sorry mess rippling outward from horrors such as the one at our feet.

I wanted to ask Faith what she meant when she said she'd seen it coming, but Sam was making quick work of the loamy soil.

We dug and dug without stopping. By the time we hit bedrock, Carlos' hands had begun to turn a dusky shade of blue. They were already cooling, even in this heat. We laid him in the earth and covered his face with a sleeve of the sweater. I couldn't push the dirt onto his eyes. No way. The hole wasn't nearly deep enough, but it was the best we could do in the rocky canyon.

Pain coated my words as I fought to speak. "He was a good man. The best. He didn't deserve this. We were going to go to Mexico." The notes of the songs careened about inside my skull like pin-balls, and I massaged my temples, remembering what Faith had said about praying. "Lord, take this kind man into your embrace and hold him there until he's healed." I didn't know what I meant. Didn't know why I said those words. Something spoke through me. We'd just buried Aunt Edna—maybe there was an open line to the afterlife.

I wanted to follow that train of thought, but a different sound found its way into my tortured brain. It was the shushing sound we knew and feared. Somewhere nearby, the Takers had come to a road. The shushing was the sound of bare toeless feet hitting the asphalt.

Snake must have felt the vibrations. He exploded into action, taking off down the trail without a backward glance.

I looked at Sam and Faith, then took off behind Snake. I couldn't keep up. I lost sight of the dog, but moments later, I began to see *them*, the gray shapes through the trees. An unseen root grabbed my toe, and I was face down in the dirt before I knew what had happened.

"Jack!" Faith's voice seemed a mile away. Hands clutched me, picked me up, helped me stand.

"I have to find out if it was Cade. If he's still alive. Maybe they're keeping him prisoner, maybe we can—"

She raised her voice. "Even if it was Cade, and they do have him, we don't know how or why." Her face pleaded with me to read between the lines. "He was probably in the car that rolled. With Hal dead, maybe he doesn't know what to do."

I wiped the filth off my lips from where I'd fallen. The gray shapes were no longer shapes. Now it looked like smooth water flowing slowly past the widening gaps in the trees. There were so many of them, I could no longer make out individual creatures.

"But if he *is* alive, he may be a scout, Jack." She smiled to soften her words. "I thought he and Hal acted weird back at the motel. And then the others came, and it reminded me of something a guy told me on the road."

"On the road?" I was having trouble following her.

Sam arrived and stood nearby, taking in the scene. Snake also came back, tongue lolling.

"A couple weeks after the rip, I met this guy named Dawk." She ducked her head. "Not Doc, like a doctor, but D-a-w-k, like a hawk." Her face went still. "I think it was some sort of nickname even before the rip, but I'm not certain."

I concentrated on dusting myself off. "Keep talking," I said. "But I think we should follow them while you do."

Sam cleared his throat. "We need to go back for the vehicles. If this is some sort of trick, it may be too late already."

My brain almost imploded. "You're right. Knowing they have humans with them changes everything. They could be after the vehicles. Especially since they totaled Hal's Challenger."

We turned and started back. "That many of them, on a rural road, it won't be hard to find and follow—"

Sam nodded. "And Colorado?"

"We're still going, but Cade—"

Faith spoke again, softly. "Dawk told me he'd noticed some of the creatures changing, just like our Turq picking up the dead, but he said he also noticed some humans pretending to befriend them, in order to use them the way humans will always do."

"That makes no sense," I said. "You can't befriend the unclothed ones. What happened to this Dawk?" I asked.

Faith shrugged. "He just went his own way. Sort of a loner. Said he was going to something called harp, in Alaska. That was too far away for me, so I stayed in Lewiston and let him move on." She wiped her eyes with her fingers. "He was a nice guy, so smart."

"I'm sorry. I've heard of that place. It's an old military research facility. I think they were studying the atmosphere or ionosphere." I didn't tell her I'd read about it and knew it was really HAARP, short for High-frequency Active Auroral Research Program. I sensed there was more to the story about Dawk.

She let out a breath of air. "It's okay. We only traveled together for a while. He taught me a lot about observation, though. How to stay safe." She glanced down before continuing. "And one thing I noticed while we were with Cade and Hal …"

I waited, tried to catch her eye.

Finally, she looked up. "Cade could have joined us at any time. He *chose* to stay with Hal." Faith looked away when she said it, as if she knew it would hurt me.

"Yeah, I got a funny feeling from him a time or two." I shrugged to let her know it didn't matter. "I'm glad you said that. And I'm glad to learn about Dawk. I hated to think of you being alone the whole time."

She nodded. "Dawk said something else." Her voice took on its poetic tone. "He said the things didn't seem real to him. Like they were a figment of someone's imagination come to life. Made up and *then* made real."

I tried to recall what Carlos had said back at the Quonset hut. Something about a hologram, but I couldn't quite grasp it. Maybe I couldn't think straight because we were passing back by the freshly turned earth where we'd just buried him. I recalled wondering how he would get around without Turq, and now it didn't even matter. And yet it did. It suddenly felt predicted. Planned, somehow.

Faith took my elbow when she saw me slowing down. Within no time we were back at the camp site.

The Chrysler and the Jeep were there. But the tires on both vehicles were ruined. Shredded. Oddly, they hadn't destroyed the little stock trailer or even broken into it.

"Probably coming back for it later," Sam said.

I nodded. "You're probably right."

Faith looked at the tires on the Chrysler. "They did that, why?"

Anger slid out with my words. "They know we don't have four extra tires for each vehicle, but they can pick them up along the road if they want. Takers could easily carry tires." I gritted my teeth, trying to control my tone. "I think your friend was onto something. It appears the Takers are being used as weapons now."

My blood felt close to boiling. I wanted to slaughter them, torch them, burn them the way Carlos had been burned.

For the first time since it happened, I didn't want to just get away or defend myself. Now, I wanted revenge.

CHAPTER TWENTY-THREE

Kill. Obey.

Sam looked at his crippled Jeep. "If we don't find a similar Jeep on the side of the road, with the big tires, then we'll have to hoof it into Amarillo and find a tire store." He rubbed his lips, frowned. "We'll have to carry our food and water on our backs, plus weapons, of course. This changes things. I haven't been on foot against them before."

I couldn't believe we were suddenly laid so low. *All my trials ...*

"I can stay with the trailer," Faith said. "I know you guys will find another car or Jeep or something. Amarillo's a big town. Anyhow, there are lots of cars on the highway like the Chrysler. Why not get those tires first, then drive on to Amarillo for the Jeep tires?"

"That's a good plan," Sam said. "Maybe we can find a car close by, roll the tires back here one by one." He chuckled. "I just want to do one thing before we go."

We looked at him in expectation.

"I want to find a place to stash most of the food." He nodded toward the trailer. "Leave them an empty trailer. In case they come back before we do, I mean."

"Good idea," I said. "We can stash it in several different places. Too bad we can't stash the cars somewhere, too."

"I'll hold 'em off as long as I can," Faith said.

"Nah," I shook my head. "I think you should go with us. I'd rather they take the food than you." Heat crept into my cheeks. I hadn't meant to declare my thoughts so boldly.

"Then I'll go with you." She looked into my eyes. "I can roll a tire, too. And when we get back, we can put the spare on and that will be four good tires."

I nodded. "There you go, being all smart again."

She smiled but glanced over her shoulder. "What was that?"

I didn't hear anything, but I trusted her ears. A sudden horrible thought occurred to me. "Maybe it wasn't the food they were after." I slowly pulled my revolver. "Maybe it was a trap. For us."

Snake came to his feet, looking toward the trees on the opposite side of the camp road. A coldness encased my body.

Sam slid his machete out of its sheath. By the time the tip cleared leather, the Takers were upon us.

He disabled the first three with the machete. Clear fluid splashed the stone. Black letters littered the patio. But it was no use. Even single file, there were too many of them. I shot half a dozen, but they just kept coming. They surrounded Sam, knocked his machete to the ground, slammed his head into a tree trunk.

The sky rippled; a scar opened.

Sam went down, scrambling for Carlos' shotgun. One of the unmarred Takers picked him up, slung him over its shoulder, went back to the dirt trail, and began to march.

I grabbed the shotgun, took out a few more. Their sin words exploded into the coming sunset light. I reloaded from my bandolier.

The black rain began to fall. There were at least ten injured Takers in various stages of "bleeding out." The sand-colored patio stones grew wet with viscous fluid and black letters.

"C'mon," I yelled toward Faith. I intended to follow Sam and shoot the ones that had grabbed him.

And then I saw the kid from the motel. He and Marla had Faith by the arms. They'd already whipped a bandana around her mouth as a gag. Her eyes were huge. It *had* been a trap. They must've sent one squad ahead—the one that killed Carlos—while the rest of them simply waited for us to return. No wonder they didn't take the food.

I raised the shotgun. "Let her go," I commanded. "I swear, I'll blow your head off."

Marla raised a small revolver and pointed it at me. "I told you I'd see you dead." Her voice hissed across the patio like a rattlesnake. "But this is even better. You took Kevin, so I'm taking *her*." She jerked her chin toward Faith as her finger pulled the trigger on the revolver.

Faith jostled her and the bullet went wide, grazing my thigh and twirling me around. White pain seared my leg. I felt myself falling. Somehow, I held onto the shotgun, afraid of pulling its triggers, afraid of hitting Faith.

I landed in a puddle of clear fluid, letters still wiggling. Wounded Takers lay here and there or dragged their mangled bodies across the stone. Words were scattered everywhere. Broken words. Jumbled.

Here and there I picked out two still intact. *KILL* and *OBEY*.

Were those sin words? They certainly weren't the same sin words I'd seen before. Those had seemed to echo past sins.

These seemed to be more like orders.

Black sludge from the sky holes pushed across the patio in wrist-sized rivulets. Some Takers were already being absorbed, their garnet eyes staring into the sunset without expression.

The pain in my leg grew worse, but I didn't think it was fatal. I used the shotgun to help me gain my feet. The black rain inched toward me, lessening as it expended its mass on the injured creatures.

I made it to the shelter of the cabin doorway, managed to hang on to the door jamb, turned, raised my gun, and aimed at the coming line just as the first flight of locusts burst from the black rain puddles, buzzing their way back into the nearest sky scar.

A wave of grayness began to eat the edges of my vision. It had been a while since I'd seen the black rain turn to locusts and carry the Takers back into oblivion. But that wasn't what caused my sudden lightheadedness.

A puddle of blood pooled around my sneaker. My pant leg was soaked. Maybe the bullet hadn't just grazed me, after all.

Forcing myself to focus, I ripped the bottom off my t-shirt and tied it around my thigh as a tourniquet. It was the last thing I remember doing before I dragged myself across the threshold and sank to the cold stone floor.

Behind me, black sludge made a barrier between the horde and the cabin.

I awoke to a strip of sunlight warming my eyelids. A hot tongue rasped across my cheek. Snake stood over me, licking, licking, licking. The underside of my body was stuck to the floor in a pool of blood lacy with frost.

A groan escaped my lips as I peeled myself from the floor. "*Snake,* help."

The stout dog crowded up under my arm. I clutched his thick neck.

Icy wind whispered through the cracked-open door. "It's summer," I said. "Why's it so cold?"

Snake began to lick my face again.

"Thank God for you, old man." I used his strength to pull myself to a sitting position. The shotgun lay where I'd fallen. I didn't know what had become of my machete, but my backpack stood in the corner of the room from the day before. The narrow strip of sunlight fell through the barely open door like a promise.

I grabbed the shotgun, pushed the door shut, then struggled up onto one knee. The other leg was no good, stiff as iron, throbbing like a ruined tooth. My whole body felt frozen.

No way I could stand. I lowered myself back down and inched across the floor backward, one butt cheek at a time. My teeth were chattering in my head by the time I grabbed one of the sturdy four-legged chairs with the CCC letters burned into the seat. Hand made by the Civilian Conservation Corps way back in the Great Depression, one of President Roosevelt's alphabet soup programs that helped pull the country back from the brink of collapse during my great-great-grandpa's day.

My great-gramps once told me his daddy had worked for the CCC to keep them from starving during the dustbowl days. Maybe he'd even built one of these chairs.

The connections were unbelievable.

I gritted my teeth to stop their chattering. "Maybe those connections will save me now."

"Snake," I yelled. "Fetch." He couldn't hear my voice, but he knew I needed something from him. He cocked his head and peered into my face. His brown eyes showed a level of concern more human than animal.

Leaning close to him while hanging onto the seat of the chair to keep myself from toppling over, I watched my breath puff out as I said, "Get the bag." I pointed to the backpack in the corner.

Snake's gaze followed my finger.

It didn't surprise me when he walked straight to the corner and dragged my pack to me across the uneven floor. That bag had been with us since day one. It had carried medicine for all of us, especially him and Carlos. The image of our friend as we laid him in the earth rolled across my mind. "All My Trials," crept in behind it.

When I saw what else Snake had dragged into the cabin, my vision blurred. I wiped my eyes and reached under the table, snagging the remains of Turq's old turquoise shirt. I stuffed it into my pack. A new talisman to join my mom's turquoise earrings, and the spare key to Dad's Mustang. His note was crumpled in there, too. The photo from Aunt Edna's house was still safe in the glove box.

Clasping the dog around the neck, I hugged him fiercely. "It always comes back to you and me, doesn't it, boy?"

I dug into the pack for antibiotics and Tylenol III. "I really need a fire," I muttered.

My eyes examined the small room. A neat stack of kindling lay bundled on the rock hearth. "First the meds, then the fire."

I shook pain pills and antibiotics into my palm, swallowed them with a sip of water from the bottles we'd brought in from the trailer, then used my trusty lighter to fire up the bundle of kindling. It caught and flared. I knew it wouldn't last but a few minutes.

After checking to make sure the flue was open—a much easier task since I was already sitting on the floor in front of the hearth—I said, "I hope it warms up in here before the kindling runs out." I glanced at the rustic chairs. "I don't want to, but I may have to."

Snake went to the door and scratched, wanting out.

I managed to scoot back across the floor.

When I got the heavy door open, he strolled into the morning light as if it were just another day. There was no sign of the Takers that had attacked us except for dark stains on the sunny patio. The locusts had cleaned up all the bodies. I couldn't see the vehicles from where I sat, but the small fire and bright sunlight were beginning to warm the interior of the cabin.

I glanced down at my leg. Sometime during the night my tourniquet had loosened, thank God, or I would probably be looking at an amputation. With much effort, I pulled myself to my feet, removed my bandolier, and worked my blue jeans down to have a real look.

My entire thigh was purple, black at the edges of the wound itself, but still oozing blood. I felt it was likely just a graze, but it was a graze that had knocked out a bullet-sized chunk of flesh. And I didn't like it oozing blood constantly.

Holding on to the wall and the backs of the sturdy chairs, I made my way to the kitchen area and opened a drawer to find a knife.

It was only a butter knife, but it would suffice.

I pushed the blade of it into the fire.

When it began to glow, I pulled it out and stuck the metal to the wound on my leg. My hand jerked, my skin sizzled, and I flung the knife across the room with a shriek. The smell of burnt flesh assailed my nostrils.

I fell backward into the CCC chair. *My God, why did I think that was a good idea?* Sweat popped out on my forehead. I tasted blood where I'd bitten the side of my tongue.

"Dumbass!" I thought. But then I looked down and decided it might not be too bad. At least it stopped the bleeding. A shallow blister now covered the wound. The Tylenol III kept it from being unbearably painful.

But when I tried to stand, my head swam like Turq's old sin words.

I lowered my butt back onto the chair and stretched my leg gingerly to make certain the bleeding was done. Then I dug into the backpack again, feeling around for a cleaner shirt to use for a bandage. The one I had on was bloody and filthy.

There was antibiotic ointment in Aunt Edna's First Aid kit, but I'd left it in the car, or was it the trailer? I vowed to check as soon as possible.

I heard a slight noise at the door.

Snake was back. I'd left the door slightly ajar, figuring he just had to go out to do his business, but I was wrong. He pushed the door open with some effort and came inside dragging a small branch.

I couldn't believe my eyes. How could he know—

It didn't matter. I took the branch, snapped the twigs off, and threw them into the dying fire. Then I used the stout end to help me stand. The shotgun lay near the kitchen chair.

"Man, Snake." I hobbled to the hearth. "How'd you know? Are you a mind reader like Faith?"

His eyes sought mine, and the words I'd uttered nearly knocked me down. *Faith. My God. They've got her, and here I sit, making myself cozy. Damn.*

"We've got to go." I rubbed Snake's head and said a prayer of thanks. "Let's grab something to eat and get the hell on the road." I glanced around at the few groceries we'd managed to save, snatched up a box of Frosted Strawberry Pop-Tarts and a pack of beef jerky, and tore them open.

Then I popped open a can of Purina dog food and slapped it onto a cabin-supplied plate. "Eat fast, boy. We've got to go find our Faith."

CHAPTER TWENTY-FOUR

In Search of Faith

While Snake made short work of his breakfast, I took my talismans out of my old pants and dropped them into my backpack, then pulled out my other pair of jeans. The dried blood on the first pair made the fabric so stiff it felt like sandpaper. The smell of the blood sickened me, even though it was mine.

I found a plain black t-shirt in my pack, ripped off the bottom, again, and tied it carefully around my leg wound. The rest of the soft old shirt went over my head.

Wolfing down the cold pastries while sitting on the CCC chair, I worked my legs into the fresh jeans, then grabbed all the other food I could carry and reluctantly poured water on the remains of the fire. Another half-bottle went into a bowl for Snake.

He met me at the door. If I hadn't put the remnants of Turq's shirt in the pack already, I felt certain he would have been carrying it between his jaws.

It was his very own talisman.

That gave me an idea. I took the turquoise shirt back out of the pack and found a way to tie it around the big dog's thick neck. Maybe it would protect my furry friend the way the turquoise light had helped protect us at the buffalo jump.

Snake stood perfectly still while I tied it on. "There ya go, buddy. Your very own good luck charm and badge of courage rolled into one."

When I pulled the shirt out, one of mom's earrings fell out, too. I scooped the earring off the floor, took Dad's Mustang key and his crumpled note, and made a little packet which went down into the pocket of my fresh jeans. I was becoming more and more superstitious. I recognized it but didn't fight it. Once I got Faith back, we could discuss it by a fire somewhere.

I pulled the cabin door open, picked up my bandolier, said good-bye to my great-great-grandpa's handiwork, and stepped out into the sunshine. The air had gone from frigid to near balmy in less than an hour. Life on the high plains.

The car was right where the Takers had left it, on four shredded tires, just like Sam's big Jeep. My gut did a slow roll. Now there was an empty spot where the food trailer had been. They must've taken it after I passed out in the cabin.

I couldn't understand why they'd had the Takers pull the trailer by hand when Cade and Marla could have simply driven the Jeep and pulled the trailer. Surely that would have been logical. They had Sam; they must have his keys.

Then it hit me.

Maybe they didn't need any other vehicles. If the Takers had shredded the tires and were now pulling a trailer full of food as I suspected, who knows what mammoth vehicles they had taken from somewhere else.

The question I really wanted answered was *who was making them do it?* Obviously not Marla and Cade. So, who *was* controlling them, and better yet *how* were they controlling them?

I stood in the sun pondering, making my little plan, waiting on a song to spur me on, wondering why it hadn't yet, when I heard the whirring sound of wings beating the air above my head.

My eyes sought the treetops at the summit of the gentle slope. "Turq?"

A tiny flash of turquoise as Snake dashed toward the stand of trees. He barked once, then plopped his butt down, his snout pointed up at the shadowy branches.

"Oh, my God, it is you!"

The whirring commenced again as the invisible became visible and a silvery Taker-sized bullet floated down from its perch.

I looked at him, my friend, hovering just above the ground.

Diaphanous wings fluttered now and then, for balance perhaps, and the only time I could focus on his strange shape was when the sunlight played nearby *just right*. The Goldilocks effect. But it was okay. If I looked at the ground, I could see his shadow in the dust.

"Hey," I said. "It's good to see you." In truth, I wanted to shuffle over for a hug like a little kid would do, but I didn't think it was a good idea. Even though he'd been rather alien before, at least then he'd had the shape of a man. Now, he had the shape of nothing I'd ever seen. What would it be like to touch him? Would my flesh burn like touching a white-hot fireplace knife, or would it freeze like sticking a wet finger to an ice cube?

I smiled, trying to determine if he had any sort of face. I couldn't tell. Looking at him didn't work. The sun would skate off and he would simply disappear into the light.

"Well," I looked down at his shadow. "Looks like we've got part of the band together again."

A gentle whir of wings was his response.

"Can you help us find Faith?"

Another whir of the wings.

"And Sam, of course." I rubbed my forehead. The Tylenol III was powerful.

Snake whined, a deep resounding whine down in his throat.

"Yep, time to go."

Turq flew up and disappeared. I thought he would be back, though. I didn't feel deserted. Maybe he would find them and lead us to them, but without his brute strength, I didn't see how much help he'd be when it came time to fight.

I refastened my bandolier. The shotgun would ride in the straps of the backpack, and the revolver would go into the holster around my hips. I'd felt silly the first time I put the holster on—like a kid playing cowboy—but after using it a time or two, it simply became another tool.

I tried using Snake's branch as a cane, but it snapped in half when I really leaned on it. Maybe I'd find a car with a real cane in it. I made a note to watch for blue handicap tags.

Not much of a plan.

"Farther along, we'll know all about it. Farther along, we'll understand why …" The old hymn rose inside my head again.

"Okay," I said, thankful for the music. "Farther along, then."

We struck out on the path, going back toward the highway in the direction the horde had been traveling. I knew Turq would have no trouble finding us again once he'd found them.

By the time we made it back up to the park entrance, I was drenched in sweat. The heat might be more than I'd bargained for. Even during the apocalypse I'd been nothing but a spoiled teenage boy tooling along in a middle-class luxury car. A brief image of the battle at the buffalo jump played in my mind but I didn't dwell on it. I was soft. I'd thought I was tough, but only with my friends and the right tools and wheels.

Wheels

That's what I needed.

I turned the corner onto the highway and saw a jumble of cars up ahead. I drank half a bottle of water, poured some on my head, and said a quick prayer. "God, if it is Your will, please let one of these cars have tires that will fit the Chrysler." I shaded my eyes against the glare of sunlight on chrome.

A black Dodge Charger sat just the other side of the tangle of metal. I could see the driver's door ajar. One of the tires was flat, but the others looked pretty good. If my Chrysler had a spare, or if this one did, I'd be in luck.

I hobbled toward it, favoring my bad leg, then crawled inside the blessedly empty front seat. There was no key anywhere, but I tried the starter button anyway. As usual, no spark at all, so I got out, climbed in the back, and pulled the rear seat down to gain access to the trunk. *Thank you, God, thank you.* I slithered into the narrow space, careful not to aggravate my leg any more than necessary, and then located the emergency release handle. Later, I would take time to say a proper thank you for this miracle, but right now I was on a mission.

Snake had the funniest look on his face when I emerged from the trunk of the Charger with the jack.

Ten minutes and lots of F-bombs later, I had the first tire off.

"Okay, Snake," I wiped a hand across my forehead. "Let's roll this baby home." I leaned over to begin the roll and my bad leg gave way and dumped me on the ground. Pain blazed up my thigh like a firework. I grabbed the bandaged wound and tried to determine if I'd started it bleeding again.

I'd have to take off my jeans to inspect it.

I glanced around. The area was deserted but being literally caught with my pants down would be the worst thing I could do right now. I lowered them anyway.

The t-shirt fabric had stuck to the broken blister, but I didn't see any blood. I pulled my jeans back up and wiped my brow again. The sun burned the back of my neck.

It took a while to roll each of the tires back to the cabin. Every time I made the return trip, I half-expected the ones I'd already brought to be gone or flattened.

But it didn't happen.

It took most of the morning, two wound rewraps, a wet strip of shirt wrapped around my neck, and more Tylenol, but I finally managed to get three tires and a donut mounted on the Chrysler.

"We did it," I told Snake as we sat in the shade and poured more water on our heads. I felt weak and dizzy, but that was nothing compared to what Faith and Sam must be going through.

I rubbed Snake's head and said a proper thank you to God for the tires and for the case of bottled water. Without it, my true self would have shone through a lot sooner.

Gazing at the sky, I wondered about Turq. It was hard not to think about how easy this task would have been with his tremendous strength, but of course he wasn't that way anymore. I yanked off a chunk of beef jerky and chewed.

My eyes continued scanning the sky.

Nothing but blue going white with heat. A few pulled-taffy clouds streaked across the distance. Cirrus, just like Mr. Smith taught us in fifth grade. The only other things in the big empty sky were the handful of scars where the Takers had come through, and where the black rains would fall when called by sin word pheromones.

I'll never get used to this silence, I thought. There should be cars and trucks on the highway, engines keeping the country supplied with food and other goods. There should be planes up above, contrails smeared from one horizon to the other. But the only ones we'd seen had been the Southwest and American jets crashed at the Midland Jet Port, and several smaller planes at county airports from Eden to Lubbock and all the way into New Mexico. In many instances there was nothing but scattered debris and scorched earth. I wondered if planes would ever fly again.

As if in response, my internal DJ cued up Creedence Clearwater Revival's "Someday Never Comes." It was another sad song about an absent father.

"CCR," I told Snake. "One of Dad's all-time favorite groups."

After a few minutes rest, we loaded our meager supplies back into the Chrysler. There was still a case of water in the trunk along with snacks and dog food.

"How about some happier music?" I asked the universe. "How about something to tell me which way to go to find Faith. And Sam." I had an image of the big man being carried by the Taker that had knocked him out. *If they are even still alive.*

My mind shied away from that image. I think my subconscious was working overtime to protect me while I struggled. It hadn't gone down the road after Faith and Sam. It hadn't let me imagine all the horrors they might be facing, especially Faith—

Snake jumped into the passenger seat, ready to go.

No, not ready to go.

He placed a paw on my forearm as soon as I climbed into the driver's seat.

"What's the matter? Timmy in the well again?" Dad's old joke fell flat. It was much funnier to realize I'd been looking directly at my dog as I spoke so he could read my lips. I felt a little foolish.

Then he jumped back out of the car, waiting on me to follow.

Oh, no. The last time I'd followed him into a wooded area, he'd found Carlos. The memory-scent of raw earth and violent death flooded my mind. No matter what he'd found, I had to know.

I pulled out the shotgun. "Lead on McDuff," I whispered. He was already halfway down the path toward the bottom of this shallow part of the canyon. I could see his hindquarters as he picked his way down the rocky slope.

Inhaling like a dog, subconsciously testing the air for the fetid smell of ruptured intestines or the heavy, maroon-tinged scent of fresh blood, my senses detected nothing but sharp green juniper and sunshine baked shale.

Several times I had to stop and lean against a stunted tree, my bandaged leg throbbing despite the pain medicine.

"Where we going?" I called out, my foot sending bits of scree cascading down the path. "What's so important I may fall and break my other damn leg?"

Snake continued picking his way down the loose trail, then I saw him veer off to the side and stop, his turquoise bandana making him easy to spot even in shadow.

But he wasn't just waiting on me to catch up, he was there, at the side of a shallow ravine, not all the way to the bottom after all.

I lowered my shotgun, breathing hard but feeling no threat. Behind my cranky thoughts, another CCR song had begun to play.

That made no sense. "Fortunate Son" was a protest song from the Vietnam war era? Why would—

—and then I saw it. The song question dried up and blew away like dust in the wind as a spear of sunlight bounced off the edge of a metal *something* crashed over on its side amidst the rock-strewn terrain.

I shaded my eyes against the bouncing glare. "Looks like a giant's toy plane." The sun only caught the metal in those places where the dull paint had been scraped away in the crash, or where the tiniest curves of glass were visible. Why would something be painted such a dull non-color? Then it hit me. It's painted in that non-reflective stuff.

"Damn, Snake. It's a drone. One of those military kinds they use to spy on people. Or kill them by remote control." I'd read all about these things on the internet, seen documentaries on the History Channel, soldiers sitting in control rooms, firing on targets across the world.

The drone was easily twenty-five feet across, maybe more. Hard to tell the way it had keeled over sideways. One wing had sheared off, and there appeared to be a long horizontal pipe system along the bottom. It looked a lot like the irrigation pipes I'd seen in the cotton fields around Lubbock and Lamesa, a hundred miles south of here, toward Eden. The pipe ran across the width of the drone from wing tip to what remained of the other wing before it had been broken away.

A piece of that wing and pipe lay some distance behind the drone.

I hobbled over to pick up the broken part. Sure enough, small metal spray heads were attached to the pipe at regular intervals. I ran my fingers over the small sprayers. The twirly parts still twirled freely. I gave one a spin with my forefinger.

Drops of moisture flew out, speckling my wrist. A sensation of warmth heated my flesh as if thin candle wax had dripped down and begun to spread out. The nerves in my hand started to tingle.

I flung the mechanism to the ground, spat on my hand, and tried to wipe off the spots where the moisture had landed. *Chemicals. What kind of chemicals? Oh, my God, what if this was how they had gained control of the Takers, by spraying them with something that seeps into their flesh?*

I glanced down at the piece of wing, then hobbled back to the drone body and checked it for markings. Way up near the nose, where a pilot would have been if he or she had been the size of a Chucky doll, I spied a bright red mark barely visible on the under-curve of the fuselage.

Leaning down, I looked under the cocked-up wing. I wanted to flip the thing over, see what was stamped on its belly, but I wasn't keen to get near those sprayers again. I shook my hand, the feeling beginning to return to normal.

Going down to one knee, I was about to lower myself onto my back when I noticed the earth beneath the wing appeared damp. *That can't be right. If it had been knocked down in the rip two months earlier, the ground would be dry by now even if the payload had been seeping out all this time.*

I rubbed my forehead. I wasn't thinking straight. This thing didn't go down in the rip, not if it had recently been used to spray Takers. Not if the twirly parts were still wet.

Snake whined from several yards away. I glanced down at my feet. Even though he'd brought me here, he seemed smart enough to avoid the damp area.

Hoping it wouldn't seep through the soles of my shoes, I leaned down and thrust my head into the shadowy area beneath the wing in one last attempt to see what insignia was stamped there.

UNITED STATES

Oh. My. God.

UNITED STATES

All in red letters. No blue. No white. Just red. No America, either. Just

UNITED STATES

That made no sense. *United States of What?*

Must be on the bottom of the wing that had been knocked off when it crashed. That's all. Had to be.

But was it? That solid red lettering bothered me. The missing America, too.

I backed up, eager to get away. *If there are still drones, then someone must still have a military. Maybe they've discovered a way to change the Takers, turn them into fighting machines, use them like Faith's friend had said. But where would a military be headquartered?*

I thought over all I knew about secret military bunkers. Cheyenne Mountain near Colorado Springs was the first thing that came to mind. It was a well-known military complex. Huge. Might as well check it out. Colorado is where we were headed anyway.

Snake and I carefully made our way back to the cabin and the Chrysler. I praised him, kissing his flat head and scruffling the loose skin of his neck and jaw. "If you hadn't found that thing, I never would have known it was there."

He stared at me with his bottomless brown eyes as if he would tell me more if he could. It gave me pause, thinking the dog probably knew stuff I didn't. It made me wonder how many other things I had walked or driven past, unaware.

This drone added a whole new layer to the mystery of our

apocalypse. I wanted to think our country was fighting back, spraying the Takers to get control, but the KILL - OBEY words that had spilled out last night hadn't been encouraging.

Besides, Turq didn't need spraying. Neither did the others like him.

A lightbulb went off in my head. Maybe that's why he had morphed into something else, to avoid their fate. And maybe that's why I never saw any of the other good ones. Maybe they had already morphed.

Still didn't shed any light on where they'd come from, though. Or why.

And it sure didn't explain how Cade and Marla fit into the picture. They weren't military. Marla wanted revenge on me, and Cade was still a follower. With a new leader.

No. There had to be more to it than just Marla and Cade. They may have been in it together, both being from Eden, but they couldn't be part of anything large enough to control whole masses of Takers. No way.

What is it, then?

Why hadn't the Takers simply killed Sam on the spot? Why bother to take him? Because he was a Marine?

Man. It hadn't taken me long to make the leap from a downed drone to a full-blown military. I might be assuming too much. Besides, even if Cade was somehow using the now-controlled Takers as protection for himself, why wouldn't he let me in on it? Was it because of my friendship with Turq? Or did he want Faith for himself? I remembered his remark about the sun shower.

I climbed behind the wheel of the Chrysler, ready to resume the search. My leg was weak and sore, throbbing tremendously after my climb.

"Fortunate Son" continued to play inside my skull. It was only noticeable when I stopped trying to figure things out. That's how the music had always been. I once thought of it as that *still, small voice* everyone talked about. I also thought of it as my subconscious. It was only since the rip that it had become overwhelming.

My hand went into my grimy pocket to make sure my talismans—and the Chrysler's key fob—were still there. They were.

I pushed the brake, then the starter button, and said goodbye to Sam's awesome Jeep. I'd ferreted out his few remaining weapons including a second Ka-Bar knife, a small but lethal machete, another handgun, and a few grenades. Then we were on the road again.

"On the road again, Snake." Willie Nelson's song sprang into my mind as I rubbed Snake's ears. "Just you and me," I said.

A horrible image of Faith tied up, writhing against her ropes, invaded my head like a vision. I could almost feel her fear, hear her screams.

My foot pressed the gas.

Soon we were flying.

CHAPTER TWENTY-FIVE

Raton Pass

Snake stood with his front paws on the console for a while. There were numerous scratches made by his claws in the smooth leather, but it wasn't bad—yet. I thought back to the firenado and our first Chrysler 300. We'd been so lucky to find another one.

My hand patted the passenger seat, and he came on up beside me. *My God,* I thought. *No Faith. No Carlos. No Turq. Not even Sam. They're whittling us down, one by one.* A cold fear began in my guts and moved up into my throat. My words turned to a prayer, "Please God, help us face this thing, whatever it is. Help us get Faith and Sam back, and Turq. Somehow." I glanced down at Snake. "And keep us safe. If it be Your will … Amen." I made the sign of the cross on my chest for Carlos.

Snake rolled his eyes toward me as if asking permission to nap. I rubbed his head, and he turned himself around and around in a tight circle and finally got comfortable.

I let my hand move down to his back, drawing strength from his companionship. We drove on through the afternoon and into the evening before I remembered I needed another tire. The donut had already lasted longer than it should have. My leg throbbed and burned, but I didn't want to overdo it on the pain meds.

Near twilight, I began to yawn. Cars were few and far between on this stretch of highway, but every now and then they would loom out of the murk like a roadblock. Fortunately, we soon happened upon another Dodge, red this time. Good thing they—and the Chryslers—had been so popular in the years leading up to Armageddon. It would have been much harder if I'd had to go into town and look for special tires.

I pulled over, took the tire off the Dodge, replaced the donut, and tried not to feel the creeping jitters that walked up and down my spine while I worked with my back exposed to the twilight. It didn't take long to complete the job. I'd had plenty of experience earlier in the day.

Afterward, I was worn out.

"Time for a snack and a nap," I told Snake. He had alternated between sleeping and sitting up, gazing out the passenger window. "We're getting close to Raton Pass, the gap through the Sangre de Cristo mountains. We crossed back into New Mexico a while ago." I couldn't recall exactly how far it was, but I thought only about three or four more hours before we neared Cheyenne Mountain. After that, depending on what we found, we would continue to Denver to check on my grands.

"Soon as I locate the exit sign, we'll find a secluded spot to park." In the back of my mind another idea had begun to form. Grab a couple hours sleep then continue. See what we could see. I kept watch on the air and sky, expecting my winged friend to show me where the Takers were marching. They couldn't be *that* far ahead, could they?

Snake didn't agree or disagree.

I skirted the front bumper of a jack-knifed tractor-trailer with the driver's door hanging open. As usual, I managed to avert my eyes from the skeletal form draped over the steering wheel. I did wonder what his trailer contained, though. We'd often joked about becoming Takers by need, but I'd begun to revise that thought. We weren't Takers anymore—now we were more like scavengers.

But not at this moment. No time for breaking into locked forty-foot trailers. Right now, it was important to catch a few winks so I could get on to Colorado. Once again, I had to force my mind away from images of Faith bound and gagged, maybe dead already. I worried about Sam, too, but not as much. I figured he had a lot better chance of surviving than Faith.

We took the exit to Capulin, New Mexico. We had left the Interstate to travel on US-87. I only took this exit because I recalled the place from one of the many times my folks and I had made the stop on the way to visit my grandparents. In the back of my mind a new worry surfaced. What if the horde wasn't headed to Cheyenne Mountain? What if they were going somewhere else?

John Denver began to play in my head. He'd been there for a while. I just hadn't paid attention. I'd been too busy watching for wrecks.

"Rocky Mountain High" grew louder as I listened.

Thank God.

Thank you, God.

Now I knew we were going in the right direction. I could see my landmark up ahead. Capulin Volcano—an extinct cinder cone volcano—was clearly visible from the road. It appeared out of the flat earth just like its name, an earthen cone. This year its sides were partially green with vegetation. I always tried to imagine it with bright lava flowing down the sides, spewing from the top, but I couldn't. It was too tame. The land too flat and sparse. There was even a gift shop near the road leading to the base of it.

The first time we stopped, the shop clerk told us we would be able to see all five surrounding states if we hiked to the top. I remembered the feeling of awe when we did it, when we looked out over all that expanse.

Memories cascaded through my head as I pulled into the parking area in front of the barely recognizable shop. All the front windows had been driven into the guts of the store by a giant pine tree that had crashed sometime during or after the rip.

Snake whined when I opened my car door and stepped out.

Shadows lay like black felt beneath the brittle branches of the once-magnificent tree. A swath of deep gray bathed the wide porch. The summer evening was still warm, but the feel of a cool breeze reminded me of last night in the frigid cabin.

Eden to Capulin to Colorado had been some of my greatest trips with the folks. We would stop at every roadside attraction and historical marker we saw.

The destruction of the gift shop seemed to echo the loss of my family. I glanced down at the Snake. "You would've loved them." He didn't agree or disagree.

The fallen tree had taken down several smaller saplings and left a hole in the nearby stand of pines. I opened the trunk of the car, delighted to find Aunt Edna's first aid kit right where I'd left it.

I tucked the kit under my arm before digging through the one food box we hadn't put in the stock trailer. I found a few Slim Jim sausage sticks, a severely bruised apple that had probably been in there for over a week, and a couple packages of peanut butter crackers. I also got two bottles of water and Snake's kibble and bowl, and then I eased myself back into the driver's seat and reversed the Chrysler right up into the pine tree opening in the roadside wood.

Perfect fit, I thought. *Created just for us.*

I wanted to explore the little shop—if I could get past the huge pine—but thought it would be better done in daylight, so Snake and I stood outside the car and shared our food. Snake finished off his kibble, and I tipped half a bottle of water into his bowl before opening the other bottle for myself.

After eating and drinking, I carefully lowered my jeans and examined my gunshot wound by the light of the rising moon. It looked pretty good. Bruised and crusty, but healing. Definitely healing. I poured the other half of Snake's water on it, followed up with antibiotic cream, then rewrapped it with the strip of t-shirt for good measure. Maybe I could find a new shirt in the gift shop in the morning. I knew they sold them. I'd had more than one Capulin Volcano t-shirt over the years.

Pulling up my jeans, I climbed back into the car and patted the shotgun seat for Snake. I put my gun and holster on the dash within easy reach, tucked the first aid kit down in the console, and swallowed my last drink of tepid water. I missed ice. And refrigeration and fresh food. But not as much as I missed the internet. And Faith. And my dad.

"Hold On," a different Kansas song, flared softly in my head like a lullaby. I pulled one of Carlos' blankets from the back seat, wrapped myself in his memory, and marveled at the white shimmer of the moon through the dark canopy of pine.

"We could almost be back in the park beside Mom's library," I murmured as I stroked Snake's smooth coat. My fingers found a few twisty scars under his fur, remnants of our last few weeks, but it was okay. He'd healed. I would, too. My hand strayed to the area of the bandage I'd just tied around my thigh. I wished I hadn't taken so many pain pills earlier in the day.

I wanted to keep driving. Find Faith. But I couldn't hold my eyes open.

In minutes, the big dog was snoring. Between that and my head tunes, I fell asleep, too. Almost as if I were at home in my own cozy bed.

Sometime later, John Denver jarred me awake with "Rocky Mountain High." Underneath it, Zac Brown's hit, "Colder Weather," became audible, but only the parts about a girl and Colorado.

I sat straight up. My leg sang all by itself. It had stiffened up—again. That didn't matter. I got out of the car, staggered to the trees, took a quick whiz, then fell back into the driver's seat.

Snake jumped out, did his business, then he also got back in the car.

"It's Faith," I said, pushing on the brake and then the starter button. "She's definitely in Colorado." I pulled the car out of our little hidey hole without a second thought about exploring the gift shop. The dashboard clock read three a.m. The moon had walked across the dome of the sky and now peeked coldly down at the western tips of the tall trees.

We made it to Raton Pass in no time at all. Beautiful in the summer, treacherous in the winter, the high mountain pass was once a part of the historic Santa Fe Trail. I liked to think of it as the gateway from New Mexico to Colorado.

"I'm glad it's summer," I said. "We've got to find more gasoline soon." We still had two five-gallon cans on top of the car, but the rest of the gas we'd managed to acquire had been stored in the stock trailer.

I pulled to the side of the highway when the needle got down below a quarter and poured in the remaining fuel while watching an amazing mountain sunrise. The morning air was crisp and cold and perfectly attuned to the rising warmth of the coming sun.

The new gas got me almost to the full mark. I kicked myself for not getting the punch tool out of Sam's Jeep. Now I would have to watch for old cars I could siphon or hit up an auto parts store in Trinidad on the other side of the pass.

Snake stayed close while I filled the tank and used my bungee cords to strap the empty containers back on the luggage rack.

We were only a few miles into the twenty-one-mile-long pass when we saw the first big wreck. A couple of vehicles had gone straight through the guard rail and into the valley below. Others were tangled together like an abstract sculpture. Must've happened at the instant of the rip.

I craned my neck to see the smashed vehicles, but they were so far down I could make out little more than twisted metal and scarred earth.

Once we passed that spot, the wrecks became non-stop. We were lucky to find a path through them. On the pass, there was no place to go if you lost control. Mountain on one side, steep drop off to the valley on the other, I worried what would happen when we came to a wreck I couldn't steer around.

I slowed to thirty, then twenty, then finally ten miles per hour, barely scraping through some of the openings between the bumpers.

Just as we came into Trinidad, relief washing through me like a stolen sip of Dad's beer, it occurred to me that someone must have been there before us. Someone had made that path. They'd brought a wrecker or tow truck and pulled cars and vehicles apart just enough to pass through. Whoever did it, I sure hoped they were friendly. Maybe they were also going to Cheyenne Mountain. It was so famous from movies and TV, maybe it had become a beacon for survivors.

Or maybe they were coming *from* there.

Then again, it could have been Cade's group.

Takers could have easily pulled those vehicles apart.

My foot found the accelerator again.

CHAPTER TWENTY-SIX

Hurry

Trinidad was a mess. We crossed the Purgatoire River on the long concrete bridge—"Crossing Purgatory, Jack," my Dad would've joked—and it became obvious the quaint historic town had been devastated. It had not been cleaned up like Eden and many others we'd passed through.

Desiccated corpses lay everywhere. Obviously, small in-ground dwelling rodents were plentiful. They always ate the faces first.

My belly tightened into a hard knot.

Now and then, I had to drive over someone. The crunch of bones is a sound that stays with you. I rolled up all the windows and kept my eyes level with the horizon. The branches of the trees bent low under their grisly weights. Not as low as they did at first, though. Bones weigh much less when they are no longer covered by flesh.

I found myself speaking out loud just to take my mind off the scene. "Gotta get some gas," I told Snake. I'd thought of trying some of the wrecked vehicles on the pass, but instinct had made me keep going. "Won't be doing the Highway of Legends tour this trip. I-25 all the way. Be there in three hours if we don't have trouble getting our fuel."

We drove on a little more, the Spanish Peaks shining untouched in the distance. Whitesnake's "Here I Go Again on My Own," began to play in my head, but softly. "Dad," I said. "Are you out there, somewhere?"

"Carry on Wayward Son," drowned out Whitesnake, and I smiled, grateful for whatever force kept feeding me these bits of encouragement. We drove past Walsenburg, the funky little town whose Main Street practically intersected the highway.

Fifty miles the other side, we came to the perfect jumble of cars.

One was an older model Buick Century parked on a mild slope. It had a worn, white vinyl top over a garnet red body. The body color reminded me of the multi-faceted eyes of the Takers.

"We can suck some gas out of that one," I told Snake. "We won't need a punch, just our hose and can." And a little pucker power, as Carlos used to joke. An image of him in his shallow grave drifted into my head, but I shoved it away, down into one of the memory boxes in my mind.

I pulled in alongside the Buick Century.

The old car had obviously come to a stop just shy of the crash. The driver was gone so it was my guess he or she had survived long enough to be yanked out and carried away. *Maybe the person got lucky and ran for cover.* That thought came out of nowhere. I couldn't recall seeing anyone survive the rip long enough to run for cover—unless they'd been underground the way we had—but stranger things have happened. So I've heard.

I pushed the button to pop the trunk, then opened my door and stepped out gingerly. Once again, my leg had stiffened up like a piece of driftwood.

Snake hopped over the seat and came out behind me. He trotted to the edge of the highway, lifted his leg on the tire of the Buick, and then stood stock still, peering into the distance, testing the air with his nose.

Glancing all around, I stretched my back muscles, massaging my leg at the same time. It was a still day, no breeze at all. Everything seemed A-OK as my old friend Cade used to say. *God only knows what the new Cade would say.*

The silence still disturbed me, even after all this time. I unfastened the empty gas cans from the roof and dug through the trunk for my hose and funnel, then I opened the little door flap to access the old car's gas cap.

"Man," I murmured. "You are a thing of beauty." I rested one hand on the top of the car as I unscrewed the cap and inserted the hose. "Someone took care of you. Dad would've been in love—"

"*Jack?*" Faith's voice floated toward me through the still air.

I whirled around, yanking the hose free. "Faith?" My eyes scanned the area. I imagined her lying hurt beside the road or inside one of the abandoned vehicles.

The hose fell to the ground as I took off, dashing from car to truck to van, searching each one, making certain there was no—

"*Jack.*" Her voice again. Calm. Deliberate. Not hurt. Not even excited, just calling me.

"Rocky Mountain High" rose in my mind.

I stopped hobbling and listened. "Faith, I hope you're telling me I'm near, and you're okay."

My John Denver song was quickly replaced by "Woodstock," the song that talked about finding a child of God walking along the road.

That was enough for me. "I get it," I said. "I'm coming."

"Hold On," by Kansas blared out of my head. *Out* of my head and into the quiet summer air. I squeezed my eyes shut. A slight pain flared in my temples. *I did that,* I thought. *I sent Faith a message.* I'd never done that before. In fact, I hadn't meant to do it at all.

"Hold on," I said. I rushed back to the Buick, picked up the hose, ran it into the fuel tank, put my lips to the free end and drew up clear liquid gold. I immediately stuck it into the red gas can and hoped for a full tank.

A few minutes later, I'd filled both cans, emptied both into the Chrysler, and even refilled the empties. That old car had a hell of a big tank.

I put the cap back on and resecured the cans onto the luggage rack. In moments Snake and I hit the highway with a renewed sense of urgency.

In my head, I pictured the iconic tunnel entrance to Cheyenne Mountain's nuclear bunker. I'd seen it several times in old sci-fi movies with Dad. Apparently, it started out as NORAD, the North American Aerospace Defense Command. Probably back in the Cold War like Aunt Edna's missile silo. After many years, it had been relegated to the alternate site for NORAD. But it still saw a lot of use, most recently as command center for Homeland Defense during the pandemic.

Hopefully, it was still in use today. "Watch for it, Snake," I said. "It won't be long now." We sailed on down the highway, skirting wrecks with a nonchalance born of desperation.

But it wasn't the mountain I saw around the next bend. It was the herd of Takers. I saw them before I heard them. An immense gray mass marching steadfastly along the highway in the distance. I rubbed my eyes; certain it was a mirage. But no. There they were. We'd found them. The air was so still, there had been no breeze to carry the *shush shush shush* of their feet to my ears.

I hit the brakes even though they were so far ahead of us they looked like a dirty gray glacier, barely moving.

What should we do? I had no idea if Cade and Marla were leading them, I could hear no vehicle engines. But every now and then I thought I could feel vibrations beneath my feet.

"You've Got a Friend" wormed its way into my brain.

"Faith must be up there," I said.

As if on cue, Snake came to attention and began to bound from one side of the car to the other, deep rumbling growls emanating from his chest.

The skin on my neck drew taut. "Settle down, boy." I tried to lay my hand on him to calm him, but he was having none of it. The glare of the sun on the windshield obscured the marching mass.

And then I heard Faith's faint voice. "*Hurry.*"

No wonder Snake was going nuts. He must know.

I put the pedal down just as the world *exploded.*

CHAPTER TWENTY-SEVEN

Bombs

Silvery man-sized missiles whistled down from the sky, arrows from an archangel's bow. Each one left a faint trace of turquoise in its wake.

Whap! Whap! Whap! The missiles smacked into the mass of Takers like a flock of folded-wing-gannets diving beak first into the ocean. Each time one of the missiles struck the gray horde, spiky sin-word-shrapnel burst into the air.

I stood on the accelerator, and the car leapt forward as if eager to join the fight. The sun glinted off the windshield, James Taylor sang "You've Got a Friend," Snake continued to bound and snarl, and all at once, the shiny-razor-wire entrance to Cheyenne Mountain shimmered in the west.

The huge block of Takers began to lose its shape, individuals scattering under the attack, but the silvery bombs stayed with them, streaking down, spearing them, exploding them in clouds of clear fluid and inky letters.

The air grew drive-in-movie dark, wet debris clouding the scene. I couldn't always make out what was happening—and then I did.

The bombs were not *bombs* at all. I watched one missile strike its target, then glide along the earth before swooping back into the high clear sky where it turned and dove back down again, folding its many wings, its human-sized insectile body—sharp as a rifle slug—plunging back into the mass, trailing its turquoise trace, hitting target after target after target.

These were the *friends* from the song.

Turq and his friends, spearing the Takers. Scattering the mob.

I cracked open my window as I eased off the accelerator. The massive sounds of drilling wings competed with the songs in my head.

Slowing the car even more, I noticed Snake growing calmer as we watched the one-sided battle.

"We're not alone," I said. "Not alone at all."

Sky holes pulsed and trembled.

Black salvation flowed down in straight sheets, covering every wounded Taker, along with the ones who couldn't get out of the way, then it erupted into thousands of buzzing locusts before winging back into the flickering rips.

The individual explosions continued to happen until the straight-down sheets of dark matter became so numerous they melted together into one tremendous downpour.

I peered through the windshield. Now I could see a host of humans and at least two vehicles. They'd been cocooned within the horde, encapsulated, protected. The Takers seemed to have been turned into bodyguards. I wondered if the spray from the drones had done that somehow.

As the Turqs continued to dive, I became aware of other humans running, covering their heads, trying to avoid the sin-word-shrapnel and the absorbing rain. And suddenly, I knew *our* role.

"We can't take on the Takers," I told Snake. "But we *can* take on the humans."

We drove straight into a wide gap. Leftover Takers scattered in all directions.

Chaos reigned.

I was almost even with the first vehicle, an older model Cadillac, before I realized one of the silvery bombs was skimming alongside us.

"Turq?"

The creature had no face, no arms, or legs, just that bullet shaped body—pointed where the head would be—and about a dozen wonderful, gossamer wings layered one on top of the other.

When I said his name, the beautiful thing sped up as if telling me to follow. It cut into the herd of fleeing Takers and made certain I could get up beside the Caddy.

That's when I saw the driver.

Cade.

I would've recognized that straight dark hair anywhere.

Thinking he probably had Faith, I swung my wheel that direction to cut him off, make him pull over, but he gunned it. I doubted my Chrysler would be able to keep up. But I had to try.

Boy, was I surprised.

My speedometer edged up to 100 mph and kept going. If something stepped out in front of us now, we were all toast. I thought of how Faith had survived the rolled and wrecked Camaro after they'd hit a Taker at high speed.

Faith.

The needle edged past 110 and on toward 120. I thought briefly of ramming the Caddy.

"Jack, no," Faith's voice, in my head.

Turq swooped in front of the Cadillac, and I saw the shock on Cade's face. He immediately slowed. It appeared to be the first time he'd seen Turq 2.0 up close and personal.

The other Turqs were still dive bombing the gray herd. Another vehicle—some sort of truck—disappeared into their midst.

Cade turned his head toward me, and I saw what appeared to be chemical burns across his face. "He's been *sprayed*," I told Snake. "I don't know what it is, but I remember how it burns." I scanned the sky to make sure no drones were in the area, then I rolled down the Chrysler's window and let off the gas to keep pace with him.

Cade seemed to know me, but his near eye rolled wildly in its socket like that of a racehorse on amphetamines.

"Pull over," I yelled. "Turq won't hurt you!" As I said it, a bright shaft of sunlight struck Turq and he disappeared—except for those flickering wings. They moved so fast they blurred the sky.

"Angel," Cade mouthed.

I couldn't hear him, but I read the word on his lips. "Pull over!" I yelled again.

He said something else and pointed toward the west. It looked like he said *Faith*. And then he let off the gas completely.

I did the same, not touching my brakes, just allowing the car to slow on its own, afraid of sliding, maybe rolling at this speed, and by the time I felt safe enough to make a U-turn, Cade was out of the Caddy, running across the highway on foot.

Just before he crossed the median, the black rain fell. He seemed to be in pursuit of something, probably hadn't even seen the injured Takers lying nearby.

Then I saw another vehicle, an old Lincoln, heading up I-25 on the opposite side of the highway. And then it was gone. Lost behind a curtain of black.

Cade leapt over the median and fell across the legs of a downed Taker. He looked like a hurdler tangled up on the track.

"Noooo!" I screamed the word and punched the gas. But I couldn't make it. In the few seconds it took to slam on the brakes, shove it in PARK, and open my door, the darkness had sluiced over the injured Takers and Cade as well.

I didn't get out, but I couldn't look away as it flowed up his legs and onto his body like thick, smothering syrup. Within seconds all that remained was his newly scarred face and frantic, rolling eye.

"Nooo," I said again, but I didn't scream it this time. There was no need. The buzzing had begun as the edges of the black liquid stilled and dried and broke into locusts.

Cade was gone. The locusts flew back into the aether, through the rippling sky holes, into the great beyond.

"Dear God," I breathed. "Why did he jump out of the car?"

Turq swooped in, forcing me to focus.

Was someone yelling my name? I looked back toward the direction from which we'd just come.

It was Sam, running toward us from the Cadillac. "I was in the trunk," he yelled. "The trunk of the Caddy!"

I stumbled out of the car. Snake followed, nearly knocking me off my bad leg.

"He saved me, Jack. Your friend saved me. He opened the trunk when the drones came. He knew what they were going to do. If I'd still been walking in the herd, I'd be dead, or at least sprayed."

I got to him in a few more steps.

He gripped my shoulders, out of breath. "They tried to spray Cade before he could help me."

His hands nearly crushed my shoulders.

"He opened the trunk and yelled at me to get in, then he ducked the drone and tried to make it back to the driver's seat. That's when they sprayed him a second time. He threw himself behind the wheel just as the drone swooped over a third time." He shook his head. "I slammed the trunk lid from inside."

"Faith?" I grasped his arms to loosen his grip. "What about Faith?"

"They've still got her," he said. "I hope to God she's all right."

Even though his face was unmarked, I could see defensive wounds on his knuckles.

Rage battled disbelief in my head. "Cade saved *you*? Is that why he ran from me—because he didn't save Faith?"

"Jack," her voice surfaced in my head again. But was it real, or simply wishful thinking?

Turq swooped in, agitated, wings fluttering. "I looked past him into the distance. "They're coming again," I said. "Drones."

Pushing Faith's voice behind my music, I ushered us back to the Chrysler, then shouted, "What about the Cadillac?"

Sam yelled back. "Out of gas!"

Snake charged ahead and jumped into the Chrysler as if telling us to hurry. All around us, small lakes of darkness were absorbing wounded Takers. The sky was filled with locusts and the coming swarm of drones. They looked like the one Snake had found, but much smaller.

Sam climbed into the shotgun seat. "We have to find that other vehicle. It was loud. I could only hear the engine. Maybe Faith is in there." He swiveled around, trying to see every direction. "They put us in two different groups. The Takers are different now, like guards. They no longer kill people, just round them up and march them along. Maybe your friend thought the Takers were helping them. Maybe they were bringing them to headquarters instead."

I nodded. "They sure seem different. More like actual robots. Snake found a big drone back in the woods near our cabin. It had the sprayer attachment." I glanced at Sam. "Any info about who operates those?"

He touched his ribs gently, as if probing for jagged edges. "Military, maybe pseudo-military. One of those groups that existed on the fringe all these years. Or maybe another country sweeping in to take over. Hell, maybe they're the ones who started it all."

A grimace crossed his face, and he ceased probing his midsection. "Whoever is doing this must have some amazing power if they're controlling the Takers."

I gripped the steering wheel tightly. "I'm headed to the Cheyenne compound." I pointed toward the northwest. "You can see the razor wire when the sun hits it just right."

He looked at me. "I think that's where everyone is converging. But Cheyenne isn't the only military bunker our government operates."

"There are more?"

He nodded. "They're in almost every state in the union. Colorado just has more than her share, because of the safety of the mountains."

"Do you think this one is where the other car was headed?"

"Yes. I think Cheyenne is our best bet." He twisted his head around, looking over the area all around us. "So Turq is an *angel?*"

I shrugged. "That's what Cade said." I glanced out the window. "Or maybe the Turqs are just weapons of the angels. Look at them in action. They're like supernatural bombs." I heard Carlos in that description and a momentary wave of bitterness coated the back of my tongue. My knuckles grew even whiter on the steering wheel.

"You were right, Jack," Sam said. "The black rain may be our salvation."

"Yeah. But it's so *random*. It absorbed Cade right along with the injured Takers." I thought of my friend's terrified eyes as he was consumed. "I just hope it doesn't get Faith."

Sam clenched his teeth and held on to the dash.

We passed shiny spots all over the highway where the blackness had poured down and then burst apart before buzzing back.

"There it is," Sam said. "The road to the entrance. It's like a switchback, the way it snakes around from the highway."

I made the turn, then immediately had to slow and swerve to avoid a pile of tumbled red rock—some the size of boulders—blocking half the narrow road. "Maybe that wasn't what I was seeing." I glanced at the entrance in the distance. Ahead, more fallen rock littered the sides of the road. The rip must've caused the boulders to tumble down the mountainside.

Even more disturbing were the vehicles all over the place. Once again, it appeared someone had pulled or pushed them apart, making a path just wide enough to pass through.

"The shiny things you saw from a distance must be the antenna farm farther up," Sam said. "It's visible from miles away." He inhaled sharply as we rounded another curve. "Jack! Look at all the *people*."

I couldn't believe my eyes.

They stood shoulder to shoulder and knee to knee, from the last curve, past the vacant military guard shack, right up to the famous corrugated-tunnel entrance. They lined the drive all along the chain link fencing on both sides.

"Should we get out? Talk to them?" Why was I even asking? Of course, we had to get out and talk to them. This is what we'd been looking for.

Sam leaned out his window, one hand shading his eyes. "That's a helluva lot of survivors." His tone sounded cautious. "People of every size, shape, and color. But they sure are quiet."

I could feel the blood pulsing in my throat, my heart pounding it through my veins in double time. "Looks like we came to the right place." A slip of song wove its way into my thoughts.

"I don't know if we should go up there," Sam said. "Not yet. Not knowing who is in charge." He sat back in his seat. "We could get trapped in all those people."

I massaged my temples, trying to make out the words to the song tickling my brain. Blind Faith again. Blind Faith.

Sam laid his bruised hand on my shoulder. "You okay?"

Still rubbing the temple near my squinty eye, I said, "I have to go up there, Sam." I looked at the sea of people waiting patiently to get up to the tunnel. To get inside. "I think that's where Faith will be."

Sam took a deep breath. "Then we go in together." He pointed the opposite direction. "First, we'll hide this car. These folks may think they're home safe. But I'm not convinced."

I maneuvered the Chrysler into a careful U-turn. "I can't believe there are so *many* people. Where were they all this time? And why didn't they even glance at us when we drove up?"

"That's what I wonder, too," Sam said. "They seem stoned, like Hal and Cade that night at the motel. My guess is these people have been in hiding. Just waiting on someone to tell 'em where to go, what to do." He gazed back at the crowd. "And we have no way of knowing how many may already be inside."

"Yeah," I said. "Or what's *happening* to them." I wanted to say more, but my music wouldn't let me.

"Someone is pulling the strings with these drones," Sam said. "And I find it a little hard to believe they came up with a way to control the Takers *after* the rip. It hasn't been long enough." He pressed his lips into a hard line. "Seems to me this was all planned in advance—"

I nodded. "Carlos thought so. On the other hand, my dad always said necessity is the mother of invention, and without any restraints, it would be easy to experiment, wouldn't it?" I thought of all those horrific Nazi experiments I'd read about in school.

"Yeah," Sam said. "You're right. And we both know the military provides fodder for a lot of things. Not just battle."

Those words chilled me. "Faith thinks God is on our side," I said. "She thinks the Takers and the rip are man-made while the supernatural stuff is God giving us the tools to fight back."

Sam didn't agree or disagree. "I hope she's okay. That other girl is pure evil." He rubbed a hand across his mouth as if to wipe away the words. "She's probably the one driving the other vehicle, but I can't imagine she'd save Faith the way Cade saved me."

He's trying to prepare me, I thought. *Prepare me for another horror story.*

CHAPTER TWENTY-EIGHT

The Mountain

We drove back down the snaking road, noticing how many of the cars appeared abandoned but not wrecked. "Looks like a lot of people drove here, then got out and walked." I *knew* there had to be more cars that had been parked in underground garages. This proved it.

Sam nodded. "Reminds me of a big music festival. Park a long way off and hoof it the rest of the way on foot." He glanced at my sore leg. "Can you hike a little distance?"

My hand went to the always-throbbing wound. "I can do it." I thought of the trek to get new tires.

Sam didn't look convinced. "I'll let you out here." He indicated a tumble of boulders beside the road. "Then I'll find a place to hide the car, so it doesn't get trapped or taken. I can make it back in nothing flat. Sound like a plan?"

I knew I could trust him, but shades of Thad leaving me in that Eden parking lot came back to haunt me. "You've Got a Friend," cued up in my head.

"Okay," I said. "But if you don't make it back, I won't know where the car is hidden."

"Oh, I'll be back. Don't you worry about that."

But I did worry about it. After all, if Cade hadn't saved him from the drones, he wouldn't be here at all. My "Friend" song grew a little louder, forcing me to acknowledge it. "Okay, Sam. We have to get in somehow. Cheyenne Mountain, the place to be."

He chuckled, but it was a dark sound. "We have to have a little faith to find our Faith, right?"

I liked the way he said *our* Faith. "Right," I said. "Just be sure to leave the key in the car, let's say folded up inside the backseat console, so that I can drive it if I have to."

Sam nodded, a look of concentration on his face. "I'll put the key there, but it might start if anyone tries the button. You know, with the key in the car. Don't worry. It will work out. I'm going to go the *opposite* direction once I get back to the highway. I'm pretty sure the cars will have thinned out by then." He glanced back at the milling crowd. "Just keep yourself safe until I return."

"I will." I stepped out of the car and pulled the bottom of my torn shirt over my holstered revolver.

Sam came around to the driver's side and slid behind the wheel.

Stepping away from the Chrysler was almost impossible. Like Thad and Eden. Déjà vu all over again as some funny guy used to say.

"I'm serious, Jack. Don't go up there and let yourself get herded inside with the rest of them." He adjusted the rearview so he could see the crowd. "These folks don't seem normal at all. They should be pushing and shoving. Someone should be yelling and trying to hurry things along. You know what I mean?"

"Yeah." I wasn't surprised he'd used the very words I'd been thinking. "Don't worry—I'll stay far from the madding crowd." I quoted an old poem my mom used to mention.

"Thomas Gray." Sam said. "*Far from the madding crowd ... they kept the noiseless tenor of their way.*" He looked in the mirror again. "That line about *their noiseless tenor* always struck a chord with me. Especially in battle. When things go noiseless, that's when the shit hits the fan."

We both gazed up the inclined road toward the noiseless crowd. Something was definitely not right. "I'll just hang out until you get back." I hobbled to the boulders. "The shotgun is there, in the front floorboard. Hey, pop the trunk, let me get some water before you go." Cold doubt gripped me again when I said that. But I grabbed a couple bottles—for Snake and me—and closed the trunk.

Even so, I found myself ambling along after him as he drove

away. If not for my sore leg, I might have *run* after him. We'd been very fortunate to have those wheels. They'd been the difference between life and death—

"*Jack …*"

Faith's voice stopped me in my tracks.

I whirled around.

"Faith?"

Nothing there. Nothing but shimmers of summer heat in the distance, and the noiseless tenor of hundreds of people breathing.

"*Don't let yourself be herded in.*" Sam's voice in my head.

But Faith's voice came again.

"*Jack?*"

"*I'm here,*" I thought. "*I'm looking for you.*"

With Snake at my heel, I made my way back to the boulders. We crouched in the shadows behind them to survey the area. All along the narrow road, large chunks of rock had fallen against the chain link fencing. In many places, it was flattened right down to the ground.

Sam and the Chrysler were long gone. Back around the first curve, probably to the highway already. I hoped he would find a place like these boulders, but larger, to hide the car. I only hoped he didn't see a clear highway and suddenly get the urge to keep driving.

My leg wanted to cramp. I tried sitting with my back against the rough rock, but that meant facing away from the crowd.

I couldn't do that.

Like a toddler, I crawled around the largest boulder until I could see the entrance. Above it, on the slope of the mountain, against the sun, a silhouette.

"*Faith?*"

I shaded my eyes. It *was* her. I'd recognize that shape anywhere. I'd dreamed about it every second of every day since we'd found her in the Eden gym.

A second silhouette appeared behind her. Friend, or foe? I couldn't tell. Faith scanned the crowd and the edge of the road, looking around, looking for me.

"*I'm here,*" I said inside my skull. "*Down here.*"

She glanced straight at me, then up at the sky.

The drones! They must have circled back.

They came in low over the crowd, a fine mist floating down. It reminded me of the cool-water misters at Six Flags Over Texas. They were planted at intervals throughout the amusement park to keep people from having heat strokes. I'd stood under them myself, many times.

I did not think these drones were issuing cool water. The herd of people moved around a bit more, shielding their eyes with their hands, but they didn't seem to be in pain, just uncomfortable. After the drones passed over them, the people would smooth down their damp hair as if they'd taken an early walk on a misty morning. What was that stuff? Why didn't it burn them like it did me out in the field? Diluted, maybe?

I looked for differences in the crowd. They happened quickly. People began to sit down. There was no more milling about, they all folded their legs and sat on their bottoms like obedient kindergartners. Crisscross, applesauce. No one was too fat to sit anymore. No one seemed too young or too old either. There were no children at all. I'd been wrong about all different shapes and sizes. There were different heights, genders, and races. That's all.

The herd had been culled just as Carlos predicted.

Suddenly, one of the drones appeared to malfunction. It dove into the crowd, not-so-fine droplets of liquid gushing from the sprayers.

Screams arose.

A tall man clawed his way to his feet, one hand attempting to hold his melting face onto his skull. Even from behind the rocks I could see the flesh sliding off his cheek bone. He staggered a short distance and collapsed. No one hurried to help. They simply gazed at him, disinterested. I noticed a lot of eyes blinking and tears streaming down faces. But they didn't seem to notice. Not at all.

Faith's silhouette disappeared from the mountain as the man writhed, screaming, on the ground. The small drones banked and flew silently back toward the mountain. I tried to see how they came and went, but the glare of the sun hid them.

The defective drone flamed out and began to smoke.

Snake shook his head and sneezed at the acrid odor. I pulled the neck of my t-shirt up, covering my mouth and nose. My eyes scanned the side of the mountain. The man on the ground continued to scream.

A slight movement caught my eye. Above the burning man, the air shivered, and a colorless veil parted. Behind that veil another dimension briefly appeared. Even with my eyes trained on the spot, I could only *sense* the movement. The world rippled and stilled. The temperature dipped and rose and dipped again. I had to assume the wind against my face was the cause of this deep and sudden chill. I was looking at a sky hole. Looking *inside* a sky hole.

The other people seemed to sense the change, too.

They stood silently and moved away from the still-writhing man.

Dark rain fell gently, not in a deluge but in a controlled shower. In less than a second the man was consumed. Just as Cade had been.

The rain stopped, and the blackness hardened and broke apart into locusts like always. They buzzed back up into the low-hanging split.

The air fluttered and sealed the ethereal wound.

There was nothing left of the man but a disturbed place in the dirt and the smell of chemically burnt flesh on the breeze.

CHAPTER TWENTY-NINE

Finding Faith

That was close, wasn't it?"

I spun around, turning my back to the chemically lulled crowd. "Faith?"

She stood lightly, like an apparition. "That rain can be an amazing weapon with its pinpoint technology." She indicated the crowd of people with her chin. "I think whoever is in control is refining it the same way they've refined the sprayers and the Takers." Her voice was singsong, like before. "The spray doesn't seem to hurt unless the drone screws up, or someone makes it dump too much on one person."

"Sam said they sprayed Cade a couple times." I looked her over carefully. "He's gone, now. Are you okay?"

She stepped forward as Snake rose on his hind legs to greet her. "I've been so worried." She ruffled the loose skin around Snake's face, but her eyes were on me.

Throwing caution to the wind, I closed the gap, wrapped my arms around her, and pulled her close, smashing Snake between us. "I knew you were here," I whispered. "I heard you calling my name."

She nodded against my cheek. "I thought you might hear me. It seemed to be all I could do." Her hands on my back pressed me closer.

Snake slipped down from between us, and we were suddenly belly to belly, thigh to thigh, chest to soft, soft chest. My breath quickened despite our surroundings.

"Thank God." Her voice was breathy but no longer an eerie singsong. "Thank God you're both all right."

Snake rumbled, his body trembling against the back of my calf.

I let go of Faith, and we parted. I wanted to ask how she got away, where she'd been, but Snake's warning grew louder. My left hand fell to his head.

"Well, isn't this touching?" Marla's voice cut through the air and into my soul. She yanked off a clear plastic face shield reminiscent of Covid days and slung it to the ground. Her head was covered by a battered hard hat, the kind roughnecks wore on the drilling rigs back home in Texas. "Thought you got away, didn't ya little girl?" Her eyes glittered with hate. "Didn't you think it was just a bit *too* easy?" She pulled back the hammer on a .38 much like my own. "It'll be just like old times, Jack." Her eyes bored into mine. "You know, back when you drove me and Kevin out into the street like d—"

She didn't get to finish that sentence.

Snake leapt forward and took her to the ground. The gun went off and the bullet went wide. Snake never flinched. He had her by the forearm, shaking her like a bony rag doll.

Marla screamed, tried to get the gun into her other hand, but Snake held firm, his weight and rage smashing her down.

On instinct, I'd shoved Faith behind me.

Now, *she* came unglued. "Hold her, Snake! Hold her!" She rushed forward, lashing out at Marla with her feet, kicking at her head and body. The gun went flying just as the knife-wielding kid from the campground emerged from the crowd holding not a knife but what appeared to be a mini flame thrower. He also wore a face shield and hardhat, and I knew at once this was how he and Marla had avoided being chemically managed by the drones.

I pulled my revolver out of my holster. It hung up in my t-shirt, and the kid laughed and swept the flame thrower in my direction. I pulled the trigger just as fire whooshed out the barrel of his weapon, but that wasn't my biggest fear. The Takers coming to his aid, that's what scared me. Dozens were headed our way, marching toward us in formation, as if called. I don't know how my bullet missed them.

To my surprise, the teen turned his weapon toward them instead of us. His hardhat had slipped down over one eye giving him a comical little kid effect.

The fire that licked toward the first Taker wasn't comical, though. It burned through the monster's skin and cloudy fluid gushed to the ground. But the fire also cauterized the wound the same way I'd done to myself back in the cabin.

Because of that, the kid had to hit another one. And another one, and another. Mixed-up letters flowed out. Soon there was a small puddle of silvery liquid reflecting the flames. The kid seemed to know to hit them quickly and move on.

He wants to avoid a deluge, I thought, recalling how the rain had fallen with pinpoint accuracy moments earlier.

As if on cue, a spot directly above the wounded Takers burst open, and a shot of black rain dropped straight onto their heads, embalming them from the outside. The other monsters fell back, human and non-human alike.

From the corner of my eye, I saw Marla bleeding on the ground, saw the Takers reaching for her, saw Faith attempting to drag Snake out of harm's way. Marla scuttered toward the kid on her hands and knees.

Overhead, a whirring of wings darkened the sky as a multitude of Turqs swept down from on high. They hovered, awaiting a signal. I snatched up Marla's pistol and checked the load. Four bullets left. I had five in mine.

The entrance to the mountain opened and the docile crowd stood and wandered toward the corrugated iron tunnel.

The Takers that had been coming toward us parted like the Red Sea. One side became herders, pressing the stoned people into the tunnel while the other side began to form a circle around us. I couldn't tell how Marla and the kid fit into things. I'd thought they were leaders, then it became clear that these Takers intended to march us *all* into the tunnel.

But isn't that why we came here—to get inside?

Sam's words came back to me. *"Don't let them herd you."*

Maybe Marla and the others had the same idea we did, and they just used the Takers as protection to get here.

I glanced at Faith. Everything was happening too fast. The kid still had the flame thrower. With Marla beside him, he seemed to be looking for the best spot to torch a few monsters and create an exit path.

But I thought he wanted inside? What changed his mind?

Eric Clapton's song "Let it Rain" slammed into my skull. I immediately aimed at the Taker behind the one nearest the kid and shot the monster in the chest. Then I used up all my rounds on the ones flanking him. I stuffed the gun in my holster, and emptied Marla's bullets into the next four.

The sky hole wavered. Streams of dark liquid rained down on the Takers I'd hit. Those that were nearby were covered, too.

The kid swung his weapon toward me, his face furious and terrified. We were surrounded by Takers and showers of blackness. *I'd been so focused on bringing down the rain, I hadn't saved any bullets for our human enemies.*

From the tunnel entrance a mechanical hum emerged. It sounded like a low rent version of the tuba-hum in the Eden High School basement. People began to scream. The buzz of the locusts breaking off from the embalmed Takers was drowned out completely.

"Burn 'em," Marla yelled. "Burn 'em *now*." She clapped her hands to her ears to block out the hum.

Overhead, the sky grew darker as the whirring of wings heralded the arrival of more and more Turqs.

"What's happening?" Faith yelled. "Why are those people screaming?"

Marla managed a laugh, hiding behind her cohort as he aimed the flame thrower at us again. "If Cade hadn't flaked out, you'd already know why." Her eyes flicked toward the entrance where the screams had momentarily stopped.

"Are they killing them to get their souls?" The words popped out of my mouth. I didn't expect an answer.

"They're turning them into slaves," Sam yelled from outside the circle. "I found some escapees down the road. Someone is creating a slave workforce. Or maybe a slave military."

He was tall enough we could see his head above the horde. His big voice carried. As I watched, he raised his arm and pointed to the sky. The day had grown so dim there were no more shadows, but I knew he was making sure I saw the Turqs.

"I know," I yelled. Then I muttered, "Why don't they dive bomb this mess and help us out?"

"I think they're waiting," Faith replied. "Like the Bible says, *God helps those—*"

"Who help *themselves.*"

As if he sensed my purpose—or read my mind—Snake tore free from Faith's grasp, and the old whirling dervish came back to life. He flew into the forest of Taker-legs snapping and snarling, teeth meeting gray flesh, cloudy letter-filled fluid flowing, reimagined sins dying in the dim light.

He attacked the ones nearest Marla and the kid first, ruining the monsters' balance, making it easy for me to give them a shove, bowl them over.

The kid swept the weapon toward Snake, scorching the earth all the way up to his paws.

Sam's automatic pistol boomed, and I sensed another sky hole flutter open behind my shoulder. I couldn't turn to look. The kid continued sweeping his weapon at everything around him and Marla.

But he hadn't counted on Faith.

I knocked a crippled Taker toward them just as Sam reached our side. He held a short machete toward me, but Faith was there first. She grabbed the rubber-wrapped handle and leapt toward the kid, letting out a warrior cry as she sliced downward, severing his forearm.

The flamethrower fell to the ground.

The Takers stepped up.

One grabbed the kid, the other grabbed Marla. Blood from the kid's severed arm spouted across the way until the Taker holding him squeezed it tight, like a tourniquet.

Kicking and cursing, Marla's voice was lost in the sudden cacophony of screams as the second batch of not-quite-as-stoned humans got an inkling of what was happening inside the tunnel entrance.

"Let it Rain" washed into "Carry on Wayward Son." I welcomed it and pushed over another crippled Taker. But I'd lost Faith. I couldn't see her anywhere. I could only hear the boom of Sam's 9-millimeter behind me. He must've brought it and the machete from the Chrysler. Even the sound of the powerful 9-millimeter was nearly drowned out by the chaos emanating from the entrance.

A bullet tore into a Taker near me, and I caught a glimpse of Snake dashing away as the one who'd been reaching for him suddenly found itself gushing fluid like a fire hydrant, its knees buckling without warning. I jumped over it, just out of reach of a sudden thin spout of rain.

Snake became even more enraged. He tore through the monsters with wild abandon, teeth flashing, guttural sounds bouncing off their shiny flesh like echoes of death.

More sky holes fluttered above us, but for once I couldn't see them, only sense them. The Turqs were firmly in place, so thick their wings had all the sky holes blocked from view.

No rain fell on Snake, or on me, as we did our best to keep up with the Takers dragging Marla and the kid toward the tunnel.

I still couldn't see Faith.

The entrance loomed. Snake dove under the action, grabbed the leg of another monster. Wings overhead moved with us, shielding us, then parted just enough to allow another quick stream of blackness to shoot down upon the leaking, injured Taker.

Snake took out another, and another, and another, tearing at their ankles before they knew what hit them. I thought I could hear Sam's gun, but the ear-splitting screams and solid hum reverberating down through the corrugated iron tunnel had swelled to jet-engine level.

I got another glimpse of Marla's stringy hair. She was caught fast between two Takers with no one to help her. The kid was being carried through the crowd ahead of her. As I watched, one of Marla's captors turned her loose and grabbed a woman staggering around holding her head. Marla began to kick and scream in earnest. She was not docile. She had not been sprayed.

"*Jack!*"

I couldn't tell if Faith's voice was in my head or in the air. "Let

It Rain" still played in my skull, but a Taker had closed in behind me. Hard-as-steel fingers clamped down on each of my shoulders. *"Snake."* I yelled out for him the way Faith had yelled out for me.

The Taker holding me was suddenly yanked backward by unseen hands, me along with it, my sore leg crumpled beneath the unexpected pressure.

I looked up just in time to see Sam double up his fist and punch the gray monster's arm hard enough to make it turn me loose. But it didn't break the skin. He backed up and drew down on the monster, but the Taker took one step forward, knocked the gun away, and waded back in John Wayne-style.

"Let it Rain!" burst out of me on bullet-quick notes.

Sam must've heard. He pulled the familiar black Ka-Bar knife off his belt and slashed the Taker's arm. Cloudy Taker-fluid flew, stick figure letters peppering the air.

I rolled to my feet and dragged my hand through the air for Sam to follow me to the front. Instead, he took the lead, slashing and stabbing everything that crossed our path. The pinpoint rain fell around us, shooting down through the gaps provided by our life-saving umbrella-Turqs.

Snake continued searching for Faith.

The Taker that yanked me backward had made us lose ground. I couldn't see Faith, but every now and then I caught a glimpse of Marla far ahead.

A brace of new screams overwhelmed my songs and my senses. Then I saw it. A Taker had hold of Faith just this side of the tunnel entrance. Sam must've seen it at the same time. The crowd had thinned, Takers latching onto humans like tickets to the ball. I rushed toward the crooked line.

Sam pushed past me like G.I. Joe come to life. I caught up just in time to see him slice the monster across the back of the neck. Hazy fluid splashed us all.

"Get her, Jack!"

I grabbed Faith's arm. She seemed quite disoriented, the machete no longer in her hand. It was all I could do to get her away from the area of the gushing Taker.

Turq opened a sky hole in the layer of wings overhead. Vengeance poured directly onto the wounded Taker.

I looked into Faith's eyes. Her pupils were huge. She seemed to be in shock. But we were so close to the tunnel entrance, I couldn't turn back. I had to know what was happening.

Sam slashed three more strangely passive Takers and the black rain covered them, too. If a Taker had one human captive in the line, it didn't seem to want another. That gave me courage.

I shoved Faith at Sam. "Get to the car, I have to see what's in there." I didn't wait for comments, just took off into the gap.

Snake tore past me. In seconds we'd made it almost to the front of the line of people and Takers. The sight at the covered entrance to the mountain made me question my senses. *Have I been sprayed?*

The kid had been carried inside the tunnel first. Hundreds of people were jammed shoulder to shoulder inside the immense curved entranceway. I paused. Uncertain, now.

A whir of wings spurred me on. I put my head down and bulled my way forward. "Carry on Wayward Son" was suddenly over-whelmed by Axl Rose screaming about "Knocking on Heaven's Door."

Oh my God, is that what I'm doing? Knocking on Heaven's Door?

A voice in my head began a prayer of thanks. For once, it seemed to be my own voice. *Thank you, God, for the strength to do this. Thank you, Turq, for helping me. Thank you, Sam, thank you, Faith, thank you, Snake, thank you Carlos.* At that point I ran out of helpers to thank so I went back to *Thank you, God, thank you, God, thank you, God…*

As the chant coursed through my mind, I became aware of slippery red blood coursing beneath my feet, running out of the gap between the not-quite-closed doors at the far end of the wide entrance tunnel.

Snake's paws scrabbled for traction in the slick red blood.

The hum once again grew so loud it shook my bones.

CHAPTER THIRTY

Inside

The chanting prayer in my head grew even louder in response to the roar of machinery. Not for the first time, I felt glad Snake was deaf.

In front of me, the line had ceased moving. The Takers stopped shoving their sheep along. Everything came to a standstill.

Snake nipped at the legs of the Takers just enough to make a gap for me to fit through. He didn't even break the skin, just made them move out of the way. They were so docile here—inside the mammoth covered passageway tunnel—that I no longer had to fight, I simply fell to my hands and knees and crawled.

It didn't occur to me *not* to go there. This was the place everyone strived toward. The place we just knew held all the answers.

Even though I had to crawl with my hands and knees in the blood. Even though any one of the monsters could have raised one toe-less foot and smashed my head like a pumpkin—I had to continue.

In seconds, the vibrations had grown so overwhelming the very air around me shivered. People clamped their hands to their ears, but they didn't cry out. If they had, I suspect the sprayers would have appeared and doused them with calm juice again.

The red river beneath me grew thicker. My hands slipped and I dipped my chin in the blood. It reminded me of the night outside the gym when I'd crashed over the concrete stop bar and skidded across the parking lot on my face.

I swiped my chin across the shoulder of my t-shirt to keep the blood from getting in my mouth, and then I was there.

I could see the source of all the screams, and all the blood.

People were being shoved through the massive doors even though they were closing. The immense hum was the sound of a giant motor attempting to shut the blast proof doors on dozens of human bodies. Flesh and bones were being pulverized in the gap. Lifeblood squirted and ran. The Takers stood behind or shoved on through. The humans were not so lucky.

From my vantage point on the ground, I caught a glimpse through the gap, as one body fell, and another was moved forward.

Through that gap, I could see the northern wall of the immense cave-like chamber. Rows of piping hung suspended from the cavernous ceiling, disappearing into the distance around a curve. The lighting here was dim but not nonexistent.

Attached to the lowest pipe—newer and shinier than the others—stiff silver rods jutted down, each one ending in a hinged metal collar.

I watched a Taker shove forward with his human-ticket. A collar clicked opened and then slammed shut with a metallic *SNAP*. The woman struggled and shrieked as blood gushed from beneath her new neckwear. One size definitely did not fit all.

The Taker stepped in line behind her and he, too, was fitted. He did not scream when the snap came. Fluid trickled from beneath his new shackle, too. Sin word letters ran down to the floor and wiggled on the bare concrete. No dark rain came to take the thing back to the sky. They were inside the mountain now. Protected from vengeance. Safe from salvation. *Inside the belly of the beast.* I didn't know where that thought originated, but it seemed right.

The next Taker shoved his human forward and a silent man went through the same clamping procedure. When the metal bit into his flesh, he also began to shriek. His fingers clawed at the collar, but it was fastened tight. None of them appeared to be aware of anything until they experienced physical pain. Then it was too late.

The man's Taker-captor stepped forward and underwent the same collaring method. The rods—attached to the ceiling pipe like arms on the turning rack at the dry cleaners—jerked and began to move forward.

I craned my neck to watch as the assembly-line slaves were pulled along. If they were conscious, they stumbled and screamed, choking and gurgling. If they were unconscious, they were simply dragged, adding to the blood flowing beneath us. I turned my head a second too late as one unconscious man was decapitated by his own weight. His head fell to one side, his body to the other.

The Taker behind him stumbled over the torso as he, too, was marched into the distance by the rack and collar.

Slowly, I backed away.

I no longer wanted to go inside Cheyenne Mountain. It was not the place where we would be saved. All these people dying to get in, all those poor stoned souls, were being murdered or transformed as surely as the Takers that had brought them here.

Thank God Snake hadn't dashed through those doors.

As I scuttled backward, I saw a Taker thrust the motel kid forward. The collar did not bite into his skinny neck. He was caught, nonetheless, as caught as a fish on the hook. So were the rest of those in line behind him. After every four were collared, the rack moved ahead and four more were moved up.

I closed my eyes as the skinny kid's feet tattooed the concrete in his attempt to keep from choking to death. Without the pressure of the Taker's hand on his severed arm, the kid bled out quickly. Once again, a limp body was dragged further along into the mountain before it fell.

Finally, the tremendous hum of the motor lessened as the big doors stopped attempting to close and reversed their direction.

I slipped and slid back toward the opposite end of the corrugated tunnel as the line began to move once more. My earlier chant of thanks rose in my skull. Now it said *Thank you for not letting me in there, Lord. Thank you for showing me, thank you for keeping me safe—*

And then I heard—

"Jack!"

It was Sam's voice.

He must be nearby. *I thought he was taking Faith back to the car.*

I called out, to let him know where I was, but the musical circus in my head resurfaced. Axl Rose's shrill voice wailed over and over about "Knockin' on Heaven's Door." *That's not Heaven,* I wailed back. *I wasn't knocking! Shut up! Shut up! Shut up!*

I stood up from my crawl and dodged my way back through the rest of the tunnel, my head spinning with images and songs.

Away from the entrance, the monsters who had no prisoners were not so docile.

Twice they grabbed me, but twice my Turq from above shot down like a rifle slug, piercing the translucent skin of the threatening Taker, then opening sheltering wings to let in a downpour of salvation.

"Knockin' on Heaven's Door" began to ease, giving way to my old standby, "Carry on Wayward Son."

I prayed that Sam and Faith were clear of this horde.

But they weren't.

"This way, Jack!" Sam's voice came from my left. Several streams of rescue poured down around him. He'd gotten good at bringing down the rain.

Then I heard Faith's voice in my head. *"Jack!"* she called. *"I need you."*

I scanned the crowd, and there she was, the mass closing in. *How did she get separated from Sam?* Gray bodies and garnet eyes swarmed around her. Most had captives already—those could be ignored—but a few were empty handed. They were the dangerous ones. They needed a human as their ticket to ride. I figured they'd been programmed to bring us all in—like sheep dogs bringing in the sheep.

Rushing into the confusion—Snake once again making a path—I reached for Faith's hand, but she wasn't there. It was like a dream. I kept reaching, and she kept getting farther away.

Behind us, the mechanical engine screeched up another level, once again attempting to close the doors. As before, people began to shriek and moan. I could imagine the cracked skulls and crushed lungs, the blood running—

"This way, Jack!" I barely heard Sam urging me on. I tried to focus. Kansas played steadily in my mind.

The sun became a memory.

I glanced over my shoulder to see what had caused the Turqs to gather, and when I turned back, everything was in shadow. Faith was gone. I screamed her name over and over to no avail. Even Sam had gone silent.

But that wasn't my only worry. The Takers had begun to comprehend the Turq's hit-and-run bullet-strategy. Each time the Turqs would dive down to puncture a Taker and let the rain through, the monsters would come back in quicker and quicker, like a noose tightening around us.

I grabbed Snake's collar to let him know I didn't want him dashing back into the mass of gray legs.

"Faith!" I cupped my hands around my mouth. "Where are you?" I hoped she could hear me even if we couldn't see each other. I opened my mind, intending to let Kansas soar over the sea of gray, instead, Clapton burst out with "Let it Rain."

Off to my left, a Turq dove into the crowd and the wings opened over that area. Streaks of sunlight filtered down, and through the sudden shower, I saw Faith.

She stood with her head thrown back, arms outstretched, turquoise-tinged sunlight enveloping her as she shouted the words to The Lord's Prayer into the gap the Turq had created.

"Hold on, I'm Coming!" the old Sam & Dave tune, ripped out of my head. It was so loud even Snake seemed to hear it. He tore from my grasp, biting and biting and biting at the calves of the nearest Takers.

We charged through them, the monsters high-stepping away from Snake's sharp teeth, their wiggling black letters tumbling down their bitten legs, their sin-words struggling to survive in the open, barely avoiding the narrow streams of saving rain until we were almost there—*how did she get so far away?*—and then our luck ran out, our timing was off, and two monsters had me like before, a tug o' war rope between two weightlifters.

I was helpless in their grip, my shoulders on the verge of being dislocated. They could easily rip me in two, a medieval torture rack on gray legs, but they didn't.

They began to work their way back toward the entrance dragging me between them. I had no gun, no knife, no weapon at all.

And then I remembered I *did* have a weapon. An awesome weapon.

"Turq!" I yelled. "*Turq!*"

In my head, I could hear Faith shouting, *"Our FATHER, who art in HEAVEN, hallowed be thy NAME, thy kingdom COME, thy will be DONE, on EARTH as it is in HEAVEN..."* and when she got to the line about "deliver us from evil," everything happened at once.

Dozens of Turqs began dive-bombing the Takers around me. They staggered away, cloudy fluid gushing.

I heard Sam call out to Snake, but I couldn't see either of them.

"The Lord's Prayer" continued in my head, *"give us this day our daily BREAD!"*

Whoosh.

Another Taker backed away, gushing.

"Lead us not into TEMPTATION!"

Whoosh.

Another man-sized missile and another Taker down.

Black rain fell and washed across the earth, slurping up sin words, coming for the wounded, but it did not fall upon me. My Turq's beating wings created a shelter. The very multitude of his long wings made them seem solid. Dim light fell through with the rain. It had a turquoise hue.

From the corner of my eye, I glimpsed the lug sole of Sam's huge boot as it planted itself in the chest of one of my captors. The monster flew backward, giving Sam just enough room to swipe the Ka-Bar at the other one holding onto me. He slashed open its middle, bringing a new rush of sin words and dark, saving rain.

Sam thrust the handle of the knife toward me. "Take this," he said. He needed both of his hands to retrieve something from his cargo pocket. I saw him pull the pin on a grenade. Probably one of those I'd found in his Jeep.

Without a word he lobbed it into the darkness, toward the madding crowd still hoping to get into the tunnel.

I opened my mouth to protest that there were humans in there, but my survival instincts took over and my jaw snapped shut as I sprang into action, slashing everything near me in my effort to get away.

"Take cover!" Sam yelled.

I fell to the ground, covering my face with my forearm as the tremendous blast filled the air with body parts. Blood and cloudy fluid rained down. Black letters flew. The shadowy darkness became a wet rain of horror.

The Lord's Prayer began again. This time, I was the one shouting it. Screaming it at the Turqs above, begging them to shelter us from the dark rain I was certain would follow the bombing.

Sam lifted me by the elbow, gave me a push, and then we were running—me, hobbling—through the melee, toward the last place I'd seen our Faith.

The Takers were already coming back, their orders sprayed onto their skin over the top of their old sin words.

Confusion settled upon me even as my music tried to drown me. *Music? Or my orders? My internal orders? Was I some kind of robot, too?*

"Let it Rain" and "Carry on Wayward Son" looped through my thoughts, clear as any mission ever given.

I slashed and slashed, forgetting everything but surviving.

Turq, my guardian angel, stayed right with me, opening his wings just enough each time I needed. So I carried on, yelling at Faith from time to time—in my head or into the air, I couldn't say which. Around me, nothing but a wavering river of gray, glistening bodies.

"*Jack*," Faith's voice floated over the scene. "*I'm here …*"

My eyes sought the Heavens, but all I saw were the undersides of Turq-wings.

"Where?" I yelled. "Where are you now?"

"*Here,*" she said.

Turq opened a gap, and there she was in the embrace of gossamer wings, streaks of turquoise wafting around her like an aura.

I couldn't believe it, I turned to Sam. "*Look!*"

But Sam was no longer behind me. Instead, a huge truck reminiscent of Tow Mater from the old *Cars* movie bulled its way through the mangled horde. The roar of its tow truck engine scoured the air, and I stared in dismay as it bounded up and out of the bar ditch and onto the narrow road.

Marla's face hung over the steering wheel wearing a maniacal death's-head grin. In her right hand, she clutched a rough length of rope that appeared to be tied to the steering wheel. The other end of the rope was threaded through the partly open passenger window and knotted around a man's neck.

An image tried to surface in my head, something from Aunt Edna's Quonset hut, but I couldn't drag it forth.

The man at the end of the rope appeared to be balanced on the running board, clinging to the door frame by the fingertips of one hand. His other hand grasped the hateful rope to keep it from choking him to death.

I couldn't see much of his face the way he was plastered to the side of the truck, but what I could see showed a black eyepatch. He looked dangerous. A thin-as-a-blade pirate so dangerous he had to be leashed.

The truck's headlights were trained on me.

Executing a clumsy tuck and roll into the shadows, I spied Sam on the other side of the road. He was crouched low to avoid the headlights. Then I heard a sharp yelp of pain, followed by a shrill, witchy laugh.

I dashed out of the shadow as the truck skated past.

Snake lay at the edge of the road, twitching.

"Nooo!"

He raised his head, still alive. If not for his Turquoise-shirt bandana, his brown body would've blended right into the dusty shoulder of the road.

Kansas music lit up the fibers of my brain like neon. I rocketed toward the disappearing truck.

Marla stepped on the gas. The pirate hung on for dear life.

In the middle of the road ahead stood Faith, her arms open wide, a gathering of Turqs forming a canopy above her.

No wonder Marla hadn't slowed when she passed me, she was focused on Faith.

The sky grew darker as more and more Turqs arrived. They

opened their wings above Faith, but instead of dark salvation, a brilliant light shined down, outlining her in turquoise.

Marla's face loomed out of the driver's window, looking back at me. Disbelief etched her features into an ugly scowl.

"Go Jack!" Sam scrambled out of the ditch and motioned for me to go after her.

I nodded and thrust my hand into my pocket full of talismans. The turquoise light had given me an idea. My fingers sorted the items until they landed upon Dad's giant Mustang key. I clenched it in the palm of my hand. The long shaft jutted from between my middle and ring fingers like the super-stout blade of a short knife.

Up ahead, the pirate wrenched at his rope. The truck swerved back and forth as Marla fought to retain control of the steering wheel.

I dashed toward the driver's side running board while Marla and the pirate struggled. I could see her scrabbling to get something from the floorboard with her left hand, but she couldn't keep the truck on the road because the pirate kept yanking at the wheel.

"Carry on" nearly blew the top of my head off.

The truck slowed and I jumped onto the running board, grabbing the giant side mirror with one hand as I jammed the point of the key into the side of Marla's face. It skated off her cheekbone and dragged a ragged trench across her flesh. She screamed like a banshee and raised a small pistol in her left hand.

Across the truck, the pirate's face was flattened against the outside of the window glass as he did his best to yank the rope free of the steering wheel.

The truck still moved, but jerkily.

I continued slashing at Marla's face and neck as she pointed the gun in my direction and squeezed the trigger. The bullet whizzed past my face and blew out the back windshield. The truck veered toward the opposite bar ditch.

Marla squeezed off another shot that ricocheted into the front windshield. Glass burst like a bomb, and she dropped the gun and threw both hands up to cover her face.

I smashed her in the jaw with my fist and lunged halfway through the driver's window to saw at the taut rope with the teeth of my

Mustang key. The frayed edges of hemp glowed blue when the rope parted.

The pirate jerked the length of it through the window-gap and flung himself clear. The heavy truck came to a slow rolling stop.

I leapt off, Kansas still playing beneath my thoughts, competing loudly with Axl Rose again, crying out the lyrics to "Knockin' on Heaven's Door." I knew the song was about someone on the verge of dying, but there was also a line in there about guns. *And Marla still had a gun in the truck.*

I whirled around and started up over the back of the tow truck. *There had to be a reason Axl kept wailing at me.*

Sure enough, Marla was bent over in the cab, face bloody, flesh torn, searching the floorboard with both hands.

My fist began to pulse. The Mustang key glowed blue. It burned like cold fire. From above, a fine turquoise light blazed. It was accompanied by the whirring of wings.

"Hey, Marla!" I punched my turquoise-limned fist through the missing back windshield just as she straightened up. The point of my key went directly into the base of her skull.

She didn't die immediately. Instead, she began to twitch. Just like Snake had twitched after she hit him with the truck's bumper.

"May God have mercy on your soul," I said. "And on mine."

I made the sign of the cross over my chest the way Carlos had always done, and then Marla fell over on the filthy upholstery, dead.

I jumped down and opened the driver's door to retrieve the gun. The turquoise key cooled in my palm. I shoved it back into my pocket.

CHAPTER THIRTY-ONE

Conduits

Knockin' On Heaven's Door" continued to blast my brain, my own internal *audio* tattoo. I tucked the gun into my pants and wheeled back toward the spot where the pirate had jumped.

I could see Sam helping Snake beside the pavement. The big dog would hobble a few feet, then shake his head and plop down to rest.

Snake looked like he would be okay, but the pirate-man lay as still as a tombstone. As I approached, I could see where he had skidded through the dirt when he jumped. I fell to my knees beside him, Axl still bleaching my brain cells with sound.

My hand brushed the pirate's face.

He wasn't dead. His skin was warm, but I couldn't feel his pulse because of the rope around his neck. The music blinded me to everything except the need to unknot the rope.

I closed my eyes and worked.

The volume went down, and I could barely hear Kansas singing about "Dust in the Wind."

No, I thought. *Not yet. He is not dust in the wind, and he is not knocking on Heaven's door. Marla, she is dust. She won't make it to Heaven, but she can knock. Let her knock. Let her.*

But the songs played and played, once again creating their own not-to-be-denied loop. "Carry on Wayward Son" blared through the loop every few seconds like an old-timey radio in a thunderstorm.

"Dad," I whispered, my fingers clawing at the scratchy hemp noose. "If that's you, open your eyes. You've got to open your eyes."

He'd landed on the "good" side of his face, and I couldn't see what lay under that awful black patch other than the gruesome scars running away from it, but the moment before he'd leapt off the truck, I'd caught a glimpse of his good eye.

It had been like looking into a mirror.

"Carry on" gave way to "Teach Your Children," and when it got to the part about folks on the road, living by a code, it jangled a déjà vu memory from The Yucca Motel when Cade had called *me* a pirate with my one squinty eye.

I stopped trying to unravel the hateful noose and pressed my blood-smeared hands to my ears.

The music went away.

I moved my hands, and the music came back. That's when I realized it wasn't *my* head music anymore. It was coming from somewhere else.

"It's you," I whispered. "It's coming from you."

The Dad-pirate groaned, and then Faith appeared, slipping her hands beneath his head, helping me remove the loosened rope.

I looked up at her face. "You distracted Marla, didn't you?"

Faith smiled. "I just did what I could. Everything is good now."

I nodded, surprised to realize I believed her. In the distance, I heard the whistle of more Turqs flying in from wherever they'd been before they morphed.

A bony hand gripped my wrist. "Jackie?" The voice was sore, almost as rough as the rope, but it was him. It was Dad. The music hummed out of him even as he spoke other words.

"Yes, it's me, Dad," I said. "It's me, and Faith."

Sam walked up, carrying Snake in his arms. With a groan of exertion, he placed the dog on the ground beside us.

Snake pushed his snout into Dad's hand. "And this is Snakeman," I said. "Remember him? He lived down the block, back when the world was right."

My pirate dad caressed the dog's wrinkly snout with his thumb. "Old Man Granger's pit? The one he kept chained?"

I nodded, a giant lump forming in my throat. "I've been looking for you," I whispered.

He opened his mouth, and Kansas poured out. This time he literally sang a few words of "Carry on Wayward Son." Faith helped him sit up. "I left you some notes," he murmured.

"Yeah, you did." I nodded. "I read the one in the Mustang, and the one in Aunt Edna's barn."

"My wayward son." He let the music fall beneath his real voice. "I never gave up on us finding each other."

Clasping his hand, I drew him to me. "I knew you were the one sending me those songs." I embraced him a little tighter. "I knew it all along."

He patted my back, pulling away to see my face. "Yes. It was me. Me, and the universe."

Before we could say more, the sheltering wings of the Turqs disappeared, and the sound of their whirring intensified ten-fold as they flew back toward the tunnel entrance.

That's when the organic bombings began in earnest.

We watched from afar as the Turqs kamikazied the rest of the tunnel entrance with their bullet-shaped near-invisible bodies. In moments, the heavy, corrugated steel lay crumpled upon the earth like so much useless tin foil.

The four of us stared in amazement.

"They're bombing the Beast." Dad's eyes sought the sky as if looking for something only he could see. "Making slaves," he muttered. "Stealing souls."

"In the tunnels?" I looked up, expecting more bombers. Or maybe more drones. Instead, a drift of musical notes floated in the air.

"Dad?" I looked at him for explanation, but he had collapsed to one side. "Dad!" I tried to pull him back up, but the ribbons of his muscles slid freely across his bones. There was very little meat to him, just sinewy limbs, and a hardness beneath the flesh.

Faith knelt on his other side. "Sir," she murmured. "Are you all right?"

No response except for a hum that emanated from his body like a tuning fork.

"Hang on, Dad, please, hang on. We've barely found you—" I didn't know what to do. Snake struggled to his feet and laid his head on Dad's chest.

Dad took a shallow breath and spoke. "Our family is gone, Jack. Except for you. And me." When he stopped talking, his chest rattled ominously.

I motioned for Faith to help me prop him up again.

Sam straightened and loped toward the highway. "Keep him talking, I'm going to get the car. Get some water."

I nodded. "Hang on, Dad. Just hang on." We sat him up a little straighter, but his head lolled over onto Faith's shoulder.

She began to hum.

It matched the vibrations coming from Dad's chest.

Snake pressed himself closer.

I felt the air shift.

Turq lit and moved toward us. Turquoise light scattered away from him as he came. His wings buzzed lightly, for balance.

When he stopped near Faith, we were awestruck. Except for Dad. His good eye stayed closed. "Slaves for the Beast," he murmured. "Souls to feed them …"

Faith tilted her head back, closed her eyes, and musical notes flowed from her pores like sweet water. Turq enclosed the two of them inside his see-through wings as if closing them into a chrysalis.

Turquoise light emanated from within the clasping, reaching out to touch Snake and me. The dog sneezed and licked his paw. I felt the warmth of a gentle sun.

The wings fluttered open, reminding me of the sky-ripples just before the saving rain. "We are stardust," Faith sang. "We are one."

I had expected her to sing we are golden, but she didn't. The turquoise light lay on her hair and skin like softly tinted diamonds, glowing.

"Heaven?" I asked.

"No."

I looked at Dad.

Both his eyes were open, his pirate eye-mask askew. His face crawled with healing light, scars melting away. "But it could be the *Stairway* to Heaven," he said.

It didn't surprise me when that song tumbled from his lips. Soon, it cloaked us in place of the turquoise. When my own eyes closed—to better hear the music—a deep sense of peace invaded my soul.

Snake made an odd noise, and I opened my eyes.

My dog stood whole and straight beside my dad. Not a mark on his stout brown body. He shook his head causing his fold-over ears to flap.

"Someday I'll teach you to talk." I caressed his head. "Like the amazing wonder dog you are."

Snake seemed to understand. He walked down the road to the tow truck and hiked his leg on the front tire. "Can't beat me," I imagined him saying. For a moment, I wondered if the healing light could have cured his deafness, but the thought faded away when Dad spoke again.

"Some dog," he said, the "Stairway to Heaven" music slipping into the background of his speech.

I nodded. "You have no idea."

Placing his hand on top of mine, he said, "I think I do. But don't forget who gave that dog to you." He looked up at the sky, and for a moment I thought he meant Turq.

Faith still sat with her eyes closed. She held her arms out in supplication again. "Our Father who art in Heaven …"

Turq rose on a whir of wings.

Angel wings, I thought. And then my attention was pulled back into Faith's Our Father prayer, and I joined her. Wholeheartedly.

When it ended, Turq had gone, and Sam was driving up the road toward us. The Chrysler looked like an old friend, but behind it came a blue Nissan SUV. Inside it, I counted three heads.

Both vehicles came to a stop.

A man and two kids cautiously stepped out behind Sam. He motioned them toward us. "Jack, these are the escapees I told you about. Drew and his children, Milo and Trina."

Drew held out his hand. "Jack. We got to know you in Kansas."

I shook his hand, unable to process what he was saying until he laid a battered spiral notebook in my palm. "Is this one of mine?" I gazed at the man's friendly face. "Where did you find it?"

He grinned. "At the old Bitty Sloan house, thank God. Otherwise, we'd still be wandering around New Mexico, wondering which way to go."

My Dad laughed, and "Carry on Wayward Son" burst out of his laughter like a strange hymn.

Drew and Trina laughed, too. It sounded just a little nervous.

Milo didn't laugh. He simply appeared confused. Until he saw Snake. Then it was love at first sight. Dog. And boy. Within seconds, Milo had his arm around Snake, and they were seated placidly beside my dad.

I looked at Faith sitting on the ground in the Lotus position. Her eyes were fixed on me. "Together, we are Our Father's instrument," she said.

That thought stunned me. "No. Not me," I said. "Just you." I blinked and turned my head away. "But wouldn't Carlos be proud?"

"Yes, he would," Faith said. "I miss him."

"Me, too. I would like to ask him what he makes of all this."

Somewhere, in the distance, there came an extremely loud whirring of wings.

"Who knows," Faith murmured. "Maybe you just did."

EPILOGUE

Drew and Trina took turns telling us, over bottles of water and packages of nuts and crackers, how they would have been herded into the tunnel—having barely escaped being misted at one point—if Milo hadn't run off into the bushes chasing what he swore was a big brown dog.

When they all dashed away from the start of the line to look for him, they were kidnapped and saved by a guy whose description sounded a lot like Cade. They said he's the one who told them about the soul factory.

"Not sure about the slaves part," Drew said. "The guy who saved us seemed to think so. I think the ones in control may still be in search of pure souls, just like you said in your notebook, Jack. But someone else is running the factory here at Cheyenne. They're using the soul-stealing aliens—Takers you wrote in your book—and us humans for something *inside* the factory." He gave a quick negative shake of his head. "Odd how they've got the things rounding us up and herding us like cattle, isn't it?"

Twelve-year-old Trina spoke up. "Probably so they can skip the drudgery of eating us to get our spirits. You know ... since they don't really *have* to eat anything." She looked at her dad to see if she should continue. It was obvious they'd already had this discussion, and recently.

She continued, "The guy who saved us said the monsters still *want* to get people's souls, but that the spray makes them think there is a better way to do it. All they have to do is get us inside the mountain."

Geez, I thought. *What a crazy theory.* But I didn't say that out loud. Everything was crazy now. Instead, I said, "Anything's possible, but at the big doors I saw other Takers being collared right along with the humans they brought in. Did your guy—I think it was my friend, Cade—say why the powers that be are doing that?"

Sam cleared his throat. "Could be collateral damage. Like any military-type operation. The powers that be sure seem to be using the Takers as herders, just like Drew said. And we're the sheep. Or cattle. Maybe it was Cade who saved them. Maybe he knew what he was talking about."

Faith looked at Dad, then at me. "I think it is some kind of government thing. I don't know about military." Her eyes flicked toward the sky. "Turq showed me another way into the mountain a few moments ago." She waited, probably thinking I would burst in with a lot of questions, but I had seen her up there. I knew what she meant. "What did you see?"

She looked at each of us in turn. "I saw people in uniforms."

My heart sank. Something in her tone told me more than her words. "Like *the powers that be* type people?"

Faith nodded. "People at work. All wearing red uniforms. One was leading an obviously sprayed Taker in chains, the other led a couple of docile humans in chains."

"Well that pretty well does away with the *stealing our souls* idea. Maybe Carlos was right, and the Takers had simply been another wave to wipe out those of us who survived the previous ones. You know, the big rip? The virus?"

"Maybe," Faith said. "We've been under attack for a while now. Culling the herd, I believe Carlos called it." She glanced heavenward. "Anyhow. The people I saw boarded a jet-black helicopter with some sort of red lettering on the side. I assume they flew away while we were dealing with Marla and the madding crowd." She smiled knowingly when she said that.

Did she hear all of my thoughts? Or just my conversations with others?

Drew cleared his throat. "We've seen those black choppers. Near Kansas. That's also where we met a man named Dawk. His theory was that these military types may be trying to *breed* humans and Takers. I don't think I believe that, though."

Trina's eyes welled up. "That's where they got my mom, in Kansas." She turned her head so we couldn't see her tears.

"I'm so sorry," I said. "They killed my mom, too." I hoped that would ease her pain, a little.

Sam spoke up. "You know, looking at these creatures, these Takers, makes me wonder if they were just sent here as weapons." He glanced back at the entrance. "Sent across the universe in that silvery liquid."

Faith opened her mouth, maybe to agree or disagree, or maybe just to ask if Dawk could be the same person she'd traveled with, but then she closed her mouth again without speaking. As if she knew the man had to be one and the same.

I told the group about the drone labeled UNITED STATES in big red letters. "It's all part of someone's plan, isn't it? I just can't decide if those someones sent the Takers and then began spraying them to control them, or if the Takers came from another dimension, universe if you will, and some government is simply taking advantage of our weakened status. We still don't know if this is worldwide or only nationwide."

Sam and Drew nodded.

"I also wonder how the Turqs' metamorphosis fits in? I'm thinking it could be like something Faith said awhile back. It could be God taking those organic weapons and turning them into tools for us. The tools we need to fight back."

"Turning swords into ploughshares," Faith murmured. She glanced upward again. "Ploughshares with nice, sharp edges when we need them."

"Still doesn't tell us what's going on inside the bowels of Cheyenne Mountain." I kept talking, on a roll now. "Maybe the whole thing originated right here in the good old US of A." I held up my hands.

Sam raised an eyebrow. "Something or someone wanted us all—Takers and humans both—inside that complex. Didn't even mind crushing a few skulls in those massive doors to get us there."

"That's messed up," Trina said. "I think they're making a whole army of alien-human hybrids. They want to take over the whole earth!"

I couldn't argue with that. But Dad's eerie words came back to me. "Slaves for the Beast … souls to feed them." I had no answers, only more questions. I dug through my old backpack from the Chrysler and offered Dad some plain Tylenol. He was so thin I was afraid to give him anything stronger.

He said he didn't even need it. Said the light had healed him.

I wanted to question him further, find out everything he'd been through, everything he knew, what it had felt like inside that Turquoise Light. But I was afraid it was too soon. Besides, just because our Turqs had laid waste to the corrugated entrance tunnel and all the Takers around here, that didn't mean there weren't a million more marching this way as we spoke. I was about to say as much when I heard Dad begin to hum "Carry on Wayward Son."

Everyone stood, gathering the remains of our snacks. Did they *all* hear it? Dad's music? It certainly seemed that way.

Faith smiled and slipped her hand into the crook of my elbow. "Guess it's time to carry on, Jack. Wherever we're going, I'm glad we're together."

I smiled back at her. Found my dad, found our Faith.

The song, "Something" began to play softly as we helped Dad to his feet.

It was my new favorite song.

ABOUT THE AUTHOR

Ann Swann has been a writer since junior high, but to pay the bills she has waited tables, delivered newspapers, cleaned other people's houses, taught school, and had a stint as a secretary at a rock-n-roll radio station. She also worked as a 911 operator and as a police dispatcher.

Her fiction began to win awards during her college days. Since then she's published several short stories, novels, and novellas.

She's always reading and always writing, but even if no one ever bought another book, Ann would not stop writing. For her it's a necessity, like breathing. Most of the time, it even keeps her sane.

Connect with Ann online at:

http://annswann.blogspot.com

AUTHOR'S NOTE

If you are still on this trip with me after that long gap between book one and book two, I thank you. I'm always curious about your take on my characters and stories so feel free to let me know what you think of this latest entry in the *Apocalypse in Eden* series by writing a review or leaving me a note on any of my social media sites.

Thanks to my hubby, Dude, always my first reader and gentlest critic. Thanks also to Dale and Charlotte Orr and Linda Wells for taking us all down into the missile silo. I knew I'd use that awesome memory someday. Thank you so much, Mike Parker, for your careful attention to my books.

Note: There really is an Eden, Texas. It's an historic little town named after an Englishman by the name of Frederick Ede, thus the name, Eden. It bears little resemblance to the apocalyptic Eden in my books.

By the way, one of my early *Taker*-readers asked where I came up with the name for Snake. Let me assure you, Snake was a real dog. He wasn't deaf—the Muse did that to him—but he was real, and he was my childhood partner in crime.

Half pit bull / half boxer, Snake was given to us as a big ol' brown-eyed pup when his owner had to move. In fact, Snakeman (he had several nicknames) became the fourth kid in our family. He got into at least as much trouble as any of us. We could *not* keep that dog in the yard when we weren't at home—he would often jump onto the tile fence and then leap onto the well house and continue right on up to the housetop. From there he would patrol the yard from on high. It was quite a sight if you weren't expecting it.

I have many such stories about The Snake, but they are tales for other times. Just know that Snakeman lived. And he was loved. Very loved.

I feel I would be remiss if I did not acknowledge some of the biggest influences on my development of this book series:

The Blob

The screenplay originated from an actual police report about a purple jelly that fell from the sky.

The Terminator

Killer cyborg from the future—my favorite movie of all time. And last but never least,

The Twilight Zone TV Series

Yes, the entire series.

I am a child of the '60s. Horror and sci-fi schlock make up the gist of my DNA. The rest is comprised of hagfish slime!

Until next time, stay cool, and as always—Carry On.

And now, here's a sneak peek at *REMAINDERS: Book Three of the Apocalypse in Eden* trilogy.

All my best,

Ann Swann

January 17, 2023

Chapter One

Head for Denver?" I asked.

Dad sat in the shotgun seat beside me. He shook his head. "Gran and Gramps are gone."

I stared straight ahead, swallowing hard around the solid lump in my throat. "Did they … I mean, were they …" I tried not to picture my gentle grandparents hanging from the oak in their front yard.

"No," he said. "They weren't tortured or eaten. They must've hurried outside when the noise began." He shook his head again. "Killed instantly. Seems the elderly were the first to go. Just like the virus before this."

He was right. Covid did hit the elderly and chronically ill first. Maybe this time someone was culling the old folks *and* the children.

I wanted to examine that further, with Dad, but it would have to wait. We now had several people with us, and two of them were children—but not little kids. Trina was twelve, and Milo, eight.

But if we weren't going to Denver, I wasn't sure where we were headed.

Sam had pulled Marla's body from the tow truck and busied himself cleaning out the cab. Funny how we'd talked about needing a tow truck to pull apart wrecks on the highway—but I wouldn't examine that too closely. It seemed evil to thank God for someone's death even if she was trying to kill us first. *Geez, Jack. You're one confused puppy, aren't you? Of course, you should thank the Lord. It was kill or be killed!*

I shook off those thoughts and glanced around.

Faith and Snake sat with Milo in the back seat of the Chrysler, and Drew and Trina had pulled their SUV up beside us so we could talk across the gap.

Sam walked over after moving Marla's body into the ditch. "I cleaned the cab the best I could," he said. "But I'll need diesel for this monster." He hooked a thumb over his shoulder toward the truck. "Looks like I've got about half a tank."

"We'll get more, soon," I said. "I doubt many survivors are tapping the big rig tanks. But I left your punch in the Jeep. We'll have to pick up another one down the line."

Sam nodded and leaned against the car. I knew I was only echoing his own thoughts. He was the expert on getting fuel, not me.

In the distance, the Turqs kept watch. Every now and then we would hear one whistle down like a missile. Then a sky hole would open, and the blackness would fall. From where we sat, it appeared the dark rain had cleaned up all the bodies, both Takers and humans. I had no idea what was going on inside the mountain, but after what I had seen at the big doors, I assumed the battle was far from over.

We'd seen several cars start up and head back toward the highway. I figured they were the unsprayed survivors, like Drew and his family. The ones, like us, who had arrived late to the party and lived to tell the tale.

Dad's voice pulled me out of my head. "When I didn't find you in Texas," he was saying, "I went on up to Denver, hoping you'd somehow made your way there. I was so frantic to locate you, I didn't even take time to bury Aunt Edna." He looked away, but not before I saw the moisture in his eye. "That still haunts me."

I touched his hand. "It's okay. We buried her. Besides, I had the same plan. To look for you at Gran and Grampa's house. I just got sidetracked a time or two."

He clasped my fingers briefly. "I want to hear all about it, and about those guardian angels you call Turqs. Especially the one that healed me."

I thought back over the last few days. "And I want to hear all about your time with the Takers. How you survived being sprayed and captured."

"It was Cade," he said. "He kept me alive. Just barely. Right there at the end."

Glancing at the road, I had to clear my throat to speak. "He turned out to be a hero just like Thad at the buffalo jump." *Except I should have known better. I'd known Cade all my life.*

No, my subconscious argued, *you thought you knew Cade. Someone shot at us on the highway. Someone in his group. Those weren't imaginary bullets. You did what you had to do.*

That much was true. Cade could have come with us at any time. But I wouldn't let Faith ride with him and Hal. I'd vetoed that in a heartbeat. Good thing, I guess, recalling how Hal's body had flown out the window when he crashed the Challenger.

Am I my brother's keeper?

Dad spoke again. "I don't think Cade knew what was happening at first." He touched the red marks around his neck. "I had traveled from Denver with a group that got sprayed by a flock of those drones. We couldn't seem to help ourselves after that." He touched his throat again before continuing:

"Then Cade came along. He was with Marla and a wiry kid with a foul mouth. They had these hard hats and plastic face shields, so they didn't get the spray." He hesitated. "I wanted to beg Cade for news of you, but that spray made it difficult to think, much less act."

Oh, man. I *had* failed my friend. I should have *made* him come with us. I should have forced him. But I didn't tell Dad that. Instead, I said, "I'm so glad he saved you. I don't know how he fell in with Marla. Unless it was through Hal. They were both mixed up in the drug scene back in Eden. I only met Marla the night I left."

Dad nodded. "When Cade saw me, he yanked me out of the group in front of the entrance and managed to keep me alive until I came back to my senses. That's when Marla found out I was your dad." His eyebrows went up. "She said you killed her boyfriend, but I didn't believe that."

"No, I didn't kill him. But she blamed me because I made them leave after she stole all of Mom's pain pills out of the medicine cabinet." I flashed back on that horrific night. "At the time, I still hoped you and Mom would come home somehow."

Dad patted my knee. "It's okay, Wayward Son." His hand went to his face, to his restored eye. "The Lord works in mysterious ways."

We smiled at each other. "I still can't believe it," I said.

He gave my knee a little back and forth shake. "I knew that wasn't your skull in the ashes." He glanced away. "When I didn't find you at your school, I went home. There were two women walking in our neighborhood, looking for bikes to ride or cars that would start."

My stomach fell as hard as if I'd just made the first loop on The Shock Wave roller coaster. "You're kidding me." We had missed each other at every turn.

Dad shook his head. "No kidding. One of them told me what had happened at our house the night you were there. They said they were the ones who had dozed off later and let the candle fall over. Caught the drapes on fire."

So at least Thad had been honest about that. But why hadn't he gone back and picked them up? The first Chrysler supposedly belonged to Mo's daughter.

I forced those thoughts out of my head for the moment. "That's when you went to Aunt Edna's?"

He nodded. "When they said how you had taken off in the night, I figured you were headed to the library or to Edna's place," he shrugged. "I'd already located Mom's car in the underground parking garage, and I'd found her ..." His throat muscles worked constantly when he said that, as if he had to swallow his sorrow to make room for the words ... "But I couldn't get to her. The creatures were everywhere."

That must've been before the clean-up-Turqs swept through and stacked all the bodies in the Comparative Religions room. I clenched my jaw, memories coating my tongue, memories that only needed the light of day to shrivel up and turn harmless. Like the Takers' internal tattoos drying up and dying when exposed to the world.

Dad continued, "After finding Edna on the porch, and no trace of you, I began to have doubts. I talked myself into thinking maybe it *was* you in the ash and the women had been trying to cover it up. I was so distraught, thinking I'd let you down …" He glanced away. "I believe my mind started playing tricks on me. I didn't even go down in the silo to get supplies. Just high-tailed it out of there, headed to Colorado."

I couldn't believe how similar our thoughts had been as we'd searched for one another. "It's okay, Dad," I attempted to ease his mind. "You were alone. You didn't have all the help that I had."

He laughed, but it was tinged with sadness. "I want to hear all about your help. About your motley crew. About your journey."

"And I want to hear what happened to the two women," I said. "But we'll have plenty of time to chat on our way to wherever we're headed." I put the car in gear. "Where *are* we headed?"

Dad shrugged. "Doesn't matter now that we're together." He patted my knee again. "Anyplace but here," he said. "*Anyplace* but here." He almost grinned, a bit of the old pirate curling up one side of his mouth.

Drew leaned out and spoke into the gap between his SUV and our car. "I say we find some tropical isle. A place untouched by all this. A place with good fishing and warm water. Maybe some mangoes and coconuts." He held up Trina's bony arm. "Something that will put a little meat back on these bones." He glanced into the backseat at his son. Milo was asleep with his arm around Snake's neck. The dog didn't seem to mind at all.

The question about kids gnawed at me again, but that would be another topic for later. For the next campfire.

Sam and Faith spoke almost in unison. "It's not tropical—"

"—but the silo still had a ton of food."

"Jinx," Faith said.

Sam stuck his big hand inside the window, pinkie finger crooked out. "You owe me a Coke," he replied.

Faith laughed and hooked her pinkie around his. "I will gladly pay you, Tuesday," she quoted an ancient cartoon which endeared her to me all over again. "Or when we hit up the next 7-Eleven." She paused, then added, "Whichever comes first."

Sam grinned. "I'll hold you to that, young lady." He straightened and turned toward the tow truck.

"On the Road Again," cued up in my head. Even Willie Nelson agreed it was time to go. "I believe Dad is right," I said. "Anyplace but here." I glanced at Faith in the rearview and she nodded.

I put the Chrysler in gear and headed north. I didn't know if there were any tropical isles where we were going, but at least we *were* going.

Suddenly, on the road again felt like home.

9 781957 344621